Cost of Victory

C R Saxon

This is a work of fiction. Names, characters, places, and incidents either are the product of the author's imaginations or are used fictitiously, and any resemblance to actual persons, living or dead, business establishments, events, or locales is entirely coincidental. The publisher does not have any control over and does not assume any responsibility for author or third-party websites or their content.

First Edition

www.hcspublishing.com

ISBN: 9781955644006

Acknowledgements

To my amazing, supportive, and totally awesome husband and alpha reader: Thank you! Thank you for helping me make this book a reality. I love you oodles!

Thank you to my wonderful beta readers – my two most loyal in particular: Tammie and Kelly. And thank you to everyone who helped get this book published.

To everyone reading this, thanks for giving my story a shot. I hope you enjoy it!

Reading and Pronunciation Guide:

Languages:

Common - Generally used by the majority of the world

Oŭndo (Ō-**o͞o**n-dō) - Considered an extinct language; origin unknown

Yemeri (Ye-mər-ē) - North Oueshi's traditional language

Yuchio (**Yo͞o**-chi-ō) - The Grassland's traditional language

Finnish - Long dead language used for words with no Oŭndo equivalent

Continents:

Chūzo (**Cho͞o**-zō) - Largest continent

Oueshi (Oi-shē) - Eastern continent

Azuté (Äh-**zo͞o**-tā) - Western continent

Kidico (**Ke**-dēk-ō) - Northern continent

Mundan (**Mo͞o**n-dan) - Southern continent

Titles:

Dinta (**Din**-tä) - North Oueshi "lesser prince"

Hei-O (**Hī**-ō) - North Oueshi "heir"

Oza (**Ō**-zä) - North Oueshi "hero"

Nuwa (**No͞o**-wä) - East Azuté "queen"

Nu (No͞o) - East Azuté "king"

Zi (Zē) - East Azuté "prince"

Nauo (Nou) - West Azuté "lesser heir"

Inoa (E-**nō**-ä) - West Kidico "general's daughter"

Mwā-tonô (Mwä-t**ō**-nō) - Unknown origin "heir of Tonō"

Tonō (T**ō**-nō) - Unknown origin - a name from legend

Kōjomȁ (K**ō**-jō-mä) - Unknown origin - doesn't mean anything nice

Names:

Aguilla (Ä-gw**ē**-yä)

Bær (Bār)

Berago (Bər-ä-gō)

Dæya (D**ā**-yä)

Eve-lyn (**Ē**v-lin)

Gongie (Gôn-gē)

Herrard (He-rärd)

Ilu (**Ē**-lo͞o)

Kumi (K**o͞o**-mē)

Leoniel (L**ē**-än-el)

Loucé (Lo͞o-s**ā**)

Ludwick (L**o͞o**d-wik)

Oya (Oi-yä)

Raonie (Rā-**ō**n-ē)

Riaderick (R**ā**-de-rik)

Rutoric (Ro͞o-tôr-ik)

Tenalia (Ta-nôl-yä)

Theon (Th**ē**-ôn)

Tuel (T**o͞o**-el)

Û-ya'īn (o͞o-yä-en)

Xhingho (ZiNG-hō)

Xhou (Zou)

Norger (Nôr-gər)

Naizu (N**ā**-zo͞o)

Contents

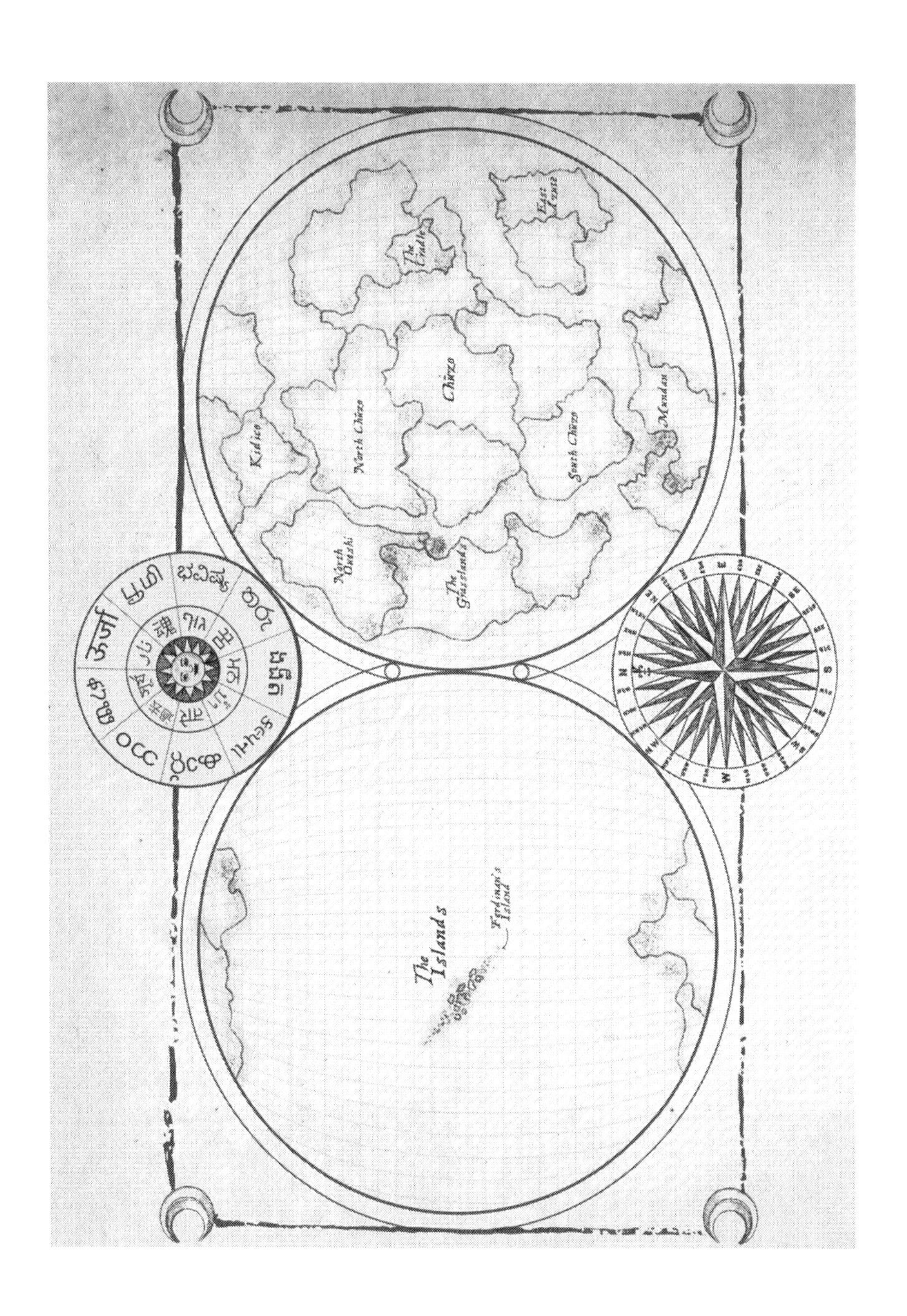

Kidico
North Chirzo
Chirzo
South Chirzo
Mandan
The Cradle
The Grasslands
The Islands
Ferdinan's Island

Chapter 1

Eight million deaths.

Eight million.

All were my fault.

All of them...

Crystal blue eyes reflected back at Ferdinan while water pooled in his bony hands. Thin lips - almost nonexistent - shook at the images surrounding his skeletal features. A glance around the room proved he was alone. But...the mirror showed countless faces.

Those eyes glared at him. They hated him. And why wouldn't they hate their murderer?

Forcing those transparent blue crystals closed, Ferdinan rinsed his mouth, splashed water on his face, and turned the handle. Silence filled the small cabin bathroom. A silence that'd end too soon. The towel acted as his shield while it dried his skin - blocking the mirror from view.

Hiding won't wash away the blood.

"I know! I know." Sidestepping, he held onto the towel until he was in the main room.

Ferdinan clenched his teeth against that horrid voice and shook his head. He didn't know where it came from or why it wouldn't leave. As much as he hated it, that voice spoke the truth. After all the deaths...

Millions...

How does a fourteen-year-old rack up such a body count?

Nothing can cleanse me.

The bunk hardly shifted under the weight of his small frame. Muscles protested, begging to run, to...no. He ignored their protests. He deserved worse than the pain of stillness - so much worse.

Every day for months Ferdinan scoured the news engines - needing to know the extent of his destruction. Eighty percent of Azuté's population died before the harvest could be brought in - leaving the other twenty to waste away from more than grief. Clenched teeth held the guilt and remorse inside.

Amazing how one child accomplished all that.

For nearly a decade, his stomach constantly bothered him, but the last few months... One failure after another. One. And another. Over. And over. No matter what he did. No matter how hard he tried... They just kept coming...

His churning insides twisted further.

Reaching into his pocket, Ferdinan pulled out his green mint tin and opened it. Inside, a dozen little capsules rolled around. All it took was one to fill his mouth and sinuses with mint - easing his unhappy stomach. Returning the tin, Ferdinan closed his eyes. There were times he wished boats swayed with the current just to have something to focus on. But that was fixed with technology millennia ago.

A sigh left him as a golden-brown hand materialized out of nowhere, grabbed his arm, and dragged him on deck. All-consuming emptiness emanated from her inescapable grip. *Oya? How did she get in my cabin?* That impossible void crawled out from where her hand touched his deathly pale skin - slowly consuming his entire frame. Never had anyone's touch felt like this - like hers. And it was... Most people were painful in one way or another and he was used to dealing with that. But this...his insides begged to be released.

Between the perfect void of her touch and their mismatched gate, being dragged across deck was odd. Though slightly taller, Ferdinan wasn't any bigger than her. Everyone considered him a skeleton. But they didn't understand, and he wasn't about to explain. Oya, however, didn't treat him differently because of it. It was like she didn't notice - leaving him uncertain.

How are you going to ruin this for her?

I wouldn't do that...

Grating laughter bounced around his skull. He cringed, pleading for the voice to go away. *I can't let them suspect.* Broken people... The shame it'd bring upon his family, his country - his Prince. No. They couldn't know.

Keep me hidden. They'll never see it coming when you kill them.

Go away!

His arm was yanked to the side as they rounded the bow. Hip length, black hair whipped around the girl like a wild mane. It was so strange. Most of it was rich and dark and beautiful, speckled lightly with sunshine and shadows. The roots, however... Over the last few months, the new growth came in an impossible blood red. Though not nearly as beautiful, it was striking.

Oya's bare feet skidded to an abrupt stop. Startled, he collided with her. She simply laughed and pointed to the horizon as he fought to escape the nothingness consuming him. This time she let him go, allowing him to finally breathe. When she spoke, it was in her native tongue. Unfortunately, he was the only one here who understood. *She'd be happier with anyone else.* But she asked him not to speak about her language - or that he'd learned it.

"*Is that it?*" The graceful sounds of her native Oŭndo waltzed through the air. Her alien green eyes were bright with crazed excitement.

That craze was an oddity Ferdinan couldn't figure out. Her eyes sparkled with it. And it ran deep – to her very core. But never bothered her. At times he found himself lost in that wildness. It was...it was almost inhuman. As if part of her soul was feral. But then she'd laugh or dance or spin and it was just that craze again. A surface glimmer of something much deeper. Something he'd never hope to comprehend.

"*Yeah...sort of.*" When she giggled at his wishy-washy response, he clarified, "*That's not the main island. It's devoted to the Artists. Just a little farther.*"

A mini jungle oasis framed by morning's colors floated past them – green, lush, and stunning. It was the perfect artistic inspiration. The main island, though lovely, was quite different. Long, white beaches crawled lazily to hug grassy fields. The buildings weren't nearly as well hidden either. Each island had its own character, making the chain the ultimate playground for those with the drive to reach them. Judging by the look on Oya's face, she'd be one of the avid explorers.

Turning her wild grin on him, she tamed her multi-toned hair with deft hands. This was the first time he'd seen anyone braid their hair. It was strangely fascinating. *I wonder what her ability is...*

Ferdinan respected her not wanting to say, but as a Scientist – a Tinkerer – he couldn't curb his curiosity. Those inhumanly green eyes suggested she was like him. But Oya insisted she didn't have a good grasp of science.

Enthralled by his thoughts, he nearly missed her attempt to leap overboard. Long, twig-like fingers caught the back of her shirt and yanked her off the rail. "*What are you doing?*"

A wild, wicked grin curled her shapely lips. "*Swim with me!*"

Cherry red head to toe, Ferdinan looked away. "*It's dangerous this far out. And…I don't like swimming.*"

"*You live surrounded by water and don't like swimming?*"

Pathetic.

Ferdinan turned purple and sunk deeper inside himself.

~

After eight days of travel, they were glad to see the beach. Ferdinan didn't even mind when his ally appeared carrying both their bags. It didn't stop him from taking his, though. Regardless of how poorly they got along, Jon was a Dinta – a lesser prince – and he was merely a Lord. Worse, the Artimus family was his country's strongest ally. There was no reason for the fifteen-year-old Dinta to carry anything of his.

Freeing his bag from Jon's grip, Ferdinan mumbled a "thank you" while blushing deeply. Seeing Jon felt like looking in a warped mirror. They shared many features – height, build, facial structure. Aside from excessive grooming, all it'd take was gaining a good thirty pounds and cutting his hair short to pass as the Dinta. At least from a distance. The most striking difference was their eyes. Rich, chocolate brown eyes matched Jon's hair, while Ferdinan's were a pale crystal blue nearly devoid of color.

Those brown eyes...they were always annoyed at him. *It's my own fault...*

Yes, it is.

^^^

Jon dropped to his knees next to Ferdinan and slammed a fist into the tile. Frustration and tears shook his voice. "I can't take this anymore...please. I tried doing as I was asked. I tried fulfilling my duty. But I'm sick of this... I never liked you. But I'm truly starting to hate you."

VVV

Shaking his head, Ferdinan banished the memory. Everything he did to bring Jon to that state... *No. I don't want to remember.*

"Have you boys gotten everything?"

How did that voice get behind him? He'd been avoiding the man the entire trip. No attempt was made to hide his rudeness as Ferdinan leapt away from the perfectly average adult. For as non-descript as Healer Bær was, the skeletal Tinkerer could easily spot the man among a throng. Just looking at the Healer was enough to set his heart into overdrive and bring black spots to his vision.

Jon sighed at Ferdinan's reaction and shook his head, "Yes, sir."

Sifting through his emotional masks, Ferdinan found the most pleasant he could manage. Unclenching his jaw let a gentle expression soften his face.

They were back at school. Time to return to normal life. Delicate golden-brown hands caught his attention as Oya waved - grinning wildly. *Normal, huh?* Maybe not completely. Not until she learned Common. *She'll be happier when she can talk to someone better than me.*

In no time, the boat docked, and they made their way down the gangplank. As the four disembarked, three enjoyed a novel sight.

Pure excitement ran barefoot down the dock and leapt onto the beach. The look on Oya's face as her toes touched the island for the first time was magical. You'd think she was peering into heaven. Calloused feet shot through sand to splash in ankle deep water. If the skeleton didn't know better, he'd say the ocean rushed toward her - wanting to play.

Ferdinan stood on the pier watching her childlike joy. As she ran and splashed, she looked like a four-year-old, not a child of fourteen. Despite himself, he couldn't stop the corners of his mouth from turning up slightly - accompanied by a twinge of envy. They were the same age, but he didn't have the freedom for that kind of joy.

Now they were here, he'd have to find shoes she liked. In the weeks he'd known her she remained barefoot, making him nervous whenever she played in the lab. *What did she do with all the shoes given to her at the hospital?*

"I don't think I've ever seen that," Bær commented.

The Healer's voice interrupted Ferdinan's thoughts - making his heart race and egging his feet closer to Oya.

Coward.

"I know I haven't," Jon grinned.

This was all the conversation they managed before she ran back and grabbed the two boys, pulling them down to the beach.

"Does she think this is new for us too?" Jon huffed.

"I don't know." A perfect void consumed Ferdinan's hand from her touch, but she wouldn't release him. Still, he smiled at her joy.

What right have you to smile?

That made him flinch - straining his expression. What right did he have? After the damage he'd done, the deaths he'd caused...what right did he have?

Leaping forward, she grinned over her shoulder, releasing their hands. Jon stopped, but he kept going, trying to escape those thoughts. A quick step was all it took for her to start a game of tag. She was an expert at dodging and weaving - changing directions on the spot with the ease and grace of a dancer.

As he attempted tagging her, Ferdinan turned, catching a glimpse of Healer Bær stepping up next to his ally. The Superintendent approached from inland. Master Dæya was Superintendent for as long as the boys had been at the school. The man was a Mind Talker – a Psych – and as troublesome as any Healer. Not only this, Dæya and Bær were brothers.

Seeing them made Ferdinan wince. Between the two, he was constantly on edge. If the Tinkerer slipped up too badly, he'd end up facing one, if not both. But they hadn't noticed. Remembering himself, the skeleton twisted his foot in the loose sand, tripped, and fell. This startled Oya, but she didn't hesitate rushing to his side.

There was no helping the involuntary jerk when she took his hand. Apologetic, he pushed himself to his feet.

"They're having fun," Superintendent Dæya commented from behind Jon.

An uneasy expression filled the Dinta's face. "It looks that way."

"How've they been, brother?" Dæya asked concerning the students gone two months longer than expected.

The Healer hesitated as uncertain eyes scanned the beach. "They're doing better."

"Ah. We'll talk later." Though brothers, the two looked nothing alike. Whereas the Healer was perfectly average, the Superintendent stood out. Dark skin gave off a beautiful, healthy glow, making the Mind Talker's dark eyes look like polished hematite. But the most glaringly obvious differences? Dæya was broad, completely bald, and covered in symbolic tattoos marking his lifetime of accomplishments.

Those Tattoos were the only difference that confused Ferdinan. If they were brothers, why didn't they both have them?

The man's accent was from North Oueshi - Jon's country. Claiming unwanted and orphaned children from around the world was commonplace. It was easy believing Bær was an older claimed child. But...once a person was claimed they were family. No questions. No exceptions. The tribe those tattoos originated from...Bær should have them too.

It wasn't until the Healer's son arrived on the islands - skin unmarked - that Ferdinan looked into it. *I'm stupid...useless.* Even thinking about it, Ferdinan rolled his eyes at himself. Why hadn't he thought of marriage sooner? It made perfect sense. The Superintendent was quick to call the Healer "brother," when Bær always hesitated-

Master Dæya's pointed cough interrupted his musings. The sun was low on the horizon but getting higher. Students were in class, leaving the island nearly deserted.

Sweat beaded on the Superintendent's brow as he stifled a grimace. "Jon Dinta, Lord Ferdinan, I want to talk to both of you. Put your bags up, then come to my office."

"Yes, sir."

When Dæya motioned them forward, Ferdinan brushed sand from his baggy clothing and signaled Oya to follow. Keeping a respectful distance, the skeleton stopped and looked at her before bowing properly to the Superintendent. She didn't follow suit. But at least she gave the man her attention. Thankfully the Healer moved to keep some distance between them. He'd never say so, but Ferdinan appreciated the respite it gave his raw nerves.

What's so scary about him? You've killed how many healers in the last few weeks?

Stop it!

"Gentlemen put your things away. I expect you in my office in twenty minutes," Dæya repeated, then turned to the girl and motioned her closer. "Welcome to our school, Miss. Please follow me."

Walking over to his schoolmates, Jon spoke up. "Um, she doesn't speak Common, sir."

"I'm aware, Jon Dinta." Scratching his head, Dæya turned to his brother. "Do you think she could handle it?"

Healer Bær's face tightened. "That's something we need to discuss."

The unspoken conversation going on between the brothers was intense. "I look forward to your report."

Oya raised an eyebrow at them. Then she giggled, "*They're close, aren't they?*"

Green eyes so intense they glowed turned on the boys, but Ferdinan held his tongue. It was the one request she made.

Winking at them, Oya trailed after the Superintendent when he motioned her to follow. *What does she find so funny?*

Jon looked exhausted watching Oya skip down the path. "Let's get this over with."

Nodding, Ferdinan followed, all the while agonizing over the last few months. *Is it possible to fix what I've destroyed?*

~

Brushing off his ally on the third floor, Ferdinan continued to the top. The door to his suite looked exactly like the other three, but those didn't constrict his heart. *It's ok. I'm not disturbing anyone. My Prince and Cep Theon are in class. Just run in and leave.*

Run in and leave? Take your time. Destroy them properly.

Covering his ears only amplified the grating laughter. Deft, bony fingers typed in his access code. It took less than ten seconds to dash through the kitchen and sitting area, throw the bag in his room, and run back out.

Don't worry, they'll die, just like everyone else.

No. I'd never do that to them!

Not giving the voice a chance to say more, Ferdinan bolted down the stairs and toward the administration building.

A soft cry floating gently on the breeze crashed against his head. *What?* It took a moment, but when he identified where it came from, he quietly moved closer.

Why aren't they in class?

Ahead was a young boy kneeling next to a weeping girl, attempting to comfort her. Slipping into the shadows, Ferdinan watched.

"I'm sorry, Tincha. You aren't ready yet. I shouldn't have made you join me." Taking her hand, the boy pulled her, but she didn't move – only sat there sobbing. "Come on, let's go inside. I'll call Master Loucé."

Thrilled laughter echoed around his skull.

Another one, huh?

Breath held, stomach twisting, Ferdinan waited for her response – knowing all too well what it'd be. *I forgot this? How did I forget everyone here?! How horrible am I?*

"Master Loucé can't bring them back! She can't make me better! It won't change anything..." Her fierce anger faded, bringing more tears to the surface.

Digging sharp fingers into his bony arm, Ferdinan swallowed hard against the rising bile.

Ah! You might've killed millions, but how many more want to die?

Biting the inside of his cheeks, Ferdinan ran. The closer he got to the administrative building, the more people were around – the more sorrow. It paled their faces and reddened their eyes, adults and students alike. *How many have I hurt? What've I destroyed? What have I done?!*

Panic drove his feet faster – taking him to the nearest restroom. Mercifully, it was empty. He had no words to describe his haunted eyes. *I did all this! I've no right to feel...like this.* Even his reflection couldn't help identify what brewed inside him. Whatever it was, it was harsh and crushing.

Eyes closed, he centered himself. Voice or not, he had to look normal. No one could see what possessed him. He couldn't let it through. Whatever that voice was, wherever it came from, if others found out...

Ferdinan banished that thought, opened his eyes, and faced the mirror. His reflection was blank, lifeless – little more than carved stone.

You think this will hide anything? They'll see the truth. They'll see you for what you are.

Despite the chastising voice, Ferdinan kept his face expressionless. Desperation still glinted in his eyes. *I'll keep my head down. As long as I don't look at anyone...* Ferdinan tried convincing himself while the voice mocked his futile efforts. *How horrible am I – forgetting everyone here? Not thinking of those who survive...*

An easily identifiable emotion filled him.

Loathing.

For as much as he hated himself before, he now loathed everything he'd become.

Even that wasn't enough.

Chapter 2

An eternity passed as Ferdinan stood by the farthest window shaking, waiting for his ally to arrive. What was taking so long? The sooner this meeting started, the sooner it'd be over and Ferdinan could get away from the threat before him. Better yet, the sooner he could sneak away and appease his aching muscles.

"Are you sure you're ok, Lord Ferdinan?"

Cringing deeper away from the Superintendent, Ferdinan swallowed hard. "I'm f-fine."

Relief blanketed them both when the secretary's voice announced the Dinta's arrival. Within moments Jon walked up and bowed to the man.

"Jon Dinta, have a seat, please." The Superintendent motioned to a chair facing his desk.

Though the skeletal Ferdinan remained standing by the window, Jon complied – frowning at the blatant disrespect.

Ferdinan's nervousness around Healers was well known among the islands. But Telepaths and Mind Talkers - Psychs of either kind – were nearly as bad. If Dæya were a Telepath, the Tinkerer wouldn't be here. The only reason he could handle being near the man was the fact that Mind Talkers had to put effort into accessing another's mind – and the one being scanned could usually feel it.

"Thank you for coming so quickly. With the assembly today, this was the easiest time to meet." Dæya gritted back a flinch, giving Jon an opening to voice his confusion.

"Assembly?"

"Yes, the assembly for Family Week assignments."

"Wasn't that a while ago?"

"A good bit happened here while you two were gone. With things settling down, we're trying to get back on track." Breathing deeply, the Superintendent started into the most important part of the meeting. "I want to thank you both. Your hard work impressed my brother and Healer Riaderick."

"Thank you, sir," Jon said as Ferdinan lowered his head.

"You especially, Lord Ferdinan." Dæya turned to the student who refused to sit. "The things you did were amazing. We can't possibly be grateful enough."

Gaze on the floor, Ferdinan hid behind his overgrown, shaggy hair. All those tattooed accomplishments were even more intimidating when trapped in his office.

Thanking you for incompetence, how generous.

"I was hired to make the second skin. It took so long I don't deserve thanks."

"You know that's not what I'm talking about." Concern took over Dæya's face. "When you asked to help your friend, I never thought it'd turn into such an ordeal. I'm truly impressed. And I'm deeply sorry for your loss. If there's any-"

"I didn't work on the blight." Ferdinan stated firmly, keeping his gaze down.

Jon tensed - face twisting.

Nodding his head, Dæya answered, "I understand. You didn't hear about the virus 'til everyone else did."

"How can you say that?" Jon yelled. "You were the only one trying to stop it!"

Burning red from head to toe, Ferdinan leaned against the window and looked outside. "I wasn't the only one."

The more people who know – you don't want that, do you? Despite all your posturing about taking responsibility.

Shut up!

"They didn't try 'til the end! You saved countless lives," Jon insisted, frustration marking every word.

^^^

He should've stopped Jon from grabbing that screen, but his ally would've pressed for answers. At least this way Ferdinan could remain heartless – could drive the Dinta further away.

Shock blanketed Jon.

He needs to leave now before he really gets hurt. *Bracing himself, Ferdinan put on a mask of annoyance and boredom – calculating his words. He'd drive away the older boy. Regardless of how much it hurt.*

VVV

"I nearly failed to fulfill the last request of an old friend," Ferdinan mumbled, curling inward, trying to escape the unbidden memory.

Surprise and concern knit Dæya's eyebrows together. "If you don't want others knowing you were involved, then we won't say anything."

◊

What? Jon thought as he looked back and forth between the two. *He nearly drove us both mad fighting that horrible disease.* "I don't understand."

"You don't *have* to understand," Ferdinan muttered, hand flicking away something near his ear. "You couldn't anyway."

Try as he might, the Dinta couldn't find a response. What haunted him for weeks was realizing how little he understood

Ferdinan. Knowing this didn't help. Neither did his abilities as a Thinker. It just left him discouraged and resenting the gent. *Why won't he believe me? None of this was his fault.*

Silence hung heavy between the three until Dæya banished it. "Concerning your schoolwork – you were gone longer than anticipated."

A grimace nearly doubled over Ferdinan. Odd twitches, constantly looking over his shoulder, covering his ears – those strange behaviors came out of nowhere, scaring Jon. When Healer Bær tried approaching the skeleton, those ticks lessened, but...

"With two weeks left in the block, I've arranged an extension with your instructors. You have 'til the end of break to finish your coursework. Exams and projects for your non-science classes are waived. The work you did the last three months adequately covers your final project. Will there be a problem with this arrangement?"

"No, sir. It's quite generous," Jon answered. Classwork wasn't difficult. A little research, then submit.

"And you, Lord Ferdinan?"

Ferdinan winced, "I don't need an extension."

"You're done?!" *There's no way. We were too stressed to focus on anything.* "When did you have time?!"

"There were so many delays."

"You did coursework on top of everything else?" Dæya blinked in awe.

Anguish cut deeper into Ferdinan's face, forcing his attention back to the window.

"Jon Dinta, I want to thank you personally for attending to Lord Ferdinan's health these past months. I know the deal you made with Bær, but Master Dimuret will happily take over. I'm concerned it's too much."

"I made a promise, sir." Jon's jaw twitched in irritation. For three months of effort, his ally looked worse than when they left. "I've no intention of telling my family I reneged on a promise to an ally."

Ferdinan swallowed hard but said nothing, flinching at something.

"If you insist. I expect regular updates on Lord Ferdinan's weight, and I'd like to meet with you every two weeks for more detailed reports." Things were getting awkward, so Dæya ended there. "I know you're both exhausted. I can't even imagine. I'd suggest attending the assembly but after, you should rest. Please take the next few days to recover. You can return to classes next week."

"Yes, sir." Rest? Could he really rest? It seemed like an impossible dream. But all Jon had to do was find his island brothers. He'd cook an elaborate meal. And they'd eat and talk. No complaining. No throwing his food away. No arguing. Just the five of them. Relaxing and laughing together. That sounded like paradise. The only way it'd be better was if his actual brothers were here too.

"Thank you for coming, Jon Dinta. I'll get in touch with you to schedule a meeting. 'Til then, contact me with any concerns."

"Yes, sir."

"Lord Ferdinan, I need to discuss something with you."

A small nod acknowledged the request, but Ferdinan didn't look up. Standing stoically, he waited for Jon to leave.

◊

"Please sit, Lord Ferdinan."

The request sounded more tired than the Tinkerer expected, so Ferdinan made his way to a chair – tripping and slamming his knees against the side table.

Flinching, Dæya paid the fall as much mind as his student did. “The incident in your literature class reached me after you left.”

“Yes, sir.” A lifetime passed since *that* happened. But there was no taking back his choice.

“I talked to Master Kezia. She was rather upset.”

“I understand, sir.”

How often do you cause trouble?

Shut up!

“I don’t think you do. I want to hear from you what happened before I proceed.”

Sighing, Ferdinan spoke, “I thought the poem we were assigned to read and interpret was odd, so I did some research... With my findings, I wrote a paper, but she wanted a report. I couldn’t lie to her and I couldn’t pass on presenting... Even though I knew I’d hurt everyone. I didn’t even apologize.”

Stunned, Dæya looked at his student. “You’re saying you’re the one at fault?”

“Yes, sir.”

“You do remember I said I talked to Master Kezia?”

“Yes, sir.” *What does he want? Give me my punishment and send me on.*

Do punishments work on someone like you?

“Hmmm. We did some research and found your aunt’s book is authentic. I sent it back to her by the way.”

“Thank you, sir.”

"Master Kezia was at fault, she admitted this to me – reluctantly, but still. I told her to apologize to you."

"She shouldn't apologize."

"She changed the nature of the assignment and wouldn't accept when you mentioned this to her. She then got angry with you for going above and beyond the requirements. She tried embarrassing you in front of the class and make you admit to something wrong. As propriety calls for, she needs to apologize in the same public manner as the offences she committed."

"I *don't* want her to apologize." Ferdinan looked away. Why didn't the man understand?

This threw the Superintendent off, knitting his eyebrows in worry. For as miserable as Ferdinan usually looked, the child was more wretched now. "Then what *do* you want?"

"I want to be done." Ferdinan pulled what looked like a small sheet of glass from his pocket and started tapping the screen. "I finished a while ago. I don't want to have to keep taking these classes."

The offered screen hosted a list of everything Ferdinan had studied. For a long moment, the skeleton stood, heart terrified to beat – to hope. Those hematite eyes looked over the information once. Then twice. Was it unbelievable he could accomplish that much? It wasn't difficult. And now...

Instead of taking useless classes, Ferdinan wanted to focus on teaching his apprentice and fulfilling the requests he received. Spending his days immersed in research and inventing and building...

Greedy child.

Ferdinan flinched. That voice was right. This was a mistake. He should've kept his head down like always. *What was I thinking? Why did I do something so stupid?*

"When did you do all this?"

When? Did it matter when? He'd been here three years longer than other students his age. But that question was surprising. It spoke volumes to how little the school kept track of him. Despite being a useless son, Ferdinan was grateful to the Duchess for this.

~

Everything hit so quickly before they left, he hadn't faced the consequences of his actions. And now they were simply ignored. *I was wrong. I did horrible things...why aren't they punishing me?* To Ferdinan's dismay, his ally was waiting when he stepped into the hall.

Jaw tight, Jon stared down the skeleton. "Let's go."

"Go where?"

Jon huffed in frustration. "The assembly? I don't know about you, but it'd be nice knowing what role we'll be fulfilling next block."

All Ferdinan wanted was to hole up in his lab and lock the door. Instead, he followed Jon outside toward the boats.

A gasp caught his attention. Looking around, Ferdinan saw an older boy a few yards away on one knee, clenching his stomach. A fellow Scientist and impossibly handsome boy named Norger, dashed forward - voice urgent.

"You ok, Gusaq?"

"Yah, give me a moment."

Jon was nearly at the boats and hadn't noticed. But Ferdinan couldn't tear those blue crystals away. He'd witnessed that look for months. Jolts of pain shook Norger too. *No. Afterall I did to keep Jon away.* Times like this, the skeleton wished he had normal hearing. Ferdinan shook his head, panting, shaking, frozen.

"The pain medicine's wearing off already?"

"Yah...*tsssk*...unfortunately."

"I'm sorry it's taking longer for you."

A strained grin took over Gusaq's lips. "I'm not too bad. At least the cure came in time."

"Yah..." Norger looked out at the ocean, soaking in the view. "You know, I've been thinking about that. I'm sure it got here on the wind."

"On the wind? Are you crazy?" Gusaq gasped again, only to laugh. "The bug would have to live in the air for weeks."

"How do we know it doesn't?"

Ferdinan fell.

His mind raced – taking in what he just heard. *No. I did my duty, I kept Jon away...*

You sent it this way.

No! I didn't hear right. I'm missing something. But he did hear correctly. It was the only fitting explanation after learning how the blight was transmitted...and what it actually was.

Stinging needles seized his shoulders, rattling him. They stopped his heart as a hand rested on his shoulder. Swinging hard at his assailant knocked away the needles. To his relief, it wasn't the dead who haunted him. To his chagrin, it was his ally – haunting him in a different way.

Ferdinan scooted to put distance between him and Jon. The skeleton didn't have to see the Dinta to know who it was. Though not the only person who's touch felt like countless needles stabbing through his skin – Jon was the only one on the islands.

Bent over – hand cradling his side – Jon's lips moved, but Ferdinan only heard grating laughter.

"What are you doing in here?!" Ferdinan forced out through clenched teeth. *Shut up! Shut up! Shut up!!*

"...we're outside... Are you alright?" Jon moved closer, but kept enough distance to avoid being hit again. "I saw you fall. What's wrong?"

"I tripped." The lie came so naturally it sounded true even to himself.

"No, you didn't. I *saw* you fall." Jon glared as he sifted through reasonable explanations. "You didn't eat the breakfast I gave you. I'll force feed you if I have to–"

"You're wrong." Erasing everything from his face but the red taking over, Ferdinan flinched at the growing laughter. "It doesn't matter. I'm tired."

With this, he pushed himself to his feet – ignoring Jon's protests. Not letting himself think, Ferdinan headed toward the boats. Mind empty, he didn't know where he was going. But it didn't truly matter. So long as he stayed away from everyone. Retrieving his green tin, he grabbed a small capsule and snapped it closed. Mint filled him as he returned the tin to his pocket. Calming, comforting mint.

A strong breeze tugged at his hair as he grabbed a boat. *The wind...*

Stupid, incompetent child.

"Don't ignore people when they're talking to you! Why're you so rude?"

Ha ha ha.

◊

"What do you want, Jon?" Irritation filled every word.

"The assembly, remember? But you could use a Healer instead." Knowing how Ferdinan would react, Jon grabbed the gent's wrist and held on tight when his ally tried fleeing. "I'm not taking you to one, but that doesn't change-"

"Don't touch me!" Ferdinan wrenched his arm hard.

Poised to yell back, pain shot through Jon's ribs where the gent punched him earlier. It hurt, but it cooled him off a bit. Ferdinan was the only person he'd met who couldn't stand being touched. No matter how hard he tried, Jon couldn't figure out why. Neither would the skeleton tell him. But then... *Even Ferdinan's own mom...* It was rare seeing the two together, but she wouldn't touch her own son. No hug. No pat on the shoulder. Nothing. It was easily the saddest thing Jon ever witnessed. "Come on, let's go."

"Where?" Ferdinan shuddered, rubbing his wrist.

"The assembly." Scared, Jon stepped closer. "You're worrying me."

The skeleton covered his ears with boney hands before shaking his head and dropping them. "I'm fine. Just go."

All but pushing Ferdinan into the boat, Jon took the oar and cast off. The row was short and the day pleasant, but the trip was strained. More than once the skeleton twitched or covered his ears. The gent didn't keep them covered long, but those boney hands were blocking something. And Jon wasn't talking.

The Thinker didn't know what to do about whatever was going on with the skeleton. *Who can I talk to? It's wrong suggesting...but...*

When they arrived, a crowd of students loitered outside the auditorium. Immediately, the skeleton tried slipping away into it.

Jon stopped him. "Where're you going?"

“There’s something I need to do. I’ll be there shortly. Save me a seat.”

“Um, ok.” Though confused, it wasn’t often Ferdinan made a request other than to be left alone. “You’re eating after the assembly, so don’t sneak away.”

Jon headed inside to find the other Science students.

Chapter 3

The Superintendent might look upon Ferdinan's sins as benign, but his cousin, his Prince, knew perfectly well what he deserved. Anticipation twisted the Tinkerer's gut into knots. Even his mints weren't enough to keep it calm. The crowd was formidable, but it wasn't difficult for the skeleton to spot his cousin. Zephyr stood out like a golden beacon of promised relief.

If he knew how many you killed, he'd punish you properly. Unless he applauds you like everyone else.

He wouldn't do that. He values life.

Unlike you.

Unlike me.

Murderers value nothing.

Ferdinan gasped. People like him shouldn't exist.

Too late, isn't it?

I don't know how to fix that.

Tripping five feet from Zephyr, Ferdinan knelt, head bowed, and addressed his cousin. Paying homage wasn't common practice on the islands. This was one of the few times in their lives they could live equally. But for Ferdinan, his Prince would always be his Prince. Regardless of what the islands were set up for, he could never set that aside.

Despite his eye twitching, Zephyr turned a smile to his companions. He tapped a thumb to his cheek and pointed it outward. "Well, my friends, it seems he's back. Please give me a moment with my little cousin."

"Pfft." Denila scrunched her nose at Zephyr - straight, black hair falling to frame her lovely face and emphasize the beauty of her deeply tanned, copper skin. Rich, dark eyes shot his Prince a knowing look. Like his cousin, she was an Athlete - a Fighter - a formidable one. Also like Zephyr, she was three years older than Ferdinan. "See you inside."

With a single command, Zephyr led him to a secluded spot. A small clearing nestled in a wooded area. Once there, Ferdinan dropped to one knee again. "My Prince."

"You disappear for three months, then come walking up like you've been here the entire time?" The golden skinned Prince tapped his knuckles against his chin before jerking them downward.

Ferdinan nodded. The strain in Zephyr's words warned him to avoid eye contact. But...he deserved worse than what was coming to him. Simply looking up - connecting with those onyx eyes - would add to what he'd earned.

Even your cousin can't stand looking at you.

Golden hands shot out a gesture Ferdinan knew too well. Depending on the context, it could mean "necessary consequences" or it could mean "death." Both were fitting. *All I have to do is let him see my sins. He'll punish me as I deserve. My Prince...he knows justice.* "I apologize, my Prince. I've not forgotten what you've held off on."

Evil child. Is there punishment sufficient for your wicked soul?

Looking at his hands, Ferdinan couldn't see the blood, but he could feel it - could smell it. And when he closed his eyes, it was always there - he was drenched in it.

◊

"I wasn't talking about that." It irritated Zephyr. Everything about Ferdinan did. As his younger cousin groveled at his feet, he felt himself growing hotter. The few words the skeleton spoke irritated him, grating on his nerves. The sounds, the selfishness they conveyed, angered the Prince to shaking. *Stop it! Why won't you try overcoming your selfishness?* "But you're right. It's best to do things in order, isn't it?"

When Zephyr grabbed the skeleton's shirt and lifted, Ferdinan finished standing under his own power – keeping his head down.

Reaching back, Zephyr readied a fist only to have a dozen knives tear through his gut. Doubling over with a groan, he gritted his teeth against the pain.

Ferdinan lunged forward. "What's wrong? Are you unwell?"

Shoving his younger cousin back, Zephyr forced himself to straighten. "You even got out of this!"

"Out of what, my Prince?"

Frustration accentuated every motion the Prince's hands spoke while his mouth searched for words. "You leave on some extended vacation while that disease works its way here. And you can't even be grateful for that."

"But...a cure. It was announced and distributed..." Ferdinan recoiled instinctively when their eyes met. Unforgivable sin danced in those clear blue crystals.

That look.

It contorted Zephyr's face.

Fire raged in the Prince's onyx eyes and he threw a punch. He felt Ferdinan's nose break. *Unappreciative! What right does someone like you have to be here? Just once you could show a little gratitude!* "Just because the cure kills the virus doesn't mean it fixes the damage."

Everything froze. What little color Ferdinan had vanished before green set in. The skeleton covered his ears and shook his head - lips mouthing something Zephyr didn't catch.

That look filled Ferdinan's face - the one which epitomized his little cousin's selfishness. It didn't matter how hard the Prince tried; he could never find another way to describe it. Those eyes held pure selfishness. Zephyr growled, unleashing a barrage of punches to his cousin's upper body. He didn't give Ferdinan a chance to recover. *How many times have I tried? Can't you think of anyone other than yourself? I'm so tired of this.*

As Ferdinan staggered back in front of the Prince, Zephyr shot a foot through his gut - knocking him halfway across the clearing. Just like propriety demanded, the skeleton forced himself to his feet again. He'd continue standing until his body gave out.

Ferdinan whispered in a language Zephyr didn't understand. Or, he didn't understand the words. But the emotion - it enraged the Prince further.

* * *

The mass of students was the only thing distracting Oya from the five glowing orbs floating in her peripheral vision. Those orbs had followed her for a while and didn't seem to be causing any trouble. So, she'd enjoy the chaos swarming around her.

The longer Oya watched students amble into the room, the more she understood the enormity of it. The ratio of seats to people was a bit overkill. Yet they arranged themselves into six distinct groups. Since she didn't belong to any particular group, Oya decided to enjoy some sun. Ferdinan would tell her anything she needed to know.

Once outside, she realized others weren't where they were supposed to be either. A grin brightened Oya's face when she saw her friend. But someone was with him.

Ferdinan didn't look happy. Neither did he look scared or angry or sad. He knelt there expressionless. Like a statue with a face carved to reflect whatever emotions the observer expected to see. All the while a smaller boy tenderized her friend. She didn't understand the words he was yelling. But a blind man could see the hate in his eyes.

Who are you, little boy?

Whoever he was, her friend was deeply connected to him. Few connections extended from Ferdinan's chest. The handful her friend had were faded and gray...save a single yellow one. But the string connecting these two... On Ferdinan's side was a royal purple. But on the golden boy's end it was...complex. Red glowed angrily while black swirled through it and a strange shade of blue sprinkled the length. This wasn't just an unbalanced relationship; it was confused and bitter and painful.

What's going on?

Not only was Ferdinan *not* defending himself, he didn't look like he wanted to. The ending blow was a knee to the gut. Ferdinan tried getting back up, but he was down after this. She heard the boy say something she was sure wasn't Common while flinging his hands around.

Kicking Ferdinan in the gut once more, her new enemy walked away.

Ferdinan lay on the ground fighting for breath. She couldn't leave him like this, but she had a bigger fish to fry and didn't know where to take him anyway. Turning, she went back to the crowd of students.

The meeting was in full swing when Oya slipped back into the auditorium. The impressively tattooed man stood on stage holding a box. Six older students stood around it – awaiting further instruction. It seemed this man was in charge. Only... *He didn't react to my words on the beach.* That was something she'd figure out later.

Jon sat near the middle. The rows behind and in front of him were filled. *Why with all the available seating is everyone right next to each other instead of spreading out?* But there wasn't anything she could do about it.

Not a soul noticed her walk along the backs of the chairs to reach him. Even Jon didn't realize she was there until she was sitting on his lap. The interesting colors consuming his face nearly made her laugh. Turning Ferdinan red was a simple task, but Jon? *I didn't know you could blush.* He stumbled on the words she blocked with a hand. Just loud enough for him to hear, she whispered Ferdinan's name in his ear, then got up and headed for the exit.

It took a minute, but he eventually jumped up and followed. Taking his arm, she dragged Jon to her injured friend. Instead of sprawled on the ground, Ferdinan now sat against a tree. She gave the boy a moment to see the skeleton's pain, then shoved him into the clearing before disappearing.

Now to track down her prey.

The boy with golden skin was a good way into the wooded area - taking advantage of a small patch of sunshine. Approaching like a shadow, she grinned, whispering in her native Oŭndo, "*Got you, little dog.*"

He didn't hear her, of course. As far as the world was concerned, she didn't exist right now. Coming up from behind, she hit him with a well-aimed strike to the head. The beast only stumbled - dazed - so she threw her fist again. This time, he crumpled. She watched his unconscious body hit the ground. *Next time I'll use a rock.*

"Let's have some fun, shall we?" She plopped down on his stomach and grabbed his head. *"Now…tell me about you."*

Reaching into his mind, she tore mercilessly through everything – hoping it hurt.

* * *

Ferdinan banished the pain from his face the moment Jon came into view.

"You're supposed to be in the assembly." Those words were weaker than expected and it hurt to breathe.

Pathetic.

Jon frowned. "I could say the same."

The slightest motion sent pain shooting through Ferdinan's body. "It's…a pointless assembly…and you know it."

"It makes everyone happy. Is that so pointless? Couldn't we all use some happiness right now?" Once Jon got closer, Ferdinan's bleeding nose and cut lip became apparent. A gash was oozing on his cheek. Alarmed, Jon shot forward. "What happened?"

Looking up, Ferdinan smiled at the lower branches. "I fell."

"From the tree? Why were you climbing a tree, you moron?"

"I wondered what it's like…" A cough forced its way out, nearly bringing Ferdinan to tears.

"I'm taking you to a Healer."

"No. You're not." It wasn't an argument; it was a firm statement of fact. *I'm so close to losing the voice. I'm so close to ending the pain. I'm so close – I won't let you ruin it!*

^^^

"That's not good enough!" he screamed at the screen.

"Ferdinan, I won't talk to someone who's yelling at me." Her voice was easily crosser than his, only it wasn't raised. "I've done everything I can. Sometimes a 'no' is a no. So, 'til I call and let you know otherwise, that's your answer."

"People are dying! Just because you don't know them - can't see them - doesn't make them any less real. Doesn't make them any less important! Or needed!"

VVV

It was hard saying what hurt worse - that memory or his body. "Take me to my lab."

"You need a bed -"

"My lab."

"Ferdinan-"

"I'm tired." The skeleton forced back the next cough, which was as painful as letting it come. But he deserved to suffer. It was the least he could do - the least he owed them.

◊

Unhappy and protesting, Jon acquiesced - half-carrying his ally the entire way. A storage closet stood at the back of Ferdinan's lab and was converted it into something short of a living area. The Dinta just eased the gent onto the stuffed sac when Ferdinan reached for a flat metallic disk. It was an invention the rest of the island and most of the world mocked. A bony finger activated the disk after placing it against his scrawny chest. A minute later the light flashed red a dozen times then green.

"What does the medical disk say?" Jon asked while the skeleton looked at the results. All he remembered was red meant bad. Just how much was wrong?

"It says I'm fine. You can leave and let me rest." A small smile tugged at Ferdinan's lips, sparking Jon to snatch it away before the skeleton could delete the results. "Give it back!"

"You're *not* fine."

"Stop grabbing things from me!" Ferdinan shook uncontrollably and was translucent. "You aren't five years old anymore."

"Then stop lying to me!"

"Your job is to be as annoying as you want about food. Not–" Coughs seized the gent, forcing tears out. At the end of his rope, Ferdinan tried one more time. "I'm asking you to give it back. Please respect my wishes."

A new hand grabbed the disk. This one golden-brown.

"Where did you come from?" Jon gasped at the sight of those wild green eyes. It looked like his ally had the same question. He hadn't heard the door open, but she managed getting into places she oughtn't at the hospital. Here was probably a piece of cake.

Words Jon couldn't hope to identify left her mouth.

Ferdinan nodded – gasping at the motion. More alien words came followed by Common. "Miss Oya, he helped me...find your language."

This was when something clicked. The ease with which those foreign sounds danced off Ferdinan's tongue was so natural, Jon hadn't noticed before now. "Wait! You can already speak it? It's only been two months!"

"Mind your own business...Jon," Ferdinan scolded weakly – batting away something near his ear.

Randomly messing with the buttons, Oya made a small screen appear on the back. She studied it intently before asking a question.

A pained gasp folded Ferdinan in half, but he managed a response. They continued back and forth until Oya removed a screen from her bag and handed it to Jon. She then said something and gave him a wink.

Looking down, Jon read, *"You can read as I talk."* The program looked amazing. "How long have you had this?"

"I created it...shortly after - *agh* - I found her language," Ferdinan admitted feebly.

"This'd be useful for her suitemates - and everyone else."

"*No,*" Oya interrupted. *"It's mine; I'll keep it 'til I'm ready to share."*

"What does that mean?"

Leaning her face in until her nose touched Jon's, she grinned and winked.

"Wait. She understands us?"

"As long...as we don't speak - *k-ka* - too quickly." Something Ferdinan wasn't in danger of doing at the moment.

"*Order and pronunciation is weird in Common.*" She looked at the disk, *"Go get something to clean his face."*

"What?"

"If you talk to anyone, I'll hurt you."

"Huh?" Jon never met anyone who made him this nervous, but that childish threat sent chills down his spine. Taking her words seriously, the Thinker left for the first aid kit kept in his lab two doors down. It didn't take long to retrieve it and start preparing a sterile cloth. Which she snatched from him.

"I've got it. You don't need to care for him."

Waving her hand dismissively, Oya set to work blotting Ferdinan's lip, moving on from there. When she was done, she let Jon patch the gash with "the goop" he'd readied for this purpose.

"*Ferdinan.*" She got both of their attention. *"The next time you fall out of a tree, I'm showing him the results."*

Horror filled Ferdinan's face. *"You can't…do that."*

"I can and I will. I won't watch a friend die from their own stubbornness."

Alarm filled every ounce of Jon as he looked between them and the screen.

"*Sleep.*" Oya covered Ferdinan's eyes and didn't remove her hand until his body relaxed and his breathing became shallow. *"Someone's waiting for you."*

"Someone's waiting?" What is she talking about?

A pier stretched over an endless purple ocean. Before Ferdinan sat an old man slumped in a folding chair. Rod in slacked hands and floppy hat pushed far enough forward to nap, the man looked like part of a painting. Was this the afterlife? But...a place like this didn't exist for a murderer like him. Footsteps echoed as he made his way to the older gentleman.

"Seems I've forgotten my fishing rod."

Reaching down, the man grabbed at thin air. A rod materialized in his hand and he offered it. Pushing back his hat revealed a much younger face than expected. There was something wrong with that face. It was as if... It was a little too perfect to be human. "Happens I have a spare. You're welcome to it. I'm afraid the fish aren't biting much."

"That's fine." Ferdinan took the rod and sat on the pier next to him.

"What's your name, son?" A friendly smile spread across the man's face.

"Ferdinan."

"Ferdinan, huh? It's nice to meet you."

"May I ask your name?"

"You may call me 'the Fisherman.'"

Ferdinan looked at him thoughtfully. "Thank you, Fisherman."

"My pleasure." The Fisherman stretched and leaned back in his chair. "What's a child doing here when he should be in school?"

Disappointment filled Ferdinan's answer. "I thought I'd be dead...but this feels more like a dream."

The man laughed. "I guess I'll disappear when you wake up."

"It'd be nicer if you woke up first."

"Ah. What makes you think this is a dream? What if we're both real and enjoying this beautiful sunset together?" the Fisherman asked.

"It's too beautiful to be real. My life isn't this lovely."

"Don't you think it should be?"

Ferdinan shrugged.

"Well then, what landed you in this predicament, Ferdinan?"

"Excuse me?"

"Bleeding internally while you make your friends watch you die?"

"I...I did some bad things," Ferdinan stated simply. *This is faster than starving to death at least.*

"Very bad?"

Ferdinan nodded.

"Evil?"

Putting down the rod, the skeleton sighed as he laid back on the pier. "Yeah."

"And you don't want to talk about it."

"No. I don't."

"That's fair." The Fisherman's smile softened. "Though, right now you've dreamed up an old man who's happy to listen and isn't going anywhere."

"One who's eager to ask questions."

This elicited another laugh. "Well, it's your choice. On one hand, I'm just an old fisherman you've dreamed up. But on the other hand, I'm just an old fisherman you've dreamed up."

Ferdinan struggled with that thought. *Am I carrying on a conversation with my unconscious?* "I'm dying now because I killed millions and hurt even more."

"Wow... Unexpected from someone so young."

"I'll die as punishment for the deaths I've caused. I don't deserve care when I denied the same for countless others."

Those words shocked the Fisherman into momentary silence. "That's quite a burden to carry."

Ferdinan placed his arms over his eyes – sealing in the tears fighting to come.

"Were you in a war?"

Ferdinan shook his head.

"Then why did you kill so many?"

"I didn't mean to," he gasped, voice high.

"You've been told it's not your fault?"

How much he hated those words was indescribable. Jon said that after every nightmare.

"That only makes it feel worse."

A sob escaped his throat as Ferdinan rolled to his side. Beating back what was clawing its way out took everything he had.

Sitting quietly, the Fisherman waited for the boy to regain control. "How about the ones you hurt, are those connected to the ones who died?"

"I've stolen so many families and friends. Even in the short time I've been back on the islands... Everyone's mourning... So many are sick."

"I see. How about your companions? Did they have a part in the deaths or injuries?"

"No." Ferdinan drowned in defeat as he scrunched into a ball.

"Then what was their crime?"

"They've done nothing wrong." Confusion filled his words.

"This is a harsh punishment for having done nothing wrong."

"What is?" Ferdinan rolled to lay on his back again.

"Being forced to let a friend die when you could easily save him. It's probably the cruelest punishment I know."

Those words sunk in deep, forcing despair to the surface. Again, he folded his arms over his face to seal everything inside. "Why did you have to say that?"

"If the cause of all of this is hurting people, I'll save you the responsibility of two more."

It was slipping through his fingers. This was all he had left to give. Ferdinan hadn't come close to atoning for what he'd done. Now, the little he could offer was snatched from him. *What more is expected of me? How many people will die because of me? How many will I hurt? How many lives will I destroy? I can't face all that... I don't want any more blood on my hands...*

...but...

She called me "friend." Can I punish an innocent person? What right do I have? Competing forces crushed him and neither could be satisfied.

"What do I have to do?"

The Fisherman reached down and poked Ferdinan's chest, only to have his hand immediately smacked away. "Did that hurt, son?"

"No," Ferdinan said as he rubbed the spot.

"I see." Getting off his chair, the Fisherman knelt beside the skeletal boy. "You have a rather nasty wound right there."

"I don't see anything."

"If you can't feel it, you won't be able to see it." The Fisherman hovered his open palm over the skeleton's chest. "It's festering and the infection's spreading."

Those words surprised Ferdinan, but disbelief shortly set in. This was a dream. "I don't feel anything."

"I can clean the wound for you."

"But not heal it?" Ferdinan asked, disinterested.

"No, this isn't something I can heal. But cleaning it will help things for a little while."

"This is a dream."

"Then what can it hurt?"

Lowering his arms and closing his eyes, Ferdinan answered with a shaky breath. “No. I deserve worse than this.”

Sighing, the Fisherman continued on, “You don’t deserve to feel this way.”

“Yes,” Ferdinan said bluntly, “I do.”

“Very well, son.” The man took Ferdinan’s hand and the sunset faded to black.

~

Pain tore through Ferdinan, escaping in a groan. Blood overwhelmed his tongue and turned his stomach. But the strange dream had ended. Everything was blurry - sights, sounds, smells - none of it made sense. Somehow, he identified the face floating in front of him. Then everything went dark.

Seems we get to dance a while longer.

Chapter 4

The remainder of Xhou's people abandoned their homes and migrated to East Azuté's capital city. Being a major port, however, aid would arrive there first. The Nuwa - his mother - requested the citizens gather there. They provided transportation. What was left of the military combed the lands, looking for stranded citizens. It was pitiful. But this was their first step toward recovery.

Tears dripped on the screen in his hands. Try as he might, Xhou couldn't stop them. All of this made him sick. Mass graves. Loss of family, wellbeing, and a way of life. His proud and noble people, in the course of a few months, became a nation of vagabonds. Corpses outnumbered the living. *Who'd do such a thing? Why? What could they possibly gain?*

Brushing his face dry, the older boy - nearly a man - went back to reading the report on the state of his country. The royal advisor detailed the projected issues in the coming months. *It'll be easier for everyone to leave. East Azuté will become as the Cradle of the World. All its glory and beauty gone. Empty. Desolate. Dead.* Even now. Thousands of years later...

The Cradle nursed humanity when they returned to the earth's surface - for generations. Whatever cursed that region...it still couldn't support life. Even birds avoided flying over as there was little to sustain them on their migrations. "How can I fix this?"

That thought ate at his insides. Running away wasn't an option for him. The remaining citizens were looking to their Nuwa - their queen and his mother - for what to do next. A year and he'd stand beside her in rebuilding their country. His baby sister was too young to do anything... That's all the family he had left. Just the two of them. His father, all seven of his older siblings...all gone.

"Papa." The screen fell from his shaking hands, allowing him to cradle his head. It was all Xhou could do to draw in a breath between the tears choking his words. "What do I do? I was never supposed to be Nu... Why did you leave this to me?"

For as passionate as his plea, silence was the answer.

Fighting to regain control, Xhou scowled at the chime echoing around the room. Drying his face and steadying his breath, he stood. There was more than his country to worry about. As Science Lead, all Thinkers and Tinkerers were under his care. One deep breath after another, he shook off the pain and put a smile on his face. Others were suffering. And there was another disaster looming over them. Luckily, his Idea Man was finally back – now to find the boy.

Considering dawn was still hours away, there was only one place that particular child would be. Disturbing someone at this hour wasn't polite... But sleep wasn't coming to Xhou, and the Idea Man was always awake.

* * *

Chewing on his lip, Jon waited. After Ferdinan coughed up a ton of blood and passed out, Oya threatened his life if he left the room. Then she sat statue-still for over a day. No one checked on them either. *Did everyone forget about me?* Yes, the Superintendent gave them the week to recuperate, but... *I haven't even seen my island brothers. Why's he such an inconvenience?*

An unladylike yawn startled him. Before his eyes, Oya returned to flesh - wiggling.

"You finally moved," he grabbed her screen.

On the hard, cold floor Oya yawned again and stretched every muscle from head to toe. *"So tired."*

"Tired? You sat there sleeping for twenty-eight hours." It scared him to no end.

"You've no idea. He's sleeping now. I should rest too."

That crazed look put Jon further on edge. Something about the glint always shining in her eyes felt off. No. It felt *wrong*. Thinking this way, feeling this way, about a girl made the Thinker upset with himself. He knew better. Girls deserved respect. They should be looked upon for the miracles they are. The miracles they possess. But...that craze was always there. It felt...inhuman... No. That wasn't right. How did it feel? Were there words? All Jon knew was seeing it always sent a shiver up his spine. "Excuse me?"

He never got an answer – only a smirk as she vanished.

Am I hallucinating? No...she did that at the hospital too. There wasn't a tiny part of this he liked.

Pacing the room, Jon noticed Ferdinan's best known invention – the medical disk. Results from the first scan were erased before he could see them. But the Tinkerer was sleeping, and Oya wasn't here to stop him. Now was the time. Placing the disk on his ally's chest, Jon commenced the scan.

When finished, it blinked red once, then yellow, then green. *Yellow?* Jon examined the results. There was nothing wrong with Ferdinan – ignoring the warning about the skeleton's dangerously low weight. Yellow advised of one problem requiring personal care, but not medical attention. Anemia, it flashed, along with a list of symptoms and suggestions to correct the problem.

"How is this right?"

Confused, Jon wandered out of the closet and into the main lab. *I saw the light flash red a dozen times. A day of sleep doesn't fix that. Is the disk broken?* No. Ferdinan was meticulous when building his devices. *But...he didn't have time to reprogram it...*

Dismissing this oddity would be easier if Ferdinan wasn't also looking better. It'd take gaining forty pounds for the gent to pass as human. But color was back in his cheeks. No pain marred the skeleton's face and he was breathing easily. *It's not possible. Recovering from being that sick without help... Is Oya a Healer? But she didn't touch him...*

For a Thinker, things not making sense was the ultimate annoyance. It didn't matter if reality was convoluted; the more complex the better – as long as an answer could be found. But this? It made as much sense as Oya's vanishing act.

A chime drew his attention to the door. Through the window above the handle, Xhou Zi's blue-black eyes widened in surprise. Jon was caught. *What's Xhou doing here?* Only two people had labs in this building, him and Ferdinan. The Science Lead had no reason to be here...unless the Zi needed something. That was the only reason anyone put up with Ferdinan. Except for Jon – who's family pressured him into "befriending" the gent. Or when political duties forced them to cooperate.

"Why weren't you at the meeting? And why're you in here? Better yet, where's my Idea Man?"

Centering himself, Jon stepped out so the older gent couldn't come in. "I'm taking care of him. He's not well."

"Ferdinan's never well," Xhou sighed dramatically, running fingers through his coarse black hair. "Let me guess, he insisted he needed to keep working and sent you to get some things?"

Jon forced a smile, grateful the Zi's guess kept him from having to lie. "You know Ferdinan."

"Still, no excuse for you skipping out. Don't you understand the emergency we're facing?"

"Huh?"

Xhou rolled his eyes. "The assembly? Our assignment?"

"Oh. Sorry, I missed the results – Ferdinan," Jon shrugged, letting Xhou fill in the rest.

"What's wrong with him this time?"

"You know it's always his stomach." Why was lying coming so easily? It never had before.

Patting the younger boy's back, Xhou smiled – worried. "Jon, I know you've more than enough stress, but Ferdinan's been sick a *lot* this year. Not that he's ever been particularly healthy, but he's gotten pretty bad. I'm concerned."

"Don't." Swallowing hard, Jon covered his curt response. "He doesn't like being worried over. It'll make him sicker. I'll give him your message and make sure he reports to you when he's better."

"I think I should see him. Don't want him dying on me," Xhou countered.

"He's exhausted."

"And yet you're here?"

"No choice."

Shaking his head, Xhou frowned. "Listen, Jon, we got assigned the Welcome Show again."

"What?" Jon groaned. That was another annoyance he'd love being rid of. "That's the fourth time since I've been here."

"I think you're a jinx. Before you arrived, Sciences hadn't gotten it in nearly two decades."

"I hate that thing. Why does it have to be random? Once every six years is better than four in ten."

"I know!" With Xhou's usual flourish, the older boy waved a hand before dramatically dropping it to his side. "Sick or not, I need to see him. He won't have to move and he's always looking for things to do, even when he shouldn't."

"Xhou." This boy was nearly as stubborn as his ally. "I need to get him to eat first. Come back after lunch."

"You mean after breakfast."

"No." Setting his jaw, Jon held his ground. "After lunch. What're you doing here now anyway?"

"Couldn't sleep. He never sleeps, so I jumped the gate blocking the bridge."

"You're as bad as *he* is! Did he learn those tricks from you?" When it came to sneaking about after curfew, Ferdinan was a pro.

"No, but I picked up a few from him."

"Go get ready for class." Jon turned back to the door. Now to find an iron rich recipe for a picky eater.

"What about you?"

"Xhou, I'm tired and my day hasn't begun. Please don't be nosy, 'cause I can't promise I'll be nice."

* * *

Alien green eyes stared at the diamond sky – searching for something she'd yet to find. But Oya couldn't waste much time. There were more important things to take care of. Delicate lips kissed the rectangular, steel locket she always wore and slipped it back under her shirt. Her other hand held something different.

Something only she could see.

A wicked grin took in the sight of a silver thread. It was quite similar to a spider's web. But she knew better. This was her link to that woman. The one with silver streaked black hair. Taking a moment, Oya wrapped the thread around her palm, strengthening her hold on the connection. She wasn't sure how, but she needed time to seek out everything connected to that woman. But for now, something else was just as important.

Winking to the glowing orbs in her peripheral, Oya climbed.

There was a dog in need of training.

Security was negligently low on these islands. Getting into buildings took little effort. Since it suited her purposes Oya wasn't going to complain, but it was good knowing not to leave anything of value out of her sight. Luckily, she owned very little.

Full of energy, she readied the little "gift" she'd prepared.

Scaling the building's walls was easy enough. There were plenty of foot holds, especially at the corners. Discovering his room didn't take long. The connection between him and her friend was one of the few Ferdinan had, making it easy to follow. The idea of protecting slime like the boy in front of her wasn't something she could fathom. Whatever was going on between her friend and this mongrel was going to end. She'd make sure of it.

Vengefully grinning at the golden boy's unconscious body, Oya inched forward. She'd show this dog fear and return the pain he caused. Reaching out, she grabbed his forehead. Luckily, language didn't matter in dreams - not for a master like her.

Let's have some fun, shall we?

~

Blinding purple light appeared - filling the void, trapping him. Laughter rang out. But Zephyr couldn't see anyone - she made sure of it. The Prince tapped his jaw and pointed. "Who's there?"

A dark blur circled him. This shadow was his one recurring nightmare. He never saw it - making it perfect for her purposes. When his heart raced, she delved in - intensifying every ounce of anxiety and uncertainty. *How much fear can you take?*

"I'll catch you and kill you!" Zephyr threatened defensively, shaking hands moving with his mouth.

Laughter rang out as blood rained down. Before his eyes lay his cousin's body, completely lifeless. The accusation of murder echoed in his mind - certain and unwavering - demanding justice and congratulating him on a task well done. Seeing his blood-soaked hands froze them in place and sent his heart into overdrive. "I've killed no one! My hands are clean!"

Fire red eyes glowed from the shadow - pure joy reflected therein. Unseen fingers snapped and a perfect double of Zephyr appeared. On the copy's face was the pure anger and hatred the dog had while beating her friend.

"What is this?!" Zephyr screamed - flinging his hands back.

Moving closer, she forced him to gaze into the nothingness those two specks of fire danced in. *Come my pet; lesson number one.* She signaled the doppelganger to replay the attack perfectly while fear chained Zephyr in place. Each blow returned the pain she removed from her friend. Punch to the face, in seeped a little. Kick to the shin, a little more. Uppercut to the gut, more.

More and more she released as each strike increased in violence. Doing what was necessary, she watched dispassionately. The emotionless portrait she presented wasn't perfect. With each blow, her eyes glowed a little more, satisfaction filling them. Not only was she returning the pain, but giving him fear - magnifying them both. If she could see her own eyes, she would've admitted how evil they appeared, gratified by another's suffering.

Cower dog and know I'm "Master" here.

The final blow landed him on his side. With it she released the last bit of pain, and filled his belly and mouth with blood.

Red soured his stomach. Heaving gave no relief as more filled him. He'd die if he stayed like this. He'd die without help.

~

Oya anchored the nightmare near the surface of his mind. Controlling his dream was too easy. Picturing it as a film in a continuous loop, she held it in place. It'd play whenever he closed his eyes. Purely for her own pleasure, she intensified the fear and pain. Even if the trash did fall asleep, it wouldn't last long.

Locking it in, she sat back - a Cheshire grin on her face.

Fully energized, she gave up on the idea of resting. There was a request to make of Jon and it was far more important than the garbage she was leaving here.

* * *

"Come on."

Jon's voice jolted him awake. Knocking the boy away, Ferdinan scooted back as far as he could. "Huh?"

"Time to wake up," Jon frowned. "Here."

You're a ray of sunshine.

To Ferdinan's surprise, Jon held out a screen with a waiting call. "I'd rather choke down your food than talk to your family."

"She's your family too. She claimed you before she accepted us." Jon pressed the device against his ally's chest, ignoring the rude comment. "Take it. Don't keep her waiting."

"She...?" Enlightenment brightened his eyes. Taking the screen, Ferdinan turned red when Jon smiled smugly.

"Consider this your birthday present, as belated as it may be."

"Birthday?" *When did that happen?*

Why would anyone celebrate your life?

Why would anyone want someone like me to exist? "You know my culture doesn't celebrate those."

"Ya, but mine does." Disappointment turned down the corners of Jon's mouth. "Talk to her while I get lunch ready."

"Stop doing this every year. It's annoying."

"You only turn fifteen once. Now, just 'cause it took me over a month to get it to you, doesn't mean you should take that long accepting it. The Oza's waiting."

It was nearly two months ago, wasn't it?

How many had you killed by then?

^^^

Cold sweat coated his skin. His insides twisted hard. Frantically, he fought to get the readings back. But nothing...

She was gone.

No.

No... She can't be gone. She was here a moment ago! She can't be gone!!

"Come back!" he yelled at the screen, legs weakening, and hands pounding on the table. "COME BACK!!!"

Rage suffocated him. The sound of shattering porcelain stung the air. Knees buckled. He melted to the floor, ears ringing.

Everything stopped existing.

How did he make the world start again?

"People are dying," he told himself in a voice as cold and hard as the one he used with Jon. "Mourn on your own time."

VVV

His throat tightened. *I failed her irrevocably that day.*

There's no fixing your mistakes for her.

"You can eat when you're finished." Concerned, Jon reached in and tapped on the flashing icon. Evelyn's face filled the screen. She was wearing a silly hat and a blanket tied as a cape.

Loose, black curls encircled that adorable face, making the small ring of green on the outside of her black irises all but glow. Saucer sized eyes shone with joy and pure innocence. Those eyes were exactly like her grandmother's. "Big Brother! Happy birthday!"

Chapter 5

"He's going to find you here." Jon handed Ferdinan a mug of iron rich soup.

"It doesn't matter... Persistent people always get what they want...eventually." Though Ferdinan took the soup, it was all he could do not to gag.

Trying to ignore the rather pungent scent, the skeleton considered what he'd learned of the families of the students from Azuté. The only reason Xhou had anyone left was because his mom and youngest sister were traveling at the time.

And Xhou was one of the lucky ones.

Here you could've killed two more.

I'm horrible... How can I think that's lucky? The least he could do was face all of them, but... *I can't let them know it was me...I'd hurt them again.*

Sitting in the shade of a tree, the two boys enjoyed silence until Ferdinan couldn't hold back anymore. "Who came? Healer Ilu?"

"What're you talking about?"

"I know you called a Healer."

"No, I didn't." Jon leaned back hard against the tree. "Miss Oya wouldn't let me leave the room. Besides, you're doing well enough...I guess you didn't need one."

"I know she didn't call one, she doesn't know how."

"She didn't leave your side for more than a day." Jon's face scrunched for a moment. "And I didn't tell anyone."

"What did she do?" *Is she a Healer? But...how does she disappear and reappear at will?*

"She sat on the floor with her eyes closed the entire time. Don't ask me why."

"Then...she didn't touch me?"

"No. She didn't move at all. It was creepy. Sat there like a statue – never even flinched," Jon shivered.

That's...not possible...

You're right. Why would anyone want to save you?

"Have you considered it?" Jon changed topics, "You know that's the first thing Xhou'll ask."

"What? The show? It isn't my responsibility, he's the Science Lead. It won't affect me much."

"What're you talking about? Of course, it will. You remember how awful it was the last two times. Do you really want to suffer through that again?" Jon pointed at the soup as a hint to start eating.

Ignoring the gesture, Ferdinan mumbled, "I'm already the school joke. It's everyone else who has something to lose."

"You aren't a joke," Jon wavered dishonestly. "Looks like he's here."

No. He wasn't ready to face that child.

How badly have you hurt him?

"There you are! I've been looking everywhere for you. Did you leave the face of the earth?" Xhou exclaimed, sliding to a halt where the two of them sat, and giving a winning smile.

"Maybe. Does it matter?" *He's as energetic as always...* Ferdinan hid his eyes and guilt behind shaggy hair. That grin…Xhou's uncle Yewaru smiled just like that every time they talked – it didn't matter how much he hurt. Until the end…

^^^

Alarms wailed, beating against his ears. Ever so slowly the man's pain-wracked body eased… Just like that, Ferdinan failed again.

VVV

The skeleton's heart twisted at the memory. *Stop! I'm not the one hurting!*

You destroyed all those people, don't pretend to feel sorrow now.

"I need to talk to my Idea Man about the show."

"I'm sorry, Xhou Zi, I'm not up for nonsense today."

"This isn't nonsense! It's important." Xhou folded his arms, pouting like a little child. "I'm surprised at you."

"What for this time?" Not only was the Lead behaving like a spoiled fool, but Ferdinan couldn't see any sign of distress about him. *Is he actually ok?*

"Acting like you don't care about Family Week. This is the crowning event of the year! It's a time to show our families what we can do! What we're made of. We can't disappoint everyone like last time. *Ugh!* What a disaster. I'm embarrassed thinking about it." Xhou covered his face dramatically with a hand.

"I *honestly* don't care." *Talking about family didn't trip him up…*

"Well I do. And so do the rest of us." He scratched his head. "My little sister's coming for this one. It'll be the only time she'll see the islands. I bet she's grown a foot since I saw her last."

Peeking through his hair, Ferdinan watched Xhou's blue-black eyes glisten at the thought. More guilt beat into the Tinkerer - sorrow shown through the Lead's mask. *I hurt him...*

You stole everything from him.

"If your point's a guilt trip, you're failing."

"Yah, I guess it'd sound like that. I want to show her how amazing we can be."

The soup cooling in his hands suddenly had Ferdinan's full attention. Xhou loved his little sister more than life itself. *I'm glad she's safe at least.* "I haven't thought about it."

Crestfallen, Xhou worked to scrape himself off the ground.

"But I'll consider it this evening. You could come up with something on your own."

"I've been trying! But the only one of us with any proficiency to perform is Jon. And no one's going to listen to a two hour solo piano act."

Guilt ridden or not, Ferdinan couldn't help but roll his eyes. "That's not what I meant. It's *ok* to think about things which haven't been done. We don't have to replicate others."

"Like what, Idea Lord?"

"Well...what kind of entertainment do you enjoy? What things do you look for to fill your time?"

Xhou considered this for a moment. "I don't much care for sitting through long performances. Don't get me wrong, the skill and precision I appreciate. It's really the only thing I admire. But everything's been done to death. What's so entertaining about watching something when you know what's going to happen?"

"Then what would you like to happen?" Ferdinan asked. *Why am I the one making a Thinker think?*

"I don't know. It'd be nice to see something new. But how does that help us?" Xhou glanced at Jon for support.

A deep sigh left Ferdinan. *Is the concept of unconfined thinking so foreign?*

High and mighty, aren't we?

"Talk to me tomorrow."

"But...we haven't..."

"I said I'd consider it this evening. I'm busy at the moment."

Xhou shot him a critical look. "Busy with what?"

Ugh... The too full mug was still making him gag. "Trying to fulfill a different, unreasonable demand."

"What?"

"Lunch. He hasn't done more than look at it," Jon chimed in.

"You can eat while we brainstorm. I won't find it rude," Xhou offered – obviously curious.

Ferdinan paled to a rather sickly alien color. Eating in public wasn't something he made a habit of. *How do I get out of this and make Jon leave me alone...?* "I want to go to my room."

"Not your lab?" Jon asked confused.

Slowly, pitifully, Ferdinan shook his head.

Liar.

That was all Jon needed. Shooing Xhou away, he and Ferdinan walked to the boats. No arguments were made, no conversation was had, while they traveled to the dorms.

Ferdinan waved Jon off at the third floor and continued up. Only, he didn't stop on the fourth. The last place he wanted to be was his suite. What right did he have to annoy his suitemates? So, he continued to the roof – waiting for the dead of night and an easy escape.

* * *

Finally! After a lifetime, Jon was about to reunite with his island brothers. A smile spread across his lips and his eyes teared up. He'd waited months. How much he missed his island family was second only to how much he missed his real one. Being in their presence, soaking up their energy and joy – this was what he needed. No more fighting and nightmares and stress. He wanted home, love, and silliness more than anything else.

Opening the door, he spread his arms wide and called out. "Gents! I'm back!"

The response from the two in the common room was underwhelming to say the least.

Why did it feel so sullen? It was only slightly lighter than his time with Ferdinan. *After everything I went through, I need their joy.* Pain contorted his face. Tuel flew overhead while Gongie jumped up and dashed over.

"Jon!" Gongie exclaimed as he hugged his sorely missed suitemate. "You're finally back. What's wrong?"

These gents aren't Ferdinan, it's fine to feel. Jon found himself breathing hard as tears stung sharply. Reaching up, he grabbed the flying Energist, Tuel, and smothered both suitemates in a painfully tight hug. "I've missed you so much! Where's everyone?"

"Ilu's with his dad and Marcus is at his session," the tiny, floating shadow answered somberly.

"Session?" Jon released them. Even if the two looked stressed, seeing thier faces brought more relief than he realized. There was always kindness and understanding in Gongie's eyes and not just because the gent was a Telepath. Whenever Tuel –

the afternoon shadow with snow white hair – came flying, he knew the five of them were going to have fun.

"Counseling sessions are mandatory for everyone from Azuté."

Surprise. Then the guilt and remorse hit. *With all that happened, I forgot everyone here. How could I forget about Marcus?*

"'All that happened?'" Gongie repeated Jon's thought. "What's happened?"

"I..." Panting, Jon wiped away his tears and cleared his mind. "I can't. I'm sorry."

Looking down worried his suitemates. It was a gesture he never made before leaving for South Chūzo. All Jon wanted was a hug and to talk, but he wasn't allowed – the Superintendent made that perfectly clear. Without hesitation, Tuel and Gongie wrapped their arms around him, obviously wondering what happened to change their island brother. Jon squeezed harder and didn't let go until the door opened.

Looking back, he saw Marcus walk in. Knives stabbed deep in his chest. Marcus was disheveled. And had lost weight. The gent's eyes were still red on the edges. Pushing away from Tuel and Gongie, the Thinker ran over and hugged the gent as tight as he had the other two.

"I'm so sorry, Marcus. I'm so sorry..." This only stirred painful memories for both of them, but Jon couldn't think of anything else. "I'm sorry I wasn't here. I'm sorry..." *We weren't fast enough for you.*

Gongie turned confused eyes on Jon as that thought floated through his mind.

* * *

A quarter moon and a trillion stars filled the surrounding black. *Fifteen millennia of human history... Why did it happen now? Why was I the one? Why did they ask me?* Standing, Ferdinan looked out over the coal sea, shoes pressed hard against the parapet wall. *Of all the people she could've asked, why me...?*

The least competent of them all.

Leaning forward, the roof's lip cut deep into his abdomen. If he went any farther, he'd be on the ground five stories below. Complaining muscles couldn't outdo his twisting heart. Hands on top of the parapet, Ferdinan took in the view below. His heart quickened.

Not from fear.

Anticipation. Excitement. Hope.

These sensations should've scared him - sent him running.

Feeling like this was wrong. Thinking these thoughts... Imagining the ground meeting him... Wanting it all to end... It was wrong. Bad. Not allowed. *I'm a horrible person. I have no right to live when I killed so many.*

What right have you to peace?

Dizziness hit, causing him to stagger. What right did he have to peace? To rest or relief? Backing away from the edge, Ferdinan focused on deeply burying his horrible desire, hoping it'd disappear. *Alone. I need to be alone.*

Aren't you always? Who'd want to be around you?

No one was nearby, but this wasn't a place for solitude. Haunted by the pain and sorrow of those he failed, Ferdinan headed to the boats. To be alone, to get away, there was only one place - only one thing offering any form of relief.

Something cold and eerie ran up his spine, forcing him to look around. As far as he could tell, no one else was about. Was he being watched? Hesitating, he strained his ears and eyes, searching for any sign of life. The feeling wouldn't go away. But neither could he find anything to substantiate the warning. *Should I go back?*

Someone knows you can't be trusted.

Wringing his hands, he chewed on his lip, trying to decide. *I can't stay here... I can't.*

The stress, the nightmares, the guilt. He needed some kind of respite. Need outweighing paranoia, Ferdinan stole a boat and pushed off.

* * *

Inhuman green eyes watched from the shadows as Ferdinan rowed out to sea. Oya knew why she was out roaming her new playground. But her friend was exhausted. So, why was he?

She wasn't the only one playing spy either. There was a presence that'd been following her since they left the hospital. Not the orbs, those were different. And not the same presence that got her to the hospital, but a new one. Whoever it was... Could "Whoever" keep up with her? One way or another, she owed "Whoever" thanks for helping with her friend.

Once Ferdinan glided away, she moved. Bare feet took one step after another into the ocean - deep into Û-ya'īn.

Waves reared up and seized her. Pushing her back. Pulling her to the bottom. Her heart froze inside her chest - but not from fear. *What is this feeling?* She tried moving, but her very soul refused. Death didn't scare her, but now wasn't the time. There was someone to build and many to protect. A promise was made she must uphold. Oya struggled and fought until Û-ya'īn understood. *I'm sorry, old friend. I know what I am, but I can't let you take me yet.*

Warmth filled her and a compromise was offered – a final gift from Û-ya'īn, her oldest friend.

Oya broke through the surface. An infinity of stars filled her view. They always intrigued her, but... Shaking her head, she forced herself back to her purpose. Negotiations between her and her oldest friend took too long; the boat was out of sight. A grin and laugh burst from her. It didn't matter how far away he was, those strings were always there. Yes, Ferdinan only had a few connections, and they were dim and muted gray, but they shot out over the water – a perfect trail.

Diving beneath the waves, she took off. Like a dolphin she flew through the water, coming up only when her lungs screamed for air. The swim was long. And the distance, exciting! When the strings finally brought her to land, her muscles were numb. The little boat was high up the beach and Ferdinan was nowhere to be seen.

This didn't discourage her. She only smirked and followed his strings inland.

* * *

Feet flew across the worn path. With each step, his muscles eased until their complaints ceased altogether. Afraid to stop, Ferdinan pushed on until there was nothing left in him to overcome. Nothing dragging him back.

ΛΛΛ

Breathing deeply, shaking from head to toe, his mind raced. All the numbers ran around his head, telling him if Grandmother could still be saved.

That unforgivable delay....

But if the agent was quick...

The biohazard room offered one solace – it was a one-man room. He was alone. No one could see him do anything.

"Why?" His insides were tearing themselves apart. Heart racing, he stood panting – looking for some acceptable way of venting his pent-up frustration. Running...no. Breaking something was rude and childish – and counterproductive to his goals. Even inside this isolated chamber, screaming would be heard this time of day. The only thing the room offered was solitude.

"I hate this!" he breathed sharply through clenched teeth. "Ugh!"

Squatting, Ferdinan found one thing he could safely attack. With everything he had, he pounded boney fists into stick legs.

VVV

The world spun and jumped and tilted around him, causing him to stagger. He skidded across the ground – panting and retching. This might've not been the best choice... But running was the only peace available. So, he ran until he had nothing left.

Pathetic.

"Gü-dé ev-ening," came out of nowhere. Soon impossible green eyes hovered above an odd grin – a Cheshire grin.

Startled, Ferdinan winced. Once his stone mask was in place, he forced himself to sit up and made his voice steady. "Good evening, Miss Oya. Seems you've caught me."

"Et sem would so."

"It would seem so, indeed," he grinned. Sentence structure was proving itself a challenging barrier for her.

Unsurprisingly, she switched to her native tongue. *"Call me 'Oya,' not 'Miss.'"*

"*My apologies. I was being respectful. Titles are normal here.*" Taking the opportunity, Ferdinan pulled his green tin out.

What does a murderer know of respect?

Mint filled his mouth and throat - calming his stomach. *Why is she here? Luyou Zah teaches languages...and is better at it. I'm a lousy teacher...* His mind stopped cold. How long had he been back and he hadn't contacted his apprentice? He really was a lousy teacher. After they finished, he'd message Elbie and set up their next lesson. But Oya... *There's nothing better I can offer her. So...why is she wasting her time with me?* Elbie didn't have a choice. Ferdinan was the only Tinkerer old enough to mentor. Even apprenticing Yuyu for two years... He was a lousy teacher to her too. How much further ahead would both young Tinkerers be if they had a decent mentor?

Oya waved a hand to draw his attention. *"I'd rather you show me a close friendship than a distant respect."*

Huh? He'd never thought of that. *"Here I'm referred to as 'Lord Ferdinan.' I promise I'll always call you 'Oya' if you never call me 'Lord.'"*

Happiness danced in her exotic green eyes. *"That's a promise I can keep. Do you run often?"*

"*I'm not supposed to.*" Sunken cheeks pinkened. Being caught was shameful.

"That's why you run at odd hours? I saw you at the hospital."

Face burning, he hid behind his overgrown, shaggy hair. *"I'm not supposed to run – but it's a hard craving to ignore."*

You can't follow a simple rule like that? How selfish are you?

Fascination danced on those shapely lips. *"Why not replace it with something else?"*

An unsteady laugh escaped him. *"Running's the compromise to what I actually want to do."*

"I see. Then what do you want to do?"

"It's forbidden."

"*That bad, huh?*" she smirked, turning crazed eyes to the night sky – as if searching for something up there.

Ferdinan blushed deeper. No one would understand and explaining wasn't an option. *"No. It'd be bad for my family."*

"Must be hard being rich and powerful."

"Huh? You aren't the daughter of a king or grand duke? I only called you 'Miss' because I didn't know your title."

Mad laughter spilled out of her making her eyes all but glow with their usual wild craze. *"I've no such lineage."*

"*Oh?*" Ferdinan thought, *"But…you must be connected to someone of importance. Everyone at this school is. After two thousand years, everyone with abilities made their way to power."*

"Interesting."

Not sure where to go with that, he changed directions. *"Are you here to work on your Common?"*

"But of course!"

Despite the heat from his face dissipating, his cheeks warmed again. *Maybe she doesn't realize I'm not needed anymore.* Something cold sat heavily in the center of his chest. *"You know, Luyou Zah is trained to teach languages. She's a better choice."*

"The girl they gave me to here? You know about her?"

"*It was easy information to find.*" And he had plenty of time on his hands during their travels back to the islands.

"Why would I want someone else? You're amazing."

What's amazing about you?

His face lit on fire. *I don't understand... Why? No one comes to me unless they need something only I can do. And...the Zah is better for everything she needs...*

"Is Luyou her title or Zah? Those words are cumbersome together."

"What? Oh, 'Zah' is her title."

"What kind of title is it?"

"It means 'princess.'"

"Ah. She likes being called 'princess.'"

"I don't know. It's just… We'll be required to use titles properly our entire lives. Aside from family and those who spend excessive time together, it's rude not to address others properly."

"Then you're close to Jon? I haven't heard you use his title."

Ferdinan chuckled. *"No. We've been stuck with each other since I was born. It probably won't end 'til one of us dies."*

'Til you kill him.

"Then he's older than you?"

"By half a year. No more stalling. If you want help with Common, we'll speak Common."

"Fine! How do you say 'meanie head' in Common?"

An exhausted chuckle escaped Ferdinan when she crossed her arms, pouting.

◊

As Oya stumbled over foreign words, she grabbed the thin gray-blue string connecting Ferdinan and Jon. With it she eased her friend to sleep. Where his heart should be was a gaping wound - weeping and bleeding. In the short time she'd known him, the infection had thrived - consuming his entire chest. *How much pain does this cause your soul? How much agony are you in, dear friend?* The clouds darkening his mind were nearly black and cracks were forming. *How do I fix this?* Taking the gray-blue string, she brushed back his hair and delved into their minds.

Ferdinan and Jon were an interesting pair, and their relationship was odd. Whether they knew it or not they'd been competing for some time. Competing out of envy of the other. The younger one's talents far exceeded the older. This left Jon fighting constantly to keep up, but always falling behind.

Ferdinan's reason was buried much deeper.

The complexities of his brain were quite the challenge to navigate after rooting round Jon's head. There was no doubt at the older boy's intelligence, but it was perfectly organized. Playing in Jon's mind was like roaming the aisles of an endless library.

Ferdinan's, however, was a galactic theme park. It was so active - so beautiful. Ideas floated around as dreams awaiting life. Each idea twinkled around her, brighter - more brilliant - than the stars in the heavens, and just as numerous.

As she roamed, pathways became available for them to travel quickly and efficiently from one place to another. Those stars met up and danced before splitting and finding other partners.

Except for one pair.

They came together and all but seemed to talk - deciding on a proper course. A light so exceedingly bright it put the other thoughts to shame exploded from the pair. Then it dimmed. The two were replaced with something rather interesting.

An assembly of gears turned in rhythm, slowly growing in complexity as more parts and pieces joined. By the time it soared toward its next destination, it'd become as amazing and beautiful as the insides of an ancient gear clock.

This is how his mind works? No wonder he comes up with such magnificent inventions!

Continuing on, Oya searched until she noticed a shadowed corner. *What's this?*

Each step closer was met with resistance. Clearing one obstacle triggered another. This was a forbidden place. One he tried forgetting. One he wouldn't let himself see. And one he didn't want others finding. She stopped her last step as the ground vanished. *You really don't want anyone here.* Placing her own stepping stone, Oya reached the hidden door with no handle. There'd been one once... *What don't you want to think about?*

She pictured a knob, grasped it, and turned. Inside sat a ragged little boy looking longingly as Jon and a group of giants played and hugged – being far more loving and affectionate than any family she'd ever seen. The happy display continued, then came another. And another after that. With each memory Jon and the giants got a little older, as did the Ferdinan beside her.

I see.

Walking forward, she hugged the Ferdinan who couldn't be more than seven. That little face was already showing signs of malnutrition and a pain that'd eat away at him until he became the boy currently sleeping beside her.

Tears filled the young child's eyes – but they didn't fall.

Chapter 6

Giving his reflection a smile, Jon adjusted his blue silk shirt and left. Last night was rough, but cathartic. It didn't help Marcus figure out what to do. His island brother's entire province was gone. What fifteen-year-old had a plan B for that? Marcus was supposed to be ambassador to one of their allies, then marry. As a younger son, the gent was looking at a rather ideal life. But now...

Did Marcus rebuild the province with a new set of people? Or was walking away from nothing and finding a new life elsewhere a better choice? As much as Jon wanted to worry over this, he had duties to tend to.

The twelfth-year suite was one floor up. And yet...

He'd promised to help his ally put on weight – promised to take charge of the gent's diet and all that entailed. But the attitude Ferdinan displayed toward his food for those months in South Chūzo...he couldn't handle it.

No. It was simpler than that. He couldn't handle the skeleton. *Why did I agree to this?* Ferdinan looked so pitiful...and he'd never live it down if his family learned he'd refused to help the gent. Besides, Jon couldn't remember the Tinkerer asking for help before.

Allowing a sigh to escape his lips, Jon activated the chime announcing his presence. The wait was longer than expected. Of the three residents, two were early risers. Though it was more likely Ferdinan hadn't slept. The Thinker was about to trigger the chime again when the door opened.

A beautiful, golden face emerged. Knowing the Prince, Zephyr finished a morning training session and was in the middle of preparing for class. For some reason his older ally looked confused...and tired.

Stepping into the shadows didn't take the gold from Zephyr's rich skin. It was as if every cell knew he was a Prince. A tiny prince... It was awkward having someone three years older look up at him.

"Jon? Can I help you?" While Zephyr talked, he tapped his heart and spread his hand out.

Does he not know? "I'm here for Ferdinan."

At the mention of his cousin's name, Zephyr's face darkened - hands clenched into fists. "He's not here."

"He walked up here shortly after classes let out." *How did he not make it up one flight of stairs?* "Could you two have missed him coming in?"

"The girls were over for an unofficial game night and didn't leave 'til curfew. It's unlikely he snuck past all of us." Opening the door wider, Zephyr invited Jon in. "Feel free to check."

"Thanks." With a bow, Jon headed to Ferdinan's room. It was empty - as promised.

Zephyr folded his arms to stifle a flinch and grimace. "I apologize for the inconvenience my little cousin caused you. These rude things are a bad habit of his. I'll tell him you're looking for him."

Why's he already causing trouble? Can't he pretend for a day? "I wasn't here to talk, so don't worry about it."

Starting at his cheek, one hand moved a pointed finger in an arch - stopping to point at Jon. "You weren't?"

With a sigh, the Thinker met Zephyr's onyx eyes. Even for an Athlete the Prince was tiny. Ferdinan and Zephyr might be cousins, but the two couldn't be more different. It was Jon and

Ferdinan who looked insufferably similar - something that annoyed them both. "Believe it or not, I was tasked with feeding him."

One eye twitched as disbelief took over the Prince's small body. Golden hands danced. "Did I hear you correctly?"

"Ya...it's a long story."

* * *

Golden-brown bare feet roamed the islands, getting to know them. This paradise was more sparsely populated than Oya expected. But those who were here weren't like any humans she'd seen. Watching them was fascinating. Not everything they did was unheard of. Many people were unexpectedly adept at normal things. There was an island devoted to art - the pieces blew her mind.

Another island was given to music. Oya loved this place. Never before did music feel like a living, breathing entity. This was the first "appropriate" music she'd ever enjoyed. The sounds it embodied moved her heart, both in joy and sorrow.

A couple islands were reserved for extreme physical training. The children using those were faster and stronger than humanly possible - even under extreme stress. But they moved thusly with seemingly little effort. *Guess I'm not the only special one.*

The most interesting island of all was a small one dotted with a dozen buildings. Children did the most fascinating things there. Though not great at science, it still intrigued her. She'd soon become acquainted with this island's resources.

There were other children who didn't belong to one specific island. They wandered and used various facilities for superhuman feats. Manipulating energy to their will was captivating to see. Lifting and moving boulders and trees - and other students. Assembling things without using their hands! That left her envious. They even held back waves from the shore and disrupted the electrical grid. However, her absolute favorite was watching them fly. *I bet my friend can help me to do that!*

Another interesting group was called "Healers." Watching them force living bodies to heal... The man who found her could do this - so could the Healer who traveled to the islands with them. But those were the first two she'd met who could.

There was another reason for staking out the Healers. Among them was a boy named "Ilu" who was supposed to classify her. According to Ferdinan at least. As this wasn't a choice she was given, she couldn't refuse. But the child couldn't classify her if he never saw her. A wicked grin stretched her lips.

The last group, however... They weren't strong or fast. Neither did they show great proficiency in arts or science. They couldn't manipulate energies or life forces either. It wasn't until she "examined" one that she realized their minds were open. They could hear or read the thoughts and feelings of those around them. Most were forced to experience this constantly, but a few had the ability to choose to listen. This made her giggle. "*How very ancient* **sci-fi**."

This place was fascinating.

Yes, she'd have fun here.

* * *

Waking up... *When did I fall asleep?* Ferdinan didn't recall feeling tired. Neither was Oya there. This was fair. Who'd want to watch someone sleep? *Why do I feel...?* What was this? Disappointment? Maybe?

You are the disappointment.

Pushing it aside he headed to the Science's island. Mind cleared and body refreshed, he focused on his next impossible challenge. Ferdinan went to the closet at the back of his lab. It was large enough to store his supplies and clothes. On the floor was a long, stuffed, lounging sac for when he slept here. The shelf nearest the door held his medical disks. Since building them was relaxing, there were always a number ready to be sent out.

Picking one at random, he held it to his chest and activated it. A light on top blinked red then flashed green after a minute. *What do I need to do?* He didn't want to know, but there wasn't a choice now.

Looking at the information on the display, Ferdinan calculated how cooperative he'd have to be. *If I gain ten pounds like they want... I have to make sure I have time before returning home.* But when would he be called home? Generally, he was allowed to go wherever he wished, but when a summons arrived, there was no ignoring it.

Are you competent enough to do this?

According to the screen, he'd lost six pounds at the hospital.

^^^

The scent of the ginger sauce turned Ferdinan's stomach. "What's this for?"

"Dinner." Jon pushed it closer.

"Why?"

"I was brought here to assist you. Which means making sure you can work. So, eat up."

"Being an interruption is hardly helping me work." Ferdinan kept his eyes averted.

Sighing, Jon brought a hand to his head. "They really didn't tell you."

"Tell me what?" As much as he didn't want to, Ferdinan took the bait.

Jon breathed in deep. "Healer Bær said once you're done here, if you haven't gained some weight, they're sending you home."

VVV

Shedding four pounds would put him back where he was... *Ok, this might be doable. I can do this. I can keep everyone happy.*

Liar.

Putting that aside, he turned his focus to something more important – only to be interrupted.

"You're awake."

Spinning in place, Ferdinan found exotic green eyes grinning at him. *"Oya! Please don't startle me like that."*

There she sat on the edge of one of his lab tables, bare feet swinging. Getting her to wear shoes was a practice in the art of futility. It left Ferdinan feeling more defeated than before. Neither would Oya leave. Safety concerns were met with giggles. Those stunning green eyes danced around his immaculately kept lab.

A sigh signaled his surrender. *How come I can't...?* "Ignore her" wasn't the right end to that question. Neither was "get rid of her," but the Tinkerer wasn't sure what the right words were. Everyone else left him alone. No one wanted to deal with him. Once his skills were no longer needed, they just disappeared until he was needed again. But not Oya. She kept coming back. Even when he told her about Luyou Zah... *Does she pity me? Is that why she keeps coming?*

Jumping off the table, Oya waltzed around the lab – playing with the various equipment scattered about.

Instead of fighting, he talked. Mostly he vented about his conversation with Xhou.

"*He's a troublesome child, isn't he?*" Sitting down, she fiddled with the chain around her neck and gazed out the window.

"*That's one way to put it.*" Talking to her eased his constricted chest. But...was enjoying a conversation with her allowed?

Do you deserve any of her time?

A Cheshire grin split her face. "*What's this show he's so worked up about?*"

There was no reason for her to be here...and it prevented her from making friends. If he didn't discourage this, he'd be hurting her – stopping her from finding happiness here. But... "*Once a year, family members with knowledge of the islands are invited for a week. The Welcome Show is the opening event. It's a spectacle showcasing the abilities of the student body...only we don't get to work with students of other classifications.*"

"*Ah. How long is it?*"

"*Two hours. Easy for the Artists, but nearly impossible for Scientists – at least since I've been here.*"

"*Really? If anything, it should be easier.*"

Stupid child.

Not sure how to take such a ridiculous statement, he continued. "*Xhou Zi wants something new. After Fifteen millennia of recorded human history, what hasn't been done?*"

A small, rubbery glob sat on a side table. It looked interesting and felt like the bouncy balls young children play with. "*What's this?*"

"A failed experiment. I was going to throw it out."

You're a failure all the way around.

"Then let's throw it." Holding it up, she signaled for him to catch.

Ferdinan gave her a grin and caught the makeshift ball.

"Does it have to be completely new or just new to these people?"

"The people coming are some of the most cultured in the world. They've seen it all." He gently returned the ball.

Giving him a grin, she caught it and threw it harder. *"Are you one of those people? One who's 'seen it all?'"*

"Yes. I can't blame Xhou Zi for wanting something new."

She raised an eyebrow at his comment, but he simply returned the ball to her.

"Is something wrong?" Ferdinan reached up, signaling he was ready.

"I want to give you something, but part of it isn't here yet."

A present for a murderer?

That turned him lobster red. *Why? "You don't have to give me anything."*

"I know I don't," she smirked patiently, *"but I want to."*

His color deepened. *Is she being nice? But why be nice to me? Is this a "thank you?" But...it's my job...I promised to help... "What does this have to do with the Welcome Show?"*

The ball flew with a *"heh." "If you're up for a trip to your little island, I could give it to you there. You'll have to wait for the rest when it arrives."*

Ferdinan stammered over words which never formed. *Why is she doing this? I don't deserve any kind of consideration.*

No. You don't.

"Don't hog the ball!"

"*Oh. S-Sorry…*" The skeleton tossed it back shakily, not entirely sure about the person before him.

◊

"*So…*" Oya caught the ball and changed topics, *"If everyone here's from a powerful family, who are you?"*

"*Huh?*" Ferdinan's face lit on fire. *"I'm the fifth child of the Grand Duke of North Chūzo."*

"Sounds…stressful."

"*Not really…the first and second have it the worst. Their responsibility is enormous.*" The ball flew back.

"*Fifth child, huh? Are you the baby?*" If Oya was going to fulfill the one task, she needed to know more about *his* world.

Those boney hands jumped up to cover his ears before falling to his side. *"No, Jon is, but I have four older sisters and two younger sisters."*

"Wow! Matriarchal society?"

"No. It doesn't matter as long as you do your job."

"*But Jon's the baby?*" That boy seemed to be a bigger part of her friend's life than either cared for. Even the little string shooting out of Ferdinan's chest was getting thicker and brighter. Looking down at her own chest, no strings could be found. But Jon had so many it was hard to focus on any one in particular - until they spread out. Ferdinan, however… There weren't many, and what were there were weak. That might be why the hole in his chest was so bad.

Ferdinan snickered as he rolled his eyes. *"Yes. And he relishes in the position."*

"They must dote on him fiercely."

◊

"You put it perfectly. His parents and all seven of his older brothers spoil him. They want him to stay the baby. And his is a matriarchal society. So...you can imagine."

Because he's a person worth keeping – unlike you.

"I don't know if I want to." Oya gave him a wink. *"Must be hard on his mother as the only woman."*

"Not really... Ruling males can't do anything without the approval of their wife or mother, whichever is the highest living matriarch. But mundane matters are usually left to the men. Women are all but worshiped there. So, tedium and high stress situations are for men to suffer through." The high regard Evelyn was receiving made him smile. Not only was she female and the adopted daughter of the Queen's first son, but she was the Oza – the hero who stopped the plague. Oueshians would recognize her for what she did.

"Sounds nice, for the women anyway. Did she have so many children hoping for a girl?"

Ferdinan laughed and chucked the ball. *Why am I laughing? Why does this feel...nice?* *"There was always the hope, but even if all eight were girls she would've had just as many. Mother Artimus loves children."*

She still loves them after meeting you?

"*Mother Artimus?*" Oya smirked at such a silly name.

"'Mother' is the highest title in Oueshi. Not calling her 'Queen Mother' is rude…but she insists I address her as 'Mother.' It feels wrong…so we've compromised with 'Mother Artimus.'"

"*Six and seven siblings, that's too much for me.*" Nodding, Oya gave the ball a wild curve and was impressed seeing him catch it without effort.

"There are a few students like my cousin, he's the only child. Most only have two or three siblings."

"Ah. Do your sisters also have abilities?"

"*No. It's rare having two children with abilities. The mutation is strange. Either you have it or you don't, but it isn't passed on easily.*" The ball in his hands became impossibly fascinating.

Don't worry, you'll never have the opportunity to curse the world with your spawn.

"Strange."

I don't want to talk about me. Why would she want to know anything about me anyway? "How about you? Tell me about your family."

Oya's wild grin faded to something much softer. *"There's my mom and dad and my little brother. We've never had much, but my parents loved us and taught us the best they could."*

"It must've been hard leaving them."

"I miss them with every cell in my body."

This wasn't something Ferdinan understood, but he was sure Jon did.

"*Think you're up for a run this evening?*" Alien green eyes all but glowed.

"I have to deal with Jon."

You mean "torture" him.

"*I'll meet you there then.*" She started to leave but spun back around. *"Jon seemed surprised that you learned Oŭndo so quickly. How many languages do you speak?"*

That question was unexpected. *"Officially, I know three modern and two ancient ones."*

"*And unofficially?*" Oya leaned back, impressed.

"At least one more than that."

"*You really are amazing.*" She gave him a grin and tossed the ball back, vanishing before he could dispute her.

With Oya gone, Ferdinan went back to the project she'd interrupted. People were still dying. Why didn't he realize stopping the disease wasn't enough? *How did I not think of this? How many people didn't have to die in all this? Why was I so stupid?* Sitting down, Ferdinan continued reprogramming his little nano-bots to rebuild cells instead of destroy them. All the while the voice mocked him.

Chapter 7

"Ha! I win!" Oya's bare feet slowed and turned into a twirl.

"Fair and square I believe." Ferdinan panted, giving her a bow.

"Ok, ok! Time for... half... of your surprise."

"I already–"

A wave of her hand interrupted him. From her pocket she retrieved a small wooden box and handed it to him.

He'd never seen anything like it. The moment she placed it in his palm he felt... It was like meeting a long-lost friend. Someone he'd been impossibly close with. They knew everything about each other - like a mother knows her child.

A broken kind of...*something*...warmed Ferdinan's heart. There was no logical reason...but he knew down to his very soul the box's contents were the most important things in the world. *This doesn't belong to me; it belongs to her.* But...this was *his.* His heart beat with an impossible warmth. *Is this what "joy" feels like?*

But...why? *Why do I feel this way? I've never seen it before...* *"What is this?"*

More than you deserve.

"Here." Taking it back, Oya showed him how to open it.

Inside was a transparent cube no more than an inch wide. Taking it out and closing the box, she placed the cube in a small indention on the lid. Flipping a switch flush with the wood made light glow out the top - forming a kind of screen.

Seeing the cube activated, Ferdinan recognized it. *This is ancient technology... How long ago did they use these? Seven hundred years give or take? So, why...?* The screen's glow called to him. Begging to be studied - understood. *No. It's pleading to be remembered...* It took licking dry lips before Ferdinan realized anticipation had quickened his breath. But...all that existed was him and the hidden knowledge that the cube wanted to share.

Wouldn't it be repulsed by you?

Most of what he saw was alien. But the Tinkerer knew enough to recognize most of these were extinct languages. Thousands upon thousands of extinct languages... *What is this?*

A golden-brown hand reached in and manipulated the screen only to touch an icon. A box appeared - offering a seemingly endless list. Delicate fingers tapped one of the many items and music filled the air. It wasn't anything he'd ever heard before. The sounds were so foreign... *What instruments are these?* The oddity only increased when singing began. Oŭndo characters danced across the light - translating the lyrics.

"What religion has this kind of music?" Both the tone and words indicated this wasn't a religious song. But only songs of worship were allowed lyrics.

"The religion of '**Nu Metal**,' *I guess."* Giggles filled the air as he tried parroting the word back to her. *"Just because there're words, doesn't make it worship."*

His chest seized. This music was far older than the cube it played from. And it shouldn't exist. *"Where did you get this?"*

"That's...an interesting story," she said. *"Its contents are old, but it'd be new to everyone here."*

"Yeah..." Ferdinan scrolled through the list - finding a language he recognized. The song changed. It sounded angry and remorseful, but he understood the words...partly. There wasn't much he could do for slang or time specific references. *"Please teach me how to use this!"*

Taking back the box, she placed it gently on the ground, music still playing – crazed smirk glowing. *"There's something else I want to teach you first."*

"And what would that be?" Intrigue coated his words but his attention was elsewhere. That cube was forbidden. Its contents – improper. *This was destroyed after the Council was formed...wasn't it?* There was no describing how much he wanted to scour it. *How does she have this? And...why is she sharing such a treasure with me?*

Mischievousness glowed at him. *"You're feeling good now?"*

"I haven't felt this well in a while."

All he saw was her Cheshire grin before a perfect void consumed his hand.

Granted he *might* have seen her spin and throw a kick if he'd known to look for it. But he was surprised by the void consuming him. Her ankle was in his grip – stopped just before colliding with his face. Her impish smirk melted away. Jumping back, he dropped her leg, banishing the nothingness she emanated. His chest constricted and his stomach twisted in knots.

"How was a Tinkerer able to react so quickly?"

Ferdinan swallowed hard. Words failed him as he watched her assemble a puzzle he hadn't realized she found the pieces to.

"I was going to teach you some basic self-defense, but I see it's unnecessary."

What do I do?! She was so fast; he couldn't stop himself from reacting. Everything was falling apart. *How do I stop this? How do I fix it? No one can know!* His racing heart and mind reached impossible speeds. Then she did something unexpected. Oya walked over to a small, flowering bush and started talking about something completely different.

"That cube's a family heirloom of sorts. I'm sure you could tell these aren't 'proper,' as deemed by that stupid Council of centuries past." Orange and red and pink flowers stood proudly, showing off their colors, but Oya picked a small yellow one.

"Why are you saying this?" Ferdinan walked over as she put the flower behind her ear. The yellow stood out beautifully against shiny black hair - but somehow only emphasized those impossible blood red roots.

"To make things even. Your face says it all. I wanted to help. And didn't mean to steal your secret… I don't understand why you'd hide something so awesome. It's common enough here. But I accept you feel threatened – in danger – by my knowing. So…if the wrong person knew what I have – how I got it. You know what'd happen. But reintroducing our past a little at a time should be safe."

What? Ferdinan sat next to her. *"No one can know. Being a Fighter is my cousin's role. I just want to create helpful things. I don't like hurting people…"*

"You may want to create, you may not want to hurt others, but you do want to fight or you wouldn't run away from it so intently." This struck a nerve - an important one from the looks of it. *"I don't want to make your life harder. But here on this little rock there're no eyes. I want to fight the person who blocked my kick."*

"Please don't ask me that." Ferdinan turned away.

"*Why?*"

"*Because...*"

"*Because?*"

"*I…I can't!*"

"*And why's that?*" A strange harshness filled Oya's tone.

"Because it's a stronger craving than running. I…I can't. I don't know if I can handle it."

"What do you mean?"

"It's a craving…giving in…"

A touch of anger colored her voice. *"You're afraid you won't be able to stop yourself? Is that why you take those beatings?"*

What? How does she know about that? "I'm afraid. But that's not why I take them."

"Then why?"

This argument was his fault. Things always ended this way... It's why no one wanted to be around him. It's why they only dealt with him when there was no other choice. But...at least she'd now finally realize how useless he was and go find friends. So...at least there was some benefit to this... A cold, hard glare drove home Ferdinan's words. *"You've no right to ask."*

Shivering, Oya jumped to her feet – looking down at him. *"Why not?"*

"It's not a simple thing." Mimicking her, he stood as well.

Proving a point, she threw a punch like lightning, which he blocked with great effort.

How is she so fast?! So strong? Is she a Fighter? But...everything else she can do...

"Here there's only you and me. It's that simple."

He narrowly dodged her next blow. And the next. And the one after that.

"Why are you doing this?" He caught her fist and twisted her arm behind her back. Utter emptiness consumed his hand and creeped up his arm.

Slithering free, she flashed him a toothy grin. "*Water may fill the belly, but without food the body will die.*"

Did she guess this as well? All these things no one knew. *Why couldn't I keep them from her? Someone I just met? Someone who knows nothing of my world? Things I keep hidden from everyone? Even myself?* The more she attacked, the more his conviction wavered. The joy of fighting! It was intoxicating - leaving him all but salivating.

She moved at near lightning speed, not giving him time to think. Only react.

Blow after blow Ferdinan countered until he blurted, "*I can't be caught!*"

Without notice, Oya stopped. "*You won't regret this compromise. Now, show me what you can do. I expect a good challenge!*"

As requested, he gave her his all. Not only was she fast, but the void that was her very being left him tensed each time they came into contact. Still, he held his own. For as fast as she was, he was faster. Gritting from the unpleasantness of her touch, he moved. Strike after strike. Was he hitting her too hard? She was smirking...so maybe not? He swung and kicked harder. *I'm hurting her. She has to be in pain...* But that grin didn't waver.

Then came a perfect opening. As she spun back - landing from her latest kick - he slipped in. Crouching low, Ferdinan rocketed straight up with her heel in his hand. The sudden force flipped her over. Landing flat on her back jarred her brain and knocked the air from her lungs.

"*Do you concede the fight!?*" he asked, chest heaving, blood rushing, adrenaline pumping. As much as it scared him, he was enjoying this. He didn't want to hurt her, but...he wanted nothing more than for her to stand and continue.

Laughter rang out – originating from the depths of her soul. It's purity...the joy filling it...brought him down from his primal desires. It drew him in until he was also laughing.

"*You win! When was the last time you fought someone?"*

"*Never. It's forbidden. But..."* He needed to be fast and sharp enough to not react to his cousin. At times his speed let him make minor adjustments to minimize the damage he'd take. *"I've seen many fights...and the things I do keep my reflexes sharp."*

"You should switch classifications with your cousin, but he couldn't possibly make it as a Tinkerer."

Ice filled Ferdinan's gut, turning his words frigid. *"I forbid that, even here."*

"I won't say it again," she grinned.

"Thank you." The bristles from Oya's callous remark eased at her concession.

"*Ferdinan.*" Reaching over, she picked up the cube and stopped the music.

You're going to fail again.

The voice jarred him - drawing his mind to something he almost realized. "*Yes?*"

"*Why's fighting your cousin's alone?"* She faced him squarely.

"He'll become General of our armies when he's an adult."

"Not you?"

"It's a position for a prince, not a lord."

It's a position of competence.

"Then you should stop him."

"Stop him from what?" What am I missing...?

"He'll never become a competent leader if you allow him to keep beating you."

* * *

Blinking, Zephyr found his arm held high above his head, a young child shrinking away from him, and Tillia's worried face not two inches from his own. *Huh?*

"Answer me!" she shouted.

"Answer what?" This startled response was all he could manage.

Releasing him, Tillia brought a hand to her chest as if pressing her heart back into place. Then she turned and addressed the dozen younger students. "Class dismissed."

Terrified children stood frozen until Tillia gently pushed the cowering boy toward the door.

She doesn't teach a class... Those are my *students.* Once the room was empty, Tillia spoke again, but she didn't turn to face him. "I've never been so scared in my life! What's wrong with you?"

"Excuse me?" Looking around, Zephyr searched for a clue- *The sun...* It was high in the sky. *But I woke up a few minutes ago... What's going on?*

"Why did you attack your students?" She turned and glared at him. "If we hadn't been nearby you would've hurt them."

"We?" Another search of the room revealed two other Fighters, both from his platoon - Bob Dosi and Tán Wern. They were nursing sore spots. "No..."

"What?" The fear in that single word threw her off.

Mouth hanging open, Zephyr thought while his hands recounted what he knew. The last thing he remembered was preparing for a run. *How did I lose half a day?* His heart raced. And his body ached from a pain not quite there... *What's going on?*

* * *

When Ferdinan finally arrived, Xhou all but jumped him with something between a hug and a death strangle – sharp talons digging deep. All the while, Oya stood on the threshold grinning. Delicate fingers tugged at the thin silver chain around her neck.

Grabbing the Lead's ear and twisting, Ferdinan forced the older boy to release him – liberating his nerves from tearing talons. "Calm down, Xhou Zi. What's everyone come up with?"

"We've been waiting on you," Jon grumbled.

Ferdinan's eye twitched. Brushing the Science Lead away, he walked to the front of the room – tripping over a stool. Oya snorted and rolled her eyes...but no one seemed to hear her. Sighing, he sat on top of the table, drawing everyone's attention. "A long, long, *long* time ago, when there were still seven continents – longer still – before the air became poison and nations weren't deeply connected, mankind learned how to combine various explosive powders and chemicals. We've been enjoying fireworks ever since."

"Fireworks aren't a good idea, Ferdinan, we'll be indoors!" Xhou exclaimed in alarm.

Quite the speaker you are.

Taking a deep breath, Ferdinan released it and continued. *Xhou can't be that stupid.* Thinkers were different from Tinkerers, but neither kind of Scientist lacked intelligence. *Is he playing the fool?* "Sun and fire were our only light. Then we made the lightbulb. For millennia now, almost every device uses a built-in light source of some kind. Do any of you know the difference between math and music?"

Jon's ears perked despite the murmurs and objections. Oya just shared this strange sentiment with him moments earlier. "Heart. Music's what happens when you give math heart. We have all the talent and knowledge needed to astonish everyone. Get out of your tiny box! The universe is nearly infinite! How is our view so small?

"Have you bothered reading the Welcome Show's description? It states we need to use *our* abilities to showcase the strengths and talents of *everyone* on the islands. We should follow it. That's what Scientists are good at, right? Following instructions. Start with the first part. We use *our* abilities, *our* talents, and *our* knowledge."

Does a pathetic child like you have any?

"No one wants to sit through a lecture on scientific theory or watch us put things together," an older girl objected.

"How many practical inventions were later used for entertainment purposes?" This silenced the murmurs. "There's someone who'll help us look past the surface and into the possibilities. She'll force you out of your comfort zone. This is my only suggestion. If you don't like it then come up with something on your own. In this room sit the best minds on the islands. This should *not* be difficult for you."

The look on Jon's face said he wondered how much people annoyed Ferdinan. "Who did you get to help us?"

Turning back to the door frame, Oya wasn't there. *Maybe stealing her words annoyed her...* Or maybe she didn't want to be introduced yet. "It hasn't been decided if we are going with my plan. Even if we do, you won't find out today."

Keep everyone in the dark. Don't let them see.

"That's a little unreasonable, don't you think?" Xhou complained.

"This whole thing's unreasonable. Forcing me to fulfill *your* responsibilities is unreasonable. Expecting one person to carry this out is unreasonable. Wasting time in this room when we should be working is unreasonable. Do you have any other complaints?" Ferdinan said coldly.

"Um...no." That left Xhou looking very much like a young child who'd been caught slacking on his chores.

Things turned out exactly as expected – much to Ferdinan's chagrin... Despite protests, he scheduled another meeting in a few days to give them the information they'd need. Grumblings came when he told them they'd be working over break. A stern look quickly put an end to that. The Tinkerer dismissed the group, but not everyone rushed out.

"Making them take time from studies and projects this late in the block is harsh," Jon frowned.

"Maybe...but I feel no sympathy..." Ferdinan grumbled – rubbing at his unhappy stomach. "I completed everything despite being gone for three months. They shouldn't have waited 'til the last minute."

You think rather highly of yourself.

"Wow. You aren't sounding like yourself, Ferdinan," Xhou pointed out.

"How am I sounding?"

"Mean. That isn't something I'm used to...at least not from you."

^^^

"These are no good," Ferdinan insisted, allowing a little anger to play in his voice. "Have you looked at them at all?"

"They were taken and shipped directly here. Those samples are less than two days old. Even if the virus is dead, there should be plenty to work with."

Doesn't she understand what "useless" means? *"Are they certain these were taken from infected persons?" The frustration from unusable samples coupled with being talked to like a spoiled child was quickly wearing on him.*

"Yes. Half of them were from persons showing symptoms. Just as you requested."

Nodding, Ferdinan connected his scanner to the com system. Though his irritation leaked through stronger than he intended, he kept the snark out of his question. "Then would you be kind enough to point out the virus?"

VVV

Getting off the table, Ferdinan sat on a stool and placed his head on the cool, steel surface. *I sound mean. That's what I get for giving in when I know better.* Yet...he almost felt calm. More so than he had in years. "I'm tired."

Evil child.

"Huh? It's not even curfew for the first years," Xhou pointed out dumbly. "Getting sick again?"

"Yes." Ferdinan stood and left the room, nearly running into Oya on the way out. As he apologized, the voice of a Scientist four years his junior reached his ears.

"What put him in such a bad mood? Normally he blends into the wall."

"Actually..." Xhou's voice sounded both thoughtful and amused. "He *looked* almost happy. I wonder why..."

What's that idiot talking about?

Chapter 8

It took some finagling to get Oya to leave him alone. It was nice that she wanted to be around him, but he still had to work. When she gave up, she vanished into thin air. Seemingly. But part of Ferdinan had a sneaky suspicion she hadn't actually left. Before he could consider it, he noticed his mounted screen was flashing.

A call request was missed two minutes ago. Knowing the person who sent it though... Thirty seconds after returning the request an older gentleman appeared on the screen. A thin line of white hair circled his head like a kotinos – only the ninety-plus-year-old man was decades too old to be winning any sports trials. Still, his face was kind. Through his eyes shone the silly disposition the man enjoyed.

This worked well for Ferdinan. There weren't many who'd help someone as young as him with what he did. But the older gentleman was eccentric enough to not care about his age. And serious when absolutely necessary.

How are you going to destroy him?

"Grampa Huey!" Ferdinan bowed to the man who wasn't his grandfather. But Huey insisted anyone younger than fifty call him this.

"Cut it out! One of these days we'll meet face to face and I'll smack you straight if you do that." Grampa Huey's voice sounded grumpy, but a big smile curled his lips, and his eyes danced.

"I'm sorry, sir. But I was raised right."

A murderer? Raised right?

"If you were raised right, you'd listen to your elder and do what I tell you!"

"Yes, sir." Ferdinan smiled softly. Seemed they had the same little "discussion" every time they spoke. Straightening to face the man, Ferdinan found himself taken in by Huey's ocean blue eyes. They were impossibly deep and rich – inescapably so. Grandpa Huey was one of the few people Ferdinan had met who also had blue eyes. This trait became increasingly rarer as the generations passed. Unlike his nearly colorless crystal blue, the older man's ocean eyes glowed, framed by dark skin.

That grin widened all the more. "Glad I caught you in such a good mood."

You do get perverse pleasure from hurting others.

Cheeks reddening, Ferdinan cleared his voice. "How may I be of service, sir?"

"You can drop the 'sir' nonsense, son." He raised a scolding eyebrow but didn't have the facial expression to pull off the look.

"Like I said, sir." A smirk fought to take over Ferdinan's lips.

"Well then, *sir,*" Huey folded his arms as if in triumph. "You got a big request this time."

"Yes, sir. What is it?" Picking up a screen, Ferdinan readied to jot down everything.

"Those silly little bars of yours you say replace food; a huge order came in for them. I'm sending the types and quantities requested."

"Thank you, sir. Is this for Azuté?"

"You don't know?" The man's surprised face spoke volumes to how much he *wasn't* kidding.

"Don't know what?"

You don't know anything.

"Boy, what's the point of having access to all the world if you don't check on home now and again?"

"Something happened in my dukedom?" *The Duchess hasn't said anything...*

"Ooo yah!" Grandpa Huey wiggled into a more comfortable position as if preparing for story time. "Your country's main crop farms failed again. Most of the livestock's been slaughtered – so that's pretty much decimated."

"Again? That's three seasons in a row... Do they know why?" Ferdinan chewed on his lip. *Not another disaster...not more blood on my hands...*

Cursing the land from here. Impressive.

No matter how he tried, Ferdinan couldn't expand his lungs.

"All official reports are being kept out of the public eye."

"But you know." *Calm down. Breathe in slowly...*

"Of course, I know, son!" Huey returned the look. "Seems the fields lost all their nutrients. I'm not sure how exactly, mind you, but I wouldn't be surprised if there wasn't someone sowing salt."

"Sabotage? You really think anyone would do that? It wouldn't hurt the monarchs, just the people."

"Oh, a few monarchs'll get it once the people get hungry enough."

"Where am I sending the bars?"

"Your dukedom. That's what's in the request."

"But...you said the main farms are down. The big cities should be needing them, not my dukedom."

"Your mother's expanded the farming. Half the lands in your Dukedom were turned over to fields and pastures. Duchess

Samultz' been sending all the crops they've produced to the main capital for distribution."

Ferdinan's teeth clenched shut. *I should've known...*

"You don't seem confused, son. She's sending *all* the food that way. After quadrupling the food production. Else why would they be needing your bars?"

"I'm not confused. I know what she's doing." Ferdinan looked down, not wanting to give anything away.

"Care to enlighten an old man?"

The Duchess wasn't trying to win support with her actions. No, her intentions fell somewhere else entirely. Ferdinan understood. If asked, he'd support this but he couldn't explain why. No one would understand. "She's doing what's best for the entire country. If a few people have to tighten their belts so others don't starve, then that's the way it has to be."

Sacrifice everyone.

"Tighten their belts? You did hear me when I said *all* the food? For three seasons."

"Yes, sir."

"Son, I don't know what's giving me more of a headache – keeping your funds under the radar or trying to understand your family."

"I'm sorry, Grandpa Huey."

"Ah! You used my name! Now that you're trying to appease me."

"I'm sorry, sir. Who made the request?"

"Anonymous."

Anonymous? Who'd help my dukedom?

Someone who doesn't want to become your victim.

"Son, why do you keep doing that?"

"Doing what?"

"There a bug flying around your head I can't see?"

Grating laughter filled Ferdinan's skull.

"Son?"

"What?!" It took yelling to realize he was covering his ears. "I'm sorry…I'm sorry…"

It wasn't often Grandpa Huey was serious, but his worry banished all joviality. "Ferdinan, are you ok?"

"I'm sorry…" *What've I been doing?* Sifting through his well-crafted masks, Ferdinan put on his most practiced smile. "I'm sorry for troubling you. Thank you for sending along that request."

There were objections as Ferdinan ended the conversation, but eventually Grandpa Huey gave up. Giving a respectful goodbye, the skeleton started up Oya's music.

It played continuously as he sent out distribution requests and called in favors to meet the amount needed. While awaiting responses, Ferdinan took a moment to check on his bots. They were replicating nicely. Next, he set to work ordering more supplies and mixing up a batch of his bars.

A twinge of guilt hit him as he realized there was something more important. Hesitantly, he reached for a screen and placed a call. The reply came hours later – when he was elbow deep in tar-like batter. Taking a moment to scrape his hands clean, Ferdinan used an elbow to tap the mounted screen.

"My apologies, Lord Ferdinan, I just received your call request." Healer Bær gave his student his full attention – unaccustomed to being contacted by the skeleton.

"There are a number of people here suffering from the effects of the virus, aren't there?" This confirmation was hardly necessary, he saw it all across the islands. There was no doubt the Healers were exhausted.

* * *

Screams shot through the door, startling the floating Theon and causing him to drop the screen he'd been working on. It took a minute to find the transparent rectangle in the soft carpet.

Nightmares again? For over a week Zephyr screamed himself awake every time he slept. It wore on both of them and severely affected the Prince's sleep. Half the time his suitemate was up and moving, it didn't look like the Prince was there. Neither did Zephyr always respond when he spoke.

Theon was halfway to Zephyr's room when the Prince's door slammed open.

Onyx eyes glared past him as if he wasn't there. "I'll kill you! What did you do to me!?"

Soaring to the ceiling, Theon hurried out of the Prince's way. He wasn't sure who Zephyr was yelling at, but the boy was exhausted. *I'll give him one more day. If he hasn't slept by then...*

Flying to the door, he slipped out into the hall as Zephyr fell to his knees. Golden hands clawed at thick black hair. *By morning. If he doesn't sleep tonight...*

Floating down the stairwell, the Energist ran into someone unexpected. Rumors spoke of the skeleton's return, but he hadn't seen Ferdinan until now. "Don't go up there."

Bowing his head respectfully, Ferdinan stepped aside for his suitemate to float past. "What do you mean?"

"Your cousin's in a state I've never seen before. Be smart. Find somewhere else to go. I know I am."

"Why tell me?"

"Being punished for the selfish, callous things you do is fine. But no one should die because he's having trouble."

Hiding his face, Ferdinan bowed properly to the older boy. "Thank you for telling me."

* * *

"Thank you for volunteering, Herrard." Healer Bær smiled as his student winced. After the miracle Ferdinan pulled off in South Chūzo, there was no question about the skeleton's abilities. However, he couldn't have people take untested medicine without their consent.

"I'm up for anything right now. This break will be a busy one. If this'll make me better faster, I'm all for it."

Bær nodded. Herrard was the perfect choice. The boy was a top-class Healer who hadn't been healing himself – focusing on the younger children instead. This seemed foolish at first, but it worked out now. If anything went wrong with the medicine, Herrard could purge it from his body. Regardless, the boy could take note on how well it worked and possible things to look for. This would be helpful here on the islands. But for those beyond an alumni Healer's reach, it was invaluable.

Before giving the injection, Healer Bær emphasized his worries. "You understand it hasn't been tried. We don't know the side effects or if there'll be any adverse reactions."

"I understand." A pained grin twisted Herrard's face. "According to legend, if I can't survive something as simple as a new medicine, I'm definitely not meant to be Kal."

Bær gave a wince of a smile. "There's something else you need to know."

"Yes, sir?"

"It's not a traditional medicine."

"Sir?" An eyebrow rose on Herrard's face, demanding an explanation.

Sighing, Bær leaned forward. "It wasn't made by Healers, it's not even organic."

This grabbed the older boy's attention. "Please, continue."

* * *

Not taking Theon's advice, Ferdinan headed up. Whatever happened to his cousin, fixing it was his responsibility first and foremost. Upon entering the suite, he was greeted by an unusual sight. Zephyr sat in the common room facing the window and didn't seem to notice him enter. Dark energy radiated from his Prince.

What's going on? Ferdinan approached, studying Zephyr's reflection in the large, scenic windows.

"My Prince?"

No response came. Blood-shot onyx eyes turned to the window as Zephyr mumbled something. Suddenly, those eyes focused, opening wide in rage as recognition hit.

"YOU!" he screamed.

What did you do to him this time?

Golden hands shot forward – one slicing under the other. It was a gesture Ferdinan knew too well. And...he deserved it. He deserved death at his cousin's hands. Yes, he'd killed millions...but his Prince suffered daily since Ferdinan was born. Simply because he was there... No matter how he tried, the skeleton always ended up hurting his cousin. Every day...because he existed... If anyone had a right to kill him, it was his Prince.

The look Ferdinan saw as Zephyr faced him was one he knew all too well. Fear and frustration boiled into rage – a rage barely contained in that small, golden frame. His cousin couldn't see anything but him right now. That face...it was the look his Prince got when no longer in control. Come morning, no memories of this night would exist for his cousin... None were being encoded now.

It'd been a while since his Prince completely lost his mind. It didn't happen as often anymore. But whatever caused it this time, ultimately, was Ferdinan's fault. It always was. But...something was different. Instead of a predator, his Prince looked like a wounded animal. *What've I done to you?*

You destroyed him.

Zephyr leapt, rushing at him, flailing wildly.

A hard blow landed, making everything dark.

◊

Oya stood above the two unconscious boys sprawled on the floor – a handful of glowing orbs dancing in her peripheral. *"How can you be so insightful, yet blind to this?"*

Picking up Ferdinan's body, she took him to bed. He was tiny. Did Jon realize how precariously balanced he was? Delicate hand hovering over his chest, she soaked up what little damage was done. Watching was fine – giving her friend a chance to do the right thing. But once she saw how barren the mutt's eyes were, waiting for him to act was no longer an option. Absolutely certain that dog would've killed her friend, she *had* to step in.

Returning to the common room, Oya squatted down next to the filthy beast. "*Why does he prostrate himself before you when he knows you'll rip his throat out?*"

Chapter 9

"We have to talk about this." Jon grabbed Ferdinan's arm - stopping his escape.

Squirming, Ferdinan fought to break free. "There's nothing to talk about."

"You're supposed to put *on* weight! You've been eating everything, haven't you?" Accusing the gent wasn't Jon's first choice. But why else was he failing in this task? Again.

"I eat it." Ferdinan finally broke free - cradling his arm.

"Then what's going on? You *know* I have to report to the Superintendent-"

"I have 'til the end of break!" Ferdinan flinched away from something Jon couldn't see. "If you'd leave me alone, I'd be fine!"

"No, you won't."

Turning away, Ferdinan headed toward the boats.

"Don't ignore me! With this...it doesn't look like you've kept your part. You'll be sent home."

"I've told you how many times?" Ferdinan turned a glare on him. "Your food's disgusting. It makes me sick. How can I gain weight when you keep making me sick?!"

He meant that literally?

"I'm tired." Hurrying away, Ferdinan grabbed a boat and pushed off.

"Great. Now what do I do?"

◊

Long after catching their breaths, they continued laying on the soft grass. Running was the only respite Ferdinan had. But racing Oya... Then their battles... The voice mocked him for smiling before he realized his lips had curled up. Forcing his face back to neutral, Ferdinan focused on the fluffy clouds. There was something about the perfect sky which made his little island feel safer – more isolated and protected.

Not even a breeze intruded upon them. The silence was strangely comfortable. This wasn't something Ferdinan was used to. Not the quiet. That never bothered him despite making those around him uncomfortable. But Oya...she seemed to enjoy it as much as him.

"Telling me which ancient languages you're willing to translate will narrow down the options immensely." Oya sat up and activated her little cube. Soon enough twisted notes danced around them – somehow bringing a wonderful sense of calm. *"You don't have to divulge all you know, but a couple...or your science people will spend the next four lifetimes trying to choose."*

"Now say all that in Common." Sitting up, Ferdinan grinned – rubbing at his complaining stomach. *How do I get out of Jon's food tonight?*

"I Common start specking now about how?" she tried.

"How about I start speaking Common now?" He waited for her to say it properly. "You have the words well enough, but I don't know how to teach you structure in a way you'll understand."

"Not fault my you out order speck of."

"It isn't my fault you speak out of order."

She rolled her eyes and repeated it before choosing a new song.

Despite the smarminess of her attitude, a smile grew on his face. The voice said nothing so Ferdinan berated himself. He had no right to any of this. Expecting anything wasn't fair to her. Once she had the language down... Something cold and hard rested on his chest. *This will all end...* He swallowed hard. Of course, it would end. He'd wouldn't be needed anymore, and she could continue on with her life. This was just another job. Only, his client was kinder than he was used to. "It seems that way because Oŭndo has no set order. Common does. Do you know how odd it is for me? Saying words in the order of importance at the time?"

"*What's so strange? Why wouldn't the most important words be placed first? It's silly wasting time with words that aren't necessary at the moment. Leaves no room for misinterpretation either."* Hands on her hips, Oya switched to her own tongue for ease of conversation. When his grin grew, she giggled and squeezed his hand.

^^^

A perfect void... That was the only way to describe the girl who abducted him and dragged him across the entire hospital. That void didn't vanish until she pushed him into a darkened room. What does she want?

Lights flicked on and Ferdinan was facing a boy not much older than himself. The child was horribly ill and asphyxiating. Rushing forward, the Tinkerer ignored the burning fire of the boy to roll him to his side.

When Ferdinan recognized what he was seeing, anger filled him. Calling healers was pointless. To die alone and not bother anyone – this is why the boy was left here.

VVV

The least important... A shaky smile hid how much that memory turned his stomach. "I'm sorry, most languages don't work that way."

Leaving that one be, she continued on. "*Well? Which ones? I can order them by language, and you can choose. Or you could, they're on that fancy glass of yours now.*"

"They are called screens. You know that." Another song started, but something was missing. It was right there. He could almost see it... And...it had nothing to do with the calm that strange music brought him...no...it was something else...

"I do." She stuck her tongue out at him and laughed a little too enthusiastically. *"How many do you think they could handle choosing from?"*

"Good question. I'll randomize them and give each person...twenty...? Yes, twenty. They should be able to pick from that many. If not, they can request another set." *The voice...*

"Sounds like a good idea to me, less than three hours of music should be doable for a person."

"*Um...*" Ferdinan hesitated but continued on. "*Most of the songs... I can't figure out what instruments they are playing.*"

Giggles escaped Oya. "*Of course, you wouldn't.*"

"And why's that?" He had to know. Reaching over, Ferdinan paused the music.

"*They don't exist anymore. That whole 'proper' nonsense.*"

Nothing's less proper than you.

"But you know what they are?"

"*I do.*" Exotic green eyes turned to the evening sky.

"And?"

If it were possible, she managed a Cheshire smirk. "*Those instruments don't exist anymore. The most commonly used you'll never find is something called a* **guitar**. *Mostly they'll be* **electric guitars**. *It was the rage for centuries.*"

"'**Electric guitar**'? *What's that?*"

Stupid child.

Laughter filled the air. Oya restarted the music then went to work scouring the cube. "**Guitars** *were instruments with six strings and were strummed with the fingers – no bow. Turning all stringed instruments electric was the fad for a while. Even some of the ones we still have today – like mandolins, violins, harps, kokyūs, huluhus, veenas, and so on.*"

Leaning in, Ferdinan looked at the picture Oya pulled up. "*How do you electrify a huluhu?*"

More giggles danced between them. "*There're instructions on the cube. Though I'm more than certain you'd figure it out.*"

Blushing, Ferdinan changed gears - making a mental note to look into these "electric instruments." "When do you want me to announce you?"

"There's nothing I can do 'til they return from this crazy long break. So, let's wait 'til then."

A laugh came up unbidden. "You *are* the mean one, aren't you?"

"Don't say that to the person who so graciously offered to help! Especially since you're all more than capable of doing this yourselves." Her tongue shot out again and she jumped to her feet, glittering. "*I'll be right back.*"

Unnatural tones swirled around him. Closing his eyes, Ferdinan laid back onto the soft grass. The voice scratched at the back of his mind...but...

When she returned, she was carrying a decent sized rectangular box. Boney hands moved across it when she placed it in his lap. Intricately carved flowers decorated the oak's surface, disbursed between flowing swirls and eddies, depicting a moving river. The design was reminiscent of artwork popular in Oueshi a century ago. It was beautiful.

After properly admiring the box, he lifted the lid – revealing a violin. An impossibly distinct violin. "Where'd you get this?"

"*Do you like it?*" She rocked on her feet.

"Where did you get this?" He repeated a second time with less awe and more ire.

At his attitude, she folded her arms and pouted her lip. "*I asked for it.*"

"Do you know what this is?" Ferdinan turned it over with utmost care. Slowly, his hands explored every inch of the beautiful instrument – taking in its very essence.

"*A violin.*" Her tone reminded him it was a pretty common thing.

"Yes, but...no. This is a Wanyuan."

"Is that a cousin to the violin?" she asked, confused at his astonishment.

"She's a luthier. Or, she was. These were worth a small fortune when she was alive! And she didn't make many."

"*I'm sorry. Was she someone important to you?*"

"She lived when my great grandfather was young."

"I don't understand the problem." Squatting down, Oya peered at the instrument.

Disbelief filled him. *How can she not?*

"I'm sorry if it isn't worth much. I thought it'd be good for you to have an outlet you didn't have to hide."

"What?" She wasn't making any sense.

"*You work hard. Once in a while we come here and run and fight. But we can't come whenever you want. I heard you're always sick. I thought if you focused your energy into something you could keep with you, you might not be sick as often."*

"What makes you...?" *Do I really want to know the answer?* Burning red head to toe, he continued on. "*This is a rare treasure. Thank you very much… But, why a violin?"*

Sadness touched her eyes. "*The violin is a most versatile instrument. It can scream and laugh, cry and sing. It can be your voice when silence is required. And it's portable."*

Blushing deeper, he looked away. She was serious and completely sincere. Even her normal half-crazed look was absent when she spoke those words. *Why...? Why would she care this much? Why is she being nice? She was there at the hospital...how can she not realize what I am? I don't understand...I don't understand...* "What makes you think I need such a voice?"

"*There're things I can't do either. This leaves us with a choice. Either we find an alternative,"* she poked him right above the heart, "*or, we let it eat away at us."*

"What can't you do?" *Seems she can do anything...*

"*Hmmm. I wonder."* Oya winked, madness touching her eyes once again.

Knowing this was all he was going to get, he changed the subject. "Do you play? Are you going to teach me?"

"No. I've no talent for such things. But learning seems to be a gift of yours." She lifted the bow from the case and handed it to him. Then she showed him how to access sheet music stored on the cube. There was a veritable library to choose from.
"Um…what's the problem with the violin?"

"I'm not worthy of an instrument of this caliber. The best violinist in the world would feel humbled holding this."

"Wow, rich people are weird. It's an instrument. I'm glad it's a nice one, but what good is it if people are afraid to touch it? Isn't it better for a novice to make horrid sounds on it than for it to sit and collect dust?"

"That's a view I've never heard before."

"How happy would you be if you only took on work at your level? I know you're more amazing than you let on. There can't be much out there. You'd sit around wasting your days waiting for a suitable challenge."

This wasn't something he wanted to acknowledge, so Ferdinan remained silent.

* * *

Screams caught Theon's attention as he prepared for class. Heaving a sigh, he leaned back - hovering in the middle of his room. *Again? …I guess I have no choice.* Ferdinan spent as many nights in the suite as he did before his three-month vacation. That left Theon and Zephyr. Getting into his suitemate's room wasn't a problem for an Energist. Tripping a latch was child's play. Waking the Prince, however, was anything but. When he'd finally succeeded, Zephyr swung - giving him a black eye.

This was a gift Theon would've returned, but the Fighter wasn't actually awake. Neither was he coherent. With no other choice, the Energist dragged him out to Healer Bær's office in Isolation – the main medical facility for the islands.

He could've taken Zephyr to one of the little clinics scattered throughout the islands, but this was too intense. It was something the Head Healer needed to take care of.

Seeing the Prince like this scared Theon. "What's wrong with him?"

"His mind's exhausted and he wasn't able to answer my questions. Doesn't look like he's slept in over a week. I put him to sleep and we're monitoring him." Healer Bær looked confused at the screen in his hands.

"Will he be able to travel home for break?" A jolt of pain hit – Theon took in a sharp breath.

"Possibly. You said earlier, he's having nightmares?" Bær asked.

Flying around during a serious conversation was rude - unfortunately. But chairs were uncomfortable, so Theon hovered just barely above the seat. "Yes. He wakes up multiple times a night screaming."

"Does his cousin know?"

"He's always the first one in there," Theon lied. *I can't also deal with that child right now.*

"Thank you for bringing him. I'm sure Lord Ferdinan appreciates it."

"Ferdinan didn't ask me to bring him."

"Really?"

"He was gone already when Zephyr started screaming."

"I see." Concern wrinkled the perfectly average man's brow. "Anything else I should know?"

"Not that I can think of..."

Nodding, the Healer jumped topics. "How're you doing? Your recovery?"

"Better." The Energist's eyes drifted toward the window. "That medicine you offered is working faster than the healing sessions, but I still get jolts of pain."

Healer Bær pulled up a new box on the screen and recorded Theon's answer. "Anything else? Before offering it campus wide..."

"No, sir. Honestly...it's a miracle in a shot."

* * *

After a short meeting with the other Science students, Ferdinan left as quickly as he could. Fifteen minutes were spent answering questions... *Were my instructions really so difficult? Pick a song out of the twenty. And don't share the music or what we are doing with anyone.*

Don't blame them when it's your fault.

If he could, he'd turn on the music, but it was time for his pupil. Ferdinan prepared mentally to give his full attention to his mentee - or as much as the voice didn't command.

As always, the six-year-old was well prepared. The child knew what each piece of lab equipment was for and how they worked. He fixed the broken ones as well.

"This is magnificent, Lord Elbarrat. You worked hard while I was gone. You've finished introductory training and are ready for the next phase," Ferdinan announced proudly. Guilt hit him hard. The only reason his pupil wasn't hurt was because the child didn't have anyone off the islands to lose.

At least Elbie's ok. Multiple times his mentee asked him to use the name "Elbie," but the skeleton couldn't bring himself to say the nickname out loud.

Twisted freak.

"Really? But..." Trailing off, Elbie ran a hand through his dark, shiny hair as mismatched eyes darted around the room. It took a moment, but one gray and one green eye returned to his mentor's gaze.

"But what?"

"You said you'd teach me your inventions after I completed the standard equipment."

"I did say that...didn't I?" Ferdinan sighed. He fetched one of the medical disks from a nearby table. "Have you finished *all* your course work? There's still a few days left in the block, but I have to know before I give this to you."

"I only have one thing left. I'll finish after our session," Elbie answered, excited that his hard work and productivity finally turned in his favor.

What a cruel joke you're playing.

Hesitantly, Ferdinan placed the disk in front of his student. "Lord Elbarrat, you are *not* to start on this 'til you've finished your last assignment. Do you understand? If you do, I'll take it back and not give you another chance."

Elbie looked at him in horror. "Yes, sir. I understand the consequences."

"Good." He sat on the table and looked down at Elbie. "I'll teach you everything about this device as soon as you figure out where I started when I assembled the circuit board. You've shown greater proficiency in understanding circuitry layout and design than other students. This'll allow you to realize something important."

"Yes, sir! Thank you, sir!" Confidence and excitement shone in Elbie's mismatched eyes.

Removing his hand from the disk, Ferdinan allowed his mentee to take it. "This is the end of our lessons for the block. Before I let you go, I have some ground rules. You can utilize any source you wish – except me."

You're a useless resource anyway.

"Huh...? May I ask why?"

"When making something new, there's no expert to ask. You figure it out from experts in other areas and help from your peers. Studies and information on similar things are priceless commodities. You'll figure this out in the same manner it'll take to develop your own equipment."

"That...makes sense."

"You'll not set foot in this lab 'til you have the answer for me."

This made the young Tinkerer a little nervous. "How about the other labs?"

"Those are fine. But my lab doesn't exist the moment you walk out the door."

"Yes, sir."

Ferdinan's expression softened, becoming friendly again. "Go finish your work. I look forward to your answer."

Sadistic jerk.

"Thank you, sir!" Elbie jumped off his chair and ran for the door, excited to get to do what he'd been waiting almost a year for. Before stepping out, concern filled him. The six-year-old looked back, hesitant to leave. He wanted this... But, giving up his advisor... A gentle, reassuring smile from Ferdinan gave him the courage he needed to take that final step out of the lab.

Enjoy crushing his dreams.

The moment Elbie left, Ferdinan slipped a small speaker inside his ear and started the music. A gray cloud hung heavy over him. He had nothing left to do. He'd perfected the second skin while at the hospital in South Chūzo. Even if the Superintendent hadn't insisted this count as his final project, he didn't have time to order what he needed for something new. So, he fiddled with the device – testing and tweaking it. He was nervous and couldn't stop. Not having anything to do... The thought made his insides shake.

The agony of nothing occupying him – and Jon's food – was wreaking havoc on his stomach. As soon as this was turned in...

A screen chimed and he leapt for it – hoping desperately for a new request.

Something to work on. Anything. Playing with Oya lessened his need to always be doing something, but only to a small degree. This project was the last thing he had.

However... The message was from the Duchess – his mother. Disappointment at a missed opportunity filled him. About this time, his door opened. There weren't many people with access to his lab: Jon, Elbie...and Oya somehow. That was about it. Though all adults had authority to override his security protocols. He was about to greet whoever it was when his eyes hit the reason for the message.

"What's wrong? You look worried." His ally's voice overcame the music to strike his ears.

"Don't be ridiculous."

Before Jon's eyes, Ferdinan's expression of fright and concern changed to boredom. "What're you reading?"

"My family's summoning me home for an event honoring my aunt."

"The Queen or the General?"

"The General."

"Ah, what for?"

"I haven't gotten that far. I'm sure it has something to do with military service. Probably her work distributing medicine and cleaning up East," he swallowed hard against the lump in his throat as a new song started, "Azuté."

"Oh ya, Samuel said something about that. Apparently, her troops cleared thousands of victims."

"She dug many of the graves herself." Ferdinan scowled at his own words and Jon's callous tone.

"This is a world recognition thing?" Jon pushed on, adjusting the cuff of his sleeve.

"Close enough. There are a number of people being recognized for their efforts in helping the affected areas. From what I know, every ruling body was invited." Somehow, it felt as if the music in his ear made this conversation easier.

"Wow. Sounds like an official party. Have fun with that."

"Thanks," Ferdinan answered, annoyed.

"Here's dinner. You better eat it all." Jon moved aside the screen to place a plate in front of him. "I have some work I need to finish up, so I can't babysit you tonight."

Ferdinan looked at the screen Jon just moved - completely ignoring the food. "I'm more than capable of feeding myself."

"It's not your ability I question."

"Get your work done. I don't know why you didn't finish before we got back."

Jon frowned. "Not all of us are workaholics."

Ignoring the Dinta, Ferdinan grabbed the screen he'd transferred all the cube's contents to. Holding this treasure in his hands... It wasn't every time, but often enough it felt like someone was pleading to him. Begging him to read and learn...and remember. *What am I supposed to remember? What have I forgotten?* He could almost hear light giggles. It had nothing to do with what he'd forgotten. Just that it wanted to be remembered...

He wasn't sure how long he stared at the endless files before his conversation with Oya floated through his head. *The "electric instruments." I'll focus on that...* Flicking through, he found the information he needed in a language he recognized. *What an intriguing concept...* Even if it was a bit odd to consider. Either way, he could put his full attention into learning about these.

* * *

"Here." Xhou handed Norger a tissue.

Taking it, Norger calmed himself enough to get his voice under control. "I don't know how you do it."

"Do what?"

"Check in with all Scientists affected by the plague weekly. That's what Master Loucé is for."

"Maybe. But I'm the Science's Lead. Being nosy is my responsibility. And my right. Got to make sure my underlings are doing well...or getting better at least." Xhou gave a goofy grin, making his younger peer smile.

"But who do *you* talk to?" Norger turned to the window, pressing his fist against a sharp pain in his gut.

"Master Loucé, at least once a week. I also have my own confidants. Don't worry," Xhou lied. Bothering others about such things... Of course, he was sad, what Azutite wasn't?

"But, still...how're you alright? I..." Bringing the tissue to his face, Norger let it soak in more tears. Only Norger could look impossibly handsome despite an hour of crying.

"Well...I'm pretty lucky. For how many people have no one left, I have two. Because mom's still alive, I don't have to rush home and figure out how to pick up a devastated country." Turning away, Xhou grimaced at his own jolt of pain. "This isn't how I pictured my life, but I got off easier than most. I stay focused on how grateful I am for that."

"You're *way* too well-adjusted."

"Tell me about it." The Science Lead smiled and escorted his subordinate out of his lab, watching as Norger walked down to the boats. "Wait!"

The exhausted boy stopped but didn't turn until Xhou was at his side.

"Let's take the bridge." Xhou walked Norger to the main island before returning to his lab.

Turning off the lights left the room cold and dim. Exactly how Xhou wanted. He was alone now. There was no one near enough to see him - to hear him. Looking around, he wished for the first time that he was a Tinkerer. *Ferdinan's lab has all sorts of things to smash!*

Trembling, his own tears fighting to come, Xhou pounded on the closest table. His hands hurt, but he kept going.

"Why?!" Dropping to his knees, he shifted to hide under the table he'd beaten.

The anger. The sorrow. The uncertainty. This was never his to deal with. Now it was his new reality. And Xhou was powerless to do anything about it. It all boiled and grew, filling him to bursting until he expelled it in a desperate scream.

* * *

Back in his own lab, Jon pulled up his screen and went back to writing. He didn't accomplish much before the eerie feeling of being watched overcame him. An investigation showed no one was there.

Turning back to his workstation, Jon nearly jumped out of his skin.

"Oya! Announce yourself next time! ...I...I'm sorry..." No matter how difficult she was, Jon had no right to yell at a girl.

Toying with the chain around her neck, Oya handed her screen to him. *"Tell me about the violin."*

Startled, he took it to see what she said. "The one you asked for? Wasn't it up to your standard?"

"According to Ferdinan, it's the best out there."

"What else would you expect?"

"Any that plays. Why such a top shelf instrument?" She leaned forward until her nose almost touched his.

Pulling away, Jon grabbed a chair for her, adjusting it to sit as high as possible. "It was repayment."

Ignoring the chair, she blinked at him. *"Repayment for what?"*

"I don't know what you did, but Ferdinan couldn't move on his own. Two days later he was up and working again. You made him better. The least I could do is fulfil your request to the same degree."

"I wasn't keeping score." Oya sat on the table, staring intensely down at Jon, causing him to waver. Amused, but annoyed, she broke eye contact so he could read her words.

"I didn't think you were." Jon looked at her earnestly. "It was my way of saying 'thank you.'"

Her face softened. *"Thank you."*

"For what?"

"For understanding his value better than he does." She moved to sit cross-legged on his worktable.

◊

Initially, Oya hadn't believed a society that worshipped women existed. But the more she talked to Jon, the more she saw it. He always placed himself so he was looking up at her – always gave her his full attention. He'd even let a couple projects get ruined because he wouldn't turn his focus from her until she left. There was no prostrating or wailing. It was the subtle things he did to show respect.

Amusingly, he was more respectful and submissive to other girls than he was to her. This indicated he wasn't certain about her, which was Oya's preference. Still, those little things added up. She now made sure he wasn't working on anything needing his attention before interrupting.

"Is there something else I can help you with?" Jon asked uncertainly.

"There is… I heard you two talking. What does it mean that he's being 'summoned home?'"

Confusion twisted Jon's face, "He's been called home to honor his aunt and attend the event being held for her and others. They did wonderful things recently and deserve recognition."

"*Who else'll be there?*"

"Representatives from all eighteen countries. I'm sure at least one of my brothers will be sent."

"*Wow. Sounds big.*"

"It is." Jon grinned, looking up at her.

"*It'll take the entire break?*"

"As far as Ferdinan's concerned. He'll be sent to Chūzo's capital with his oldest sister. They'll probably spend a couple weeks at the palace coordinating and preparing for traveling allies. The celebration will take a week. Then, he, Zephyr, and any other students in attendance will travel back to the islands."

Oya frowned at that information.

"I'm sorry, but I doubt you'll be invited."

"*Huh? No!*" She waved a delicate hand around nonchalantly. "*That's not an event I belong at.*"

"Then what's wrong?"

"*The palace. His cousin'll be there.*"

"Where else would a prince be?"

I shouldn't release him from his punishment 'til after the break. "*Ferdinan shouldn't go there.*"

"It isn't for us to decide," Jon responded, taken aback.

"*I see.*" Bringing a finger to her lip, the wheels in Oya's head turned as she looked for a solution.

"Why?"

"*Hmm?*"

"Why? The palace is a second home for him."

"You've known him your whole life and you haven't realized." Oya let her disappointment rain down on Jon. It made him visibly quiver. *"What good is an ally who lives within arm's reach if you don't even try!?"*

"I'm sorry...but... What did I do wrong?"

It wasn't just fear filling those chocolate brown eyes. Regret sighed out of her...but this wasn't a problem. Reaching out a hand, she did what she'd done dozens of times to random people on these islands. Stopping the formation of a memory was easy. She didn't even have to delve deep. This was probably the most useful thing she'd learned about the mind. A gentle swipe and everything after she'd said "I see" was gone.

For a moment, Jon sat frozen. Then, he blinked. "Why?"

"*Hmm?*"

"Why shouldn't he go to the palace? It's a second home for him."

"That's something you'll have to learn for yourself." A hint of lunacy showed through her wink.

Chapter 10

A second message surprised Ferdinan after the ship departed. Mother Artimus requested his presence. From North Oueshi he'd travel home with Xingho, Raonie, and Evelyn. There he'd meet up with his family and continue onto Chūzo's capital. *Why the sudden change?* Facing any Artimus... After all those things he'd said to Jon at the hospital – why would they want him? But he was excited to see how Evelyn was doing. It hadn't been long since he left her to the Artimus's care. And she was happy when they talked over the screen, but...

^^^

Ferdinan hid the pain his words caused him. "And this woman...she's the most wonderful of all. Like your own grandmother, she loves everyone unconditionally. This woman everyone calls 'Mother...' She's the only person who can compare to how amazing your grandmother was. She's the only reason I've ever been jealous of Jon."

Smiling sweetly, he kicked himself inside for this last thought. It came unbidden and slipped out before he could stop his tongue. But he couldn't deny the truthfulness of it.

VVV

Gloom filled him just thinking about it – a gloom as deep as the angry music screaming in his ear. He didn't deserve to see her. Regardless, he couldn't turn down an order from Duchess Samultz. And there was something he hadn't done yet... Quickly he sent a confirmation message and informed the porter of the change.

If nothing else, getting off the boat a day sooner was nice. Being trapped in tiny cabins - unable to run - wasn't something he was fond of.

The skeleton removed three of the four shirts he wore and kicked off his shoes. Grabbing a blanket, he laid down on the cot and closed his eyes. The harsh tunes did little to keep him from drifting off to sleep - deep and dreamless.

* * *

Might as well get this done. The extension on coursework was nice, but that meant what precious time Jon had with his family would be tainted. Luckily, he had four days before arriving to get as much done as possible. Since one of the tasks was picking a song, he could listen while programming.

More than once he had to skip the "music."

These songs...they were...they grated against his nerves. How was any of this noise music? Better yet, how would any of it help them with the Welcome Show?

One "song" played after another. Even the ones not bad enough to skip weren't exactly enjoyable. Altogether, the music was pretty distracting. An hour and a half should've been more than enough time to finish this program and allow him to start on the next, but... *Ugh...! Where did he get this?*

Jon considered shutting the whole thing off. Listening to anything while working was a bad idea. Then...

Soft thunder rolled through a foggy night and out of the earpiece. Jon braced himself. If the other songs were any indication, singing would start soon. Ya...the voices... There was no way any of this was worship music. It sounded wrong. But...even if it was, why not get better singers? And the instruments! Whatever they were playing always stepped up -

becoming harsher and more grating than the voices…if that was possible.

But…the song continued, and no singing came.

It sounded…

Piano keys struck…meshing beautifully with strings…

It…

Those keys danced high, then slowed to a deep waltz. Mournful…yearning… Tears filled Jon's eyes. All he could think about was the first time he stepped on a boat without his family. Long days and weeks and months of tears and isolation. Would he ever see them? Then…he finally made it back home only to leave again. It was harder the second time. And the third. And fourth…

Past and present swayed around each other. When had that heartache lessened? When did it become bearable…and how?

The music slowed – every note poignant…unmistakable. Like a sapphire on white silk.

It…it captivated him. Especially that piano. His parents' faces came to mind as did each brother. That ache… Those notes dredged up every second of longing…of loneliness… Pausing the song, Jon dried his face. Minutes passed.

For all his years of piano…nothing had made him feel like that… If sorcery was a song, this was it. But…he wanted to keep listening. It was amazing. Music that elicited such emotions…why hadn't he heard it before? Jon needed to know. Pulling up the information attached to the file… The symbols…there were two sets. One looked similar to what appeared on Oya's screen when he spoke. The other didn't look too far off from one of the languages he knew… "B-be…e…Be-e-t-t-th…"

Sucking in a breath, Jon steadied himself. He only knew one ancient language, but...he should be able to figure this out. Trying it out in his mind a few times, Jon gave it another go. "Be...Be-e-t-thoe-van. Be-e-thō-van... Who's that?"

That was a word he'd never seen before, but he was curious. The music...he wanted more. Copying the symbols, Jon pulled up another screen and started a search for their language of origin. He then took note of the song. There were still a few more to listen to...but, he didn't want to abuse his ears any further.

* * *

Pounding woke Ferdinan. But not the pounding of drums beating against his ear canal. *Knocking...? Who knocks?* Stumbling to the door, he found his cousin on the other side.

Zephyr pushed passed him – not waiting for an invitation.

"May I help you, my Prince?" Ferdinan asked, rubbing the sleep from his eyes. A backhand woke him the rest of the way. Remembering himself, he went down to one knee.

"That's better," the Prince spat, closing the door.

Exhaustion paled Zephyr's face and darkened his bloodshot eyes. He'd been notified of his Prince's time in Isolation. But it didn't look like his cousin's stay did much good.

"What did you do to me?" Zephyr's hands accented his words until he brought one down hard on Ferdinan's face.

"What's been done, my Prince?" he asked, ignoring his throbbing eye.

"Everything was fine! Then you get back, and..." Shivering, his Prince pulled out a thin, collapsible rod concealed in his pocket. A swing extended it to the length of his arm. It didn't look like much, but Ferdinan knew it was basically a metal whip. "You *will* tell me, and you *will* reverse it."

"I'm sorry, my Prince. I'm sorry."

"*Agh!* Is this some kind of rebellion? You're torturing me for keeping you in line?" Zephyr raised the rod high above his head. "If you're tired of discipline, improve your behavior!"

A cacophony of notes ground in the skeleton's ears - drowning out the whistle of that swinging rod. Ferdinan ducked his head so it hit his back instead. Cold metal stung. It split his shirt and bit deep into bare flesh. Mouth clenched tight; the Tinkerer didn't make a sound.

Again, the rod rose high above its wielder's head and with another demand of "Tell me!" it came down with all of Zephyr's considerable strength. Ferdinan shifted so each strike hit his back or shoulders. He could take as much as any Fighter...as long as nothing vital was hit. But even strategic positioning couldn't stop most blows from further splitting shirt and skin.

Calculations ran through Ferdinan's head. *How much longer before I'll have to stop him?* Soon, the blows became weaker and less consistent. Zephyr staggered to the side. *When did he last sleep?*

"Why won't it stop?" Fear and anger blanketed Zephyr at the sight of his reflection. "I'm nothing like you! Stop looking at me!"

Head bowed deeply, Ferdinan focused on Zephyr's feet. "I apologize."

The rod came down again and again... Until the Prince couldn't swing anymore. Despairing and exhausted, Zephyr sunk to his knees. A *clank* rang through the room when the rod fell and rolled away, freeing the Fighter to bury his face in his hands and weep.

What have I done to you? Because the Queen was from Oueshi, his cousin was freer with tears than most people in North

Chūzo. Even so, Ferdinan never saw his Prince cry in terrified frustration.

Moving closer, he knelt beside the Fighter and did his best to assess and comfort his Prince. He couldn't guess what his cousin was feeling, but his own heart wrenched. *I can never fix the pain I've caused.*

Once the tears dried up, Zephyr stumbled to his feet, pushing Ferdinan down. "You'll tell me.... I'll make you..."

Ferdinan cringed and waited for a worse beating to commence. Instead the door opened and then closed. Risking a glance, the Tinkerer raised his head. Zephyr was gone. Whatever the Prince was going to do, he didn't want to know.

Struggling to his feet, he staggered stiffly to the door and locked it. His skin burned. He felt blood oozing down his back and arms. Patching himself up here wasn't ideal. A scalding hot shower to clean and disinfect the opened gashes was his first task. *I brought this upon myself.* Even knowing this he didn't dare turn off the music. Last thing he needed right now was that voice's commentary.

Luckily, not *every* hit broke skin. The problem was, one laceration or a dozen, he couldn't do much on his own. Tending to his shoulders and arms was easy enough, but without his personal medical supplies, his back was out of the question. He'd sleep on his belly tonight and hope it was enough...until disembarking tomorrow evening.

At least there was music to distract him.

* * *

"Ozar!" Jon yelled and ran down the gangplank – leaping into his brother's arms.

"Ah! Baby brother!" The impossibly tall man squeezed him tightly, leaving just enough to let him breathe. "I love you! Our niece told us all about your little adventure. I look forward to hearing the tale from you."

"Of course!" Jon half-wrung his brother's neck returning the hug. Tears blurred his eyes. And that haunting song floated through his mind... "I love you, too! I've missed home so much!"

"Home's missed you." Ozar slowly lowered Jon until his feet touched the ground.

When the man stood back up, the Thinker found himself facing the lower part of his brother's chest. This was weird. It wasn't long ago he stared into Ozar's belly button. *Have I really grown this much?*

"Where's Ferdinan?" Ozar's deep, black eyes scanned the crowd.

"You mean he's coming with us?" *Why didn't he say anything?*

"Ya, mom's request was granted. She wants to discuss what he knows concerning Evelyn."

"Really?"

Jon asked his mom to have Ferdinan brought here, but he didn't know if it'd happen – especially with the Tinkerer being summoned home for such an important event. Worse, there was no reason he could give beyond the gent enjoying time with Evelyn. But Oya's words gnawed at him. He couldn't ignore them. *I'm glad it worked.* "I'll get him."

Jon was halfway up the plank when the skeleton appeared – a bag in one hand and a box in the other. Ferdinan moved stiffly, as though trying to keep everything above the belt still.

"Would you like a hand?" Surprisingly, the gent didn't argue or put up a fight. The box... "Where did you get this?"

"It was a gift."

"Really?" *I thought she wanted the violin for herself...*

"Strange, isn't it?"

"A little... What happened to your eye?"

"I was clumsy."

Jon raised an eyebrow. "Why're you walking funny?"

Straight faced, Ferdinan returned the gesture as if the question was entirely ridiculous. "Those beds are far from comfortable."

"Ah...true." Jon stretched his neck, holding the beautifully carved box securely. "Ozar's waiting."

Though Jon ran back down, Ferdinan moved more conservatively. It was truly amazing. The two brothers standing side by side couldn't look any different. Ozar was broad and heavily muscled with coarse, black hair and midnight deep eyes. The man also made Jon look deathly pale by comparison - which was saying something considering how pale Ferdinan looked next to Jon. Rich, dark skin all but shone in the evening sun - unlike the two boys who were washed out by it. It didn't help that Jon and Ferdinan never got any darker despite living on islands and spending a good bit of time outdoors.

If Jon didn't look almost exactly like Father Artimus, Ferdinan would suspect the Dinta was a claimed child. And Jon wasn't the only one. Of the eight brothers, five were like Ozar - the spitting image of their mother. Only two took after their dad - though Samuel had a bit more of Mother's features than Jon. And one shared no genetic relation.

Heavy drums kicked in, drowning out everything, forcing Ferdinan to lower the volume. *I should turn it off...* Something cold and heavy formed in his gut at that thought. Turning it off... That... Shaking his head, Ferdinan ignored the sensation he couldn't identify and focused on one he could. He was scared. Even Jon noticed something was off back at the hospital and his ally didn't pay much attention to him. Here... Dozens of eyes watched him constantly. And that voice wasn't the only thing he had to worry about.

Following behind, he stopped a good distance from the man. The last thing Ferdinan needed was a death hug – they were painful enough without a flogged back. Screaming joined drums and metallic notes. *I should turn it off...but...* Bowing, he greeted his older ally. "Thank you for your hospitality, Ozar Hei-O. You didn't have to wait for me."

Unlike Jon and the other Artimus boys who were Dintas, Ozar was heir. And it didn't make sense... With no female offspring, heirship should've fallen to the eldest son, but Ozar was second in line.

"Don't be preposterous, little brother! We're going to the same place." He stepped forward, offering the usual Artimus greetings.

Holding up a shaky hand halted the man. Ferdinan didn't know when it happened, but Jon's family claimed him as a ninth son. He didn't ask to be. Neither did he like it. But you don't say "No" to your strongest ally concerning something like that. Normally he wouldn't be so blatantly rude to the heir of an allied country, but today wasn't a normal day. "Please...it was a difficult trip."

One look at the boy's clammy, pallid complexion was all the Hei-O needed. "I understand."

After Ozar's impossibly deep voice finished reverberating through his bones, the Hei-O led them to the waiting vehicle. Rude or not, Ferdinan slipped inside while the brothers played with the luggage. The extra time didn't help him find a comfortable way to sit. Leaning forward to rest boney elbows on knobby knees was the best he found.

At least the Artimuses were a family of giants. The roomy car meant he didn't need to worry about being bumped or pushed. When the two princes finally got in, Jon sat close to his big brother. The car took off. So did Jon and Ozar's ramblings. It was a good thirty minutes before either realized Ferdinan hadn't made a sound.

"You're looking tired, little brother." Ozar studied him with concern.

Despite being half a year younger, they called Ferdinan "little brother," while Jon held the title "baby brother." It was weird. But he'd rather be called "little" over "baby" any day. "The trip was rough; I didn't get much sleep."

"Then lay down and nap 'til we arrive." The giant offered generously.

Ferdinan couldn't accept that invitation.

But, despite all his efforts and the cacophony in his ear, sleep eventually seized him.

Chapter 11

The brothers grinned when Ferdinan slumped over, completely out. Neither would the skeleton wake up when they arrived. Knowing the family was dying to see their baby brother, Ozar sent Jon ahead and he carried Ferdinan to the room shared by all the unmarried boys. Ferdinan requested his own room every time he visited, but letting a child sleep alone...it was wrong. Even though it'd make him happy... They couldn't bring themselves to grant his request.

Ozar laid Ferdinan gently on the bed prepared for him then left to find the rest of the family. *We'll let him sleep.*

Their baby brother's customary mauling always made the Hei-O grin. Though, Evelyn mixed into the chaos tightened his chest. She was so tiny... But she laughed and did well to hold her own. Those green-ringed dark eyes latched onto him – face brightening. Prying herself out of the pile, Evelyn ran over – looking all around.

"I'm sorry, Evelyn, but he's sleeping. You'll have to wait 'til he wakes up."

"Ahh! But I want to play with my big brother!" Dark barrel curls bounced as she protested.

"I know, but it's important to let him rest. He didn't look well."

Running back to the pile, she jumped in, searching for Jon's head. Getting out was a losing fight with five giants and a little girl smashing him.

"Alright, my children, that's enough," Mother laughed. Slowly they disentangled themselves, taking care not to hurt Evelyn.

Jon knelt, making himself eye level with the adorable little girl. "Evelyn Oza, what're you trying to tell me?"

"Is Ferdinan sad again?"

The Artimus boys looked between each other at her innocent question.

"Why would you think that?"

"Uncle Ozar said he didn't look well."

"Ah." Jon hugged her. "It was a hard trip. He was so tired; he fell asleep while fighting to stay awake. We should let him rest."

"Really? He's ok?" she smiled. "When can I play with him?"

Jon looked to the bright sky past the picturesque window. "If he wakes up, he may be up for playing after dinner. But he might sleep all night."

"OH!" Her dark eyes nearly popped out of her head as she remembered her earth-shattering news. "Pa-papa is teaching me to cook!"

"Really? I better keep practicing or you'll get better than me," Jon winked.

It was heartwarming watching the two. Jon was better with young children than Ozar expected. Someone tugged at his cuff. Looking down, he found Xingho's hand fussing at a spot on his new shirt - concern marring his older brother's face.

"What's on your sleeve?"

That caught their mom's attention. Soon he had two people examining his shirt. Evelyn held everyone else's attention with a story about her adventure to find new shoes. It was a tale she insisted everyone hear. A look from mom signaled Xhingho to keep everyone occupied. Mother then gestured for Ozar to take advantage of the girl's distraction.

They slipped out of the room and hurried to where Ferdinan slept.

* * *

Oya roamed the main island. Both her suitemates left for break. An adult tried putting her with some girls who stayed, but she discouraged such intentions. Strangers weren't going to invade her new home. Neither would she leave the home she now had. She enjoyed a victory walk around the beach only to realize something.

She was **VERY** bored.

Delicate hands ran through her hair. It was so long the dark strands stayed between her fingers even with her arm stretched out as far as it'd go. Years of growth... She studied the familiar black. It shone with a light it seemed to produce. Dropping her hand freed the hair to sway in the breeze.

Change is part of life...and death. Bare feet skipped down the beach and to the end of a pier. Kneeling, she faced her reflection.

Choppy waves leapt up to meet her, making her grin. *"Hello, old friend, could you be calm a moment so I might see properly?"*

The waves stilled and the surface became a mirror.

"Thank you." Her new look...

Oya couldn't say she was displeased. It was interesting. *How did this happen? Why did it...?* Lowering her head made her roots visible. Her hair wasn't growing in dark anymore. And those long blood red roots were looking weird. *There's no turning me back, is there?* It wasn't just her hair. Her eyes changed too. They used to be black with gold specks, matching her hair. Those eyes were her favorite feature... But...the green was completely unnatural. *At least it's a fun green.* Her hair, on the other hand, was simply annoying.

Sticking her tongue out at her reflection, she decided. Giggles filled her. Rolling up her pant leg, Oya freed the dagger she'd fashioned from a shell. Laying on her belly, head hanging off the pier, she winked at her reflection, grabbed a chunk of hair, and cut off the black. Bit by bit it was discarded. The last reminder of a life she'd never see again.

* * *

"You didn't notice when you carried him in?" Mother asked as they rushed up the stairs.

"No."

"Was he in pain?"

"No." Ozar shook his head. "He was a little pale, but looked fine."

Entering the huge room, they found Ferdinan sleeping. Mother Artimus went straight to her youngest son while Ozar turned on a floor lamp, moving it close. Gently, so she wouldn't wake him, Mother rolled Ferdinan to his side.

Horror turned Ozar's insides. "He wasn't like that at the docks..."

"Call Samuel. Tell him to return from town."

"Of course."

Running out, Ozar did as commanded. As expected, his younger brother was confused by the sudden call. Normally Samuel stayed away until Ferdinan settled in. But the boy needed a Healer whether he wanted one or not.

By the time he returned, Ferdinan was lying on his belly – awake and cringing. Mother had cut and peeled back four shirts and was gently tugging at a thick cloth. Blood soaked every inch of it.

Ozar locked the door then moved over to help. The stick-thin boy struggled futilely. If he couldn't escape mom – he didn't stand a chance against them both. "He'll be here soon, Mom."

"Thank you, darling. Please hand me the water."

That cloth was thoroughly stuck. Wetting it down, Mother waited for his skin to release the fibers more willingly. Still, progress was slow. Not an inch at a time. Yet...even when mom got too ambitious, Ferdinan didn't make a sound. This had to hurt.

"Ozar, more light."

"Of course."

Ferdinan struggled in vain again. Light filled the room. So did a couple muffled gasps.

"What happened to you? Who did this?" The Hei-O leaned in closer – studying Ferdinan's bruised and torn skin. If this was all, it'd be gruesome enough. But there were numerous scars marring his back and sides. The sight stole Ozar's breath. Countless scars stretched over protruding bones...

◊

A knock broke past the angry music screaming in Ferdinan's ear and stopped his heart. *How did I fall asleep with this still playing?* But...even the most grating song was more pleasant than that voice. Anything to keep it away...

Before the Hei-O opened the door, Mother Artimus put her hands on his shoulders to hold him in place. Even the endless falling of her touch wasn't enough to distract him. *...no...*

"No!" In walked a man who looked like an older version of Jon – only with slightly darker skin and curlier hair. "You can't call him!"

"Son, you need Samuel's help. You don't want this becoming infected."

"Please...! Don't touch me..." Ferdinan buried his face in the sheets, shaking. There was no outdoing their strength or weight. Because of their touch, he couldn't think...and his lungs wouldn't work.

Ferdinan was completely helpless – a half-squashed bug watching the shoe hover above for another go. He couldn't claim this was a fall. And...any scan the Healer did would show the remnants of everything else. The skeleton knew how well the body documented everything it experienced.

Samuel approached the trembling boy cautiously. "What happened to him?"

"He won't tell me." Mother's voice choked back tears.

"Ferdinan, do you give me permission to heal this?" Samuel asked, voice soft and calm.

"NO!" Struggling and falling and failing... Like Oya, Mother Artimus's touch was unique to her. And, like Oya, it was intense. Fire. Blades. Lightning. There were so many ways people's touch felt. But it was ones like this – ones which didn't hurt – that were the most jarring. "Don't touch me!"

"I understand," Samuel sighed. "But I'm healing you anyway."

Anguish escaped Ferdinan's lips. Raging fire consumed his body as the Healer scanned him.

"Most of the damage is superficial. But there're a number of stress fractures on his ribs and shoulders."

No...please stop...please... Drums kicked in and the screeching metal of electric instruments. Even if he used every ounce of strength there was no getting out. *Why did I come here?*

I should've gone home. I should've requested permission to turn them down...

"Ozar, I think Evelyn would love a sleepout with the family."

"I understand." Ozar hurried out.

"Ferdinan," Mother said, moving her impossibly tall body to the floor and bringing her eyes even with his. "I need to know who did this."

Trembling, Ferdinan shook his head, face rubbing against the sheets. Betraying his Prince and country... No. He was horrible. But he'd never willingly hurt his people. This was his fault. He wouldn't let his Prince fall for something he caused.

"I need to know what to tell your mother–"

"NO!" Ignoring the endless fall and consuming fire, he pushed himself up. But both adults restrained him easily. "Stop! You can't do this! Let go of me!"

"Calm down. Ferdinan, I can't heal you if you're moving so much."

"I don't want you to! Let me go!"

A new voice cut through the scene. "What's going on?"

"Jon! Darling, you need to go back downstairs." Mother instructed urgently. Ozar must've forgotten to lock the door.

Jon didn't listen. Instead he observed, trying to understand the scene before him.

Seeing the Thinker, Ferdinan stopped fighting... *Let me melt into nothingness.*

"Is this what she meant?" Jon asked.

Ferdinan stiffened. "I don't know what you're talking about."

"Ya. That's what I thought." Jon secured the door. "Mom, Evelyn's asking for you."

"Tell her I'm busy right now, but I'll be down later."

"I can take your place." The Thinker fell to his knees beside her and took Ferdinan's arm – adding stinging needles to everything else assaulting the skeleton. Jon was tiny next to her. "I'll help Samuel."

"Thank you, but I need to talk to him."

Jon gave his ally a long, hard look. "He isn't going to talk right now."

"Do you know anything about this, my child?"

"Nothing! Because this...!" Jon stopped before he really started yelling.

That allowed Ferdinan to free himself from the stinging needles and an endless fall. He didn't try getting away, just wrapped twig arms around his head. *I'm going to fail again. I'm going to hurt my family...my country...why is everything falling apart?*

Samuel's voice interrupted his sufferings. "Ok, Ferdinan, prepare yourself."

Nausea and fire attacked. Ferdinan was infinitely grateful he hadn't eaten today.

A Healer's ability to heal someone used the patient's energy. All it took was touching a person and the Healer could reach out to every cell and force the injured body to repair itself. Small injuries were innocuous. But larger ones like his flogged back...well, it was rather unpleasant.

Ferdinan tore his mind away – focusing on the music screaming in his ears. He wrapped it around himself like a blanket...burying his head...

* * *

"Mom?" Jon peeked around the door of her study. Samuel made Ferdinan sleep after a partial healing, then sent him off. The rest of the family was in the middle of "safari" – a silly little game of Evelyn's her new family was happy to indulge her in.

"Come in, son."

"You haven't called his family, have you?"

"Not yet. I don't know what to say..."

Being the smallest in a room...it was comforting. This is how it should be. At school, he was always bigger than those around his age. He'd even caught up with most of the oldest students. Being able to stand before his mom and feel tiny again... To feel like he was no longer required to hold up the world... "Can I talk to you? So much happened this block... I'm confused...I don't know what's right anymore."

"Come here." She held her arms open and hugged him before offering a chair.

Where do I begin? There was so much... It wasn't even half a year. How did all that happen in so little time? And he was forbidden from talking about it...

But this was his mom. He needed to tell someone, and she needed to know. Arbitrary rules encouraging Ferdinan's twisted desires or fears or whatever drove the gent... Those didn't matter. He didn't care. Jon *needed* to talk to someone. And he trusted his mom more than anyone else.

"Shortly after the block began, Ferdinan got a call." Once he started talking, it all came out. Starting from before they left for the hospital and ending with the warning Oya gave him. His mom listened patiently, soaking in every word.

Chapter 12

Once the family fell asleep, Ferdinan was moved to a guest room – where he was never left unattended. Samuel tried healing his little brother a couple times. Every time the boy fought him – ultimately reopening the partially closed skin. This left Jon or Mother tending Ferdinan's back.

It took longer this way but was probably for the best. Healing made Ferdinan unbearably ill. The skeleton was too malnourished for a complete session anyway. Leeching what little his bones and organs had wasn't preferable.

The only thing their little brother did to acknowledge them was eat when Jon told him to. But he wouldn't look at them. Or talk to them. Neither did he eat much and was in visible pain afterwards.

Then there was the screaming…every night.

What happened to my little brother?

The door creaked open and Jon motioned him to the hall.

"What is it?" Samuel closed the door behind him.

"Can he have visitors?"

"As long as he doesn't move too much. Why?"

"Evelyn *really* wants to see him. It'd be good for him. We aren't getting anywhere like this…and…I know he won't ignore her."

"If you think it'll help."

"I think it will."

Nodding, Samuel changed topics. "Are nightmares normal for him?"

"For the last few months... I don't know about before."

"Thank you."

Jon rushed off and Samuel returned to the room. Opening the blinds and windows made it more welcoming for a visit. If Ferdinan took any notice, the boy didn't show it. Soon little feet pounded up the stairs. The door flew open and Evelyn ran in, screaming joyfully. She didn't see the horror on Ferdinan's face – she was too busy charging him. For a tiny five-year-old, she effectively knocked the skeleton to the floor with a tackle.

The brothers exchanged glances. Not a sound left Ferdinan, though pain contorted his face.

"Big brother! They wouldn't let me play with you! They said you were sick. Do you feel better? Can we play? Wow!" She poked at his razor-sharp collar bones – making him wince.

Boney fingers shot for the top button of his shirt. "I'm sorry. Not yet."

Grinning triumphantly, Jon leaned on the back of a chair. Those were the first words Ferdinan said in days. But talking to Evelyn wasn't the same as acknowledging either brother.

"Lady Evelyn, I apologize." Ferdinan grimaced when he lifted and carried her to a small table by an open window. "I'm not up for playing, but I'd love hearing how you like it here."

Warmth and joy sung in her eyes. "I got to ride on a boat! Oh! And my bed is bigger than a house! And everyone's so friendly! I even got new shoes a couple days ago!"

The brothers watched Ferdinan listen intently to her. He returned all the excitement she gave him. A soft, gentle smile never left his lips despite her rambling for hours. Not once did he interrupt her. *Who is this boy by the window?* He wasn't at all like the child Samuel knew.

"Oh! Oh!" Evelyn bounced in her chair. "How long 'til I become a giant too?"

An odd grimace washed over Ferdinan's face. "That's not exactly how family works..."

"Huh? But I'm part of a giant family now. You said they all grew so big because of love..."

Being confronted with his own words left Ferdinan visibly flatfooted, but the Healer couldn't figure out why. Talking about genetics left Evelyn confused. So, the skeleton changed gears completely. "Your Uncle Rigel isn't a giant. Neither does he look like Mother or Father Artimus or any of their other sons, right?"

"Yah..." A smile brightened Evelyn's face. "He's still big, but not like everyone else. And his black hair is straight like mine."

"Exactly." Nervous energy forced crystal blue eyes around the room - avoiding Jon and Samuel. Whatever he was thinking, the skeleton was having trouble picking his words. "Rigel Dinta was claimed like you and... He looks different because of something called DNA. DNA is a material inside everybody that makes them look the way they do. It's something you have when you're born and it doesn't change. If your family is the one who gave you that DNA you'll look like them, but if your DNA doesn't come from your family, you won't look like them. Does that make sense?"

Long moments passed with Evelyn's head in her hands and lips scrunched to the side. Even Samuel and his baby brother waited eagerly for her answer.

Sitting up straight, Evelyn shook her head. "No."

Samuel, Jon, Ferdinan – all three of their reactions were comical at her blatantly honest answer. *Why didn't we think to explain this to her?* In the Healer's defense, Evelyn was five and knew the family she lost. There was no need explaining the differences in their looks...they thought. And, ultimately, it didn't matter. She was their family now.

"Um..." Leaning forward, Ferdinan tapped a finger against the little table.

Why is he struggling with this? It took Samuel a minute to understand. Ferdinan was used to Scientists, Tinkerers in particular. Explaining concepts considered basic for even the youngest Scientists to a normal child must be difficult. Samuel wanted to see what solution the skeleton found. But his baby brother tugged at his shirt – wanting his attention.

"Can he be left unattended?" Samuel whispered.

Jon nodded and motioned him out of the room – not speaking until the door was closed. "He won't do anything that'd upset her."

"Oh?"

"Um... It's like he feels compelled to keep children safe and happy." Jon's lip twitched. "Or those who act childlike."

"Really? For how long?"

"I noticed when he started mentoring three years ago."

"He's always been protective of his little sisters..." Samuel mused.

Jon wrung his hands – trembling slightly. "S-Samuel, you've seen people die, right?"

That was the last question he expected from his baby brother. "Why would you ask that?"

"...um...I..." Jon's eyes darted to the door. "How did you get over it?"

"Did you see someone die?" Of all things, this was one Samuel didn't want his baby brother knowing yet.

"No." Jon stared at the closed door. Pain filled those chocolate brown eyes. "But Ferdinan did. Two of his volunteers didn't make it. He stayed in their rooms after they went into a coma. He stayed 'til..."

"...ah..."

"Do you feel responsible for the ones you couldn't save?"

"Sometimes." Samuel hugged his baby brother. "Is that part of his problem?"

"Ya." Jon scratched his head.

A million concerns flooded the Healer's mind – but he'd need time to sort through them. "Could Evelyn get him out of the room?"

"If you tell her what you want him to do, she can get him to do it." Jon started back in but stopped abruptly. "'*Part* of his problem?'"

"There're some ugly things in the world. Things I hope you never learn about." Samuel's chest constricted. He wished Ferdinan didn't know them.

"I don't understand."

"Good."

* * *

Nothingness. It swam above her. And all around. It swirled lazy inside her. No shape. No feel. No smell. It was simply the empty void of nothing.

Oya laid on the couch staring at that nothing. She stared past it. Or didn't stare at all...as that would've required focusing her eyes.

Boundless imagination.

Excessive energy.

Countless square miles of island to explore.

But she was consumed. Trapped by this nothing - held prisoner.

Why was she so utterly bored? Bored nigh to tears...if her inhuman green eyes could cry. *When was the last time I didn't have anything to look forward to...or out for?*

Sleep...she didn't need it. Any more time in the sun and she'd become a cooked lobster despite skin used to a lifetime outdoors. Even watching the little orbs dance around her had lost its amusement. *Maybe rolling over will offer a different view to enjoy?* But she was already intimately familiar with the couch's imperfections. The seemingly random pattern in the carpets was solved. And all the ceiling's dots were counted. *I haven't numbered the carpet threads yet...* It'd take moving some furniture but should be easy enough.

On thread 13,856, a chime sounded. Looking around, she saw a small light on her screen blink. *Oh yah...those silly glass things do that when they want something.*

Grabbing it, Oya deciphered the symbols. *A call? Maybe...?* Uncertain, she tapped it like she'd seen others do - this was the first time her screen did this. A familiar and sorely missed face appeared. "*FERDINAN*!"

"*Shhh...*" He gestured for quiet - backing up a bit to reveal a small, sleeping girl in his arms. "*She won't let me put her down. She's woken up every time I've tried.*"

"What a special little girl to make you smile like that." Oya already knew this. That yellow string was impossible to ignore at the hospital. Yellow wasn't a common connection. But very little was common when it came to her friend.

"She is. Very special." Ferdinan spoke softly, smiling at the sleeping child.

Delicate fingers reached up and played with the chain around her neck. *"To what do I owe this great honor? Not only a call, but you're even speaking Oŭndo!"*

"I was thinking you'd like some conversation before practicing Common… Wait! What happened to your hair?" Ferdinan did a double take when he realized there was no black or length left.

"*Do you like it? I got bored.*"

"*I thought you might be… The style suits you…but please don't play with sharp implements while I'm gone.*"

Sticking out her tongue, she wiggled her fingers around her head. "*I'll have you know there're 473,842 dots on the ceiling. I've found non-lethal ways of keeping myself busy.*"

"*I'm sorry. I should've called sooner. Students are more willing to work when they've got nothing better to do…*"

"*Twelve days is a long time to fill.*"

"*Practice your Common with those who stayed on the islands.*"

"No! That's our little pastime. I'd never cheat on you like that."

Ferdinan went five shades of red. "*Please, others are in here.*"

"*Fine. Has anyone chosen a song yet?*"

"*That's partly why I called. Two people have. What should I tell them now?*"

Oya sniggered. "*Make the song their own.*"

"*Umm…I'm not sure what you mean. If I don't understand, I doubt the others will.*"

"Explore the song and what it means to them. Consider how it represents their assigned classification. Are there any changes they'd make? Do they want it put to dance? Played live? Set to a puppet

show or synchronized eating…? I don't know. Be creative. Like you are with your magnificent inventions."

"Those aren't all that great."

"They're amazing! So many astounding ideas! You not only think of them, but design and build them! I'm completely envious! One of these days you'll teach me, even if I can't understand."

A deeper shade of red encompassed his face and he batted at something she couldn't see. *"You're smart. With a little effort you'd understand easily. They aren't amazing. It isn't difficult."*

"Depends on who you ask."

"What're you two talking about?" Jon's voice called from off screen. "How did you make his face that red?"

She grinned and answered in Common. "Know you really want do to?"

A sly grin grew on Ferdinan's face, but he kept his eyes on her. "Do you really want to know?"

Oya leveled-up the mischievousness of her own voice and repeated the sentence properly.

"Never mind." Laughter rose from somewhere in the room, and Jon grumbled something she didn't catch.

"I have a song for you."

"What?"

"I can't play an instrument…or sing. But I can make music more 'interesting.' Here." The struggle to make it work was rather epic. But with some help from her friend, she managed.

◊

That short, blood red hair bobbed around enjoying every extra beat. Watching Oya's joy filled him with a strange warmth he wasn't used to. Yet his heart ached. Ferdinan didn't deserve her bright face or to hear her cheer his name enthusiastically... But it felt amazing enough to distract him from the lightning in his arms. *What does the original sound like?* He knew this language. And the message was nice. It felt like the Artist was talking to him.

"*Thank you. I enjoyed that. Do you have the original? I'm interested to see what you did.*"

Demand the world.

That wild, Cheshire grin didn't waver as she battled getting the original to play. The song was lengthy, but the words held more power with the slower beat. If you didn't know what you were hearing, the altered version was more enjoyable...but...

She giggled – watching him listen. *"Which did you like better?"*

"Oh, uh...they were both nice. Do I have the program?"

Great answer.

"*Yes. If you transferred everything from the cube.*" Mischievousness filled her eyes. *"Have you been practicing? Do I get to hear anything yet?"*

"Ah, yeah... I haven't had a chance since arriving, but..."

Lazy.

"But...?"

"I'll correct my mistake." Blue crystals dropped to the floor. He failed at everything. Before the voice could agree, Ferdinan turned on the earpiece for music to drown it out.

Oya laughed. "*That's not a mistake, just a setback. Setbacks happen. But...don't place it above more important things.*"

"More important things?" He looked down at the little girl in his arms, acutely aware of the lightning emanating from her.

^^^

Ferdinan took Evelyn's small hand – stifling the grimace her lightning touch caused. "Your father and grandmother didn't survive. You won't see them again."

Slowly those words sunk in. It took time for her to understand them. When she did, her teeth clenched and tears welled – magnifying the green ring around her irises. "But..."

"I'm sorry. My incompetence killed them. I wasn't fast enough... You gave everything...and I failed you. I'm sorry." Ferdinan lowered his head, too ashamed to face her.

"No. I get to see them when I'm all better... I'll see them when I go home..."

Crystal blue eyes hidden, he shook his head slowly.

"I told them I'd come back once I helped!" Her tears were moments from falling.

"I'm sorry. I stole them from you..." Ferdinan's voice cracked.

Murderer.

He flinched at the accusation. The truth.

Shooting lightning dug in deeper as she burst into sobs.

Wrapping her in his arms, Ferdinan held on while she wailed. Each cry cut deeper into his soul.

vvv

That memory – he'd never forget...no matter how much he wanted to. *"No, I won't. Thank you for your permission to slack."*

"Don't get too used to it. That permission ends with the end of break." She wiggled a finger off the tip of her nose.

* * *

"Dad?" Jon walked up to Father Artimus, who'd recently returned from the capital and was now playing in the kitchen.

Father covered the bowl and smiled brightly at his son. "Jon!"

Of all the Artimus boys, only Jon and Samuel looked like their dad. While Samuel had darker skin and a more pronounced curl to his hair, Jon was a carbon copy. It was nice knowing how you'd look in fifty years. "What makes you such a good chef?"

"That's a tall question if I've ever heard one." Tired eyes smiled at his last-born son as he guided Jon to the table.

Pulling out a chair, the Thinker sat down. "I'm sorry."

"Knowing your audience is the first step. Practice goes a long way… But with eight boys I've had endless opportunities." Father Artimus patted his son's shoulder and sat down next to him. "What's actually bothering you?"

"Mom told you I was tasked with feeding Ferdinan, right?"

"I do recall hearing such a thing." A toothy smile split the older man's face, easing his son's stress.

"He hates everything! The only time I haven't heard complaints is when I leave raw vegetables nearby…" Jon scratched the back of his neck. "I don't know what to do. I made him weigh in before we left and he'd dropped two pounds. For months he's said my food's disgusting – that it makes him sick."

"Hmm…" Leaning back in his chair, Father considered his response. "I think he's telling you the truth."

"*Ugh!* Don't say that!"

"Think. What did he eat before you started feeding him?"

"Nothing?" Jon rolled his eyes.

"So, his stomach isn't used to real food, let alone rich or spiced." When Jon sat mouth agape, Father continued on. "Hand me the screen from the wall."

Obediently, he retrieved it - waiting while his dad typed in something.

"Here." Returning the screen, Father Artimus instructed, "Read the articles I've pulled up. You'll find them helpful."

The first article was surprising. "When did this happen?"

"Before you were born. Famine hit the Grasslands pretty hard a few years in a row. They insisted on remaining secluded. Half the population died from starvation before we got in and assessed their needs. Another quarter died after supplies arrived...before we figured out the right foods to offer. It was scary."

"Is that why Samuel's so fascinated by the Grasslands?" Jon smirked, but was doing so wrong?

"Partly, I'm sure."

"Do you think Ferdinan knows about this?"

"He's a wealth of information. Why do you ask, son?"

"There're some things he outright refuses to eat, despite being tasteless and nutritionally sound."

Another smile crossed Father's face. "I'll prepare Ferdinan's food while you study."

"Thanks, Dad." Jon jumped up and gave his dad a hug. "I'll track you down with any questions."

"Samuel's a good resource too. You may find things in there he's told you, and you've forgotten."

Jon blushed. "I don't remember forgetting anything."

A hearty laugh escaped Father, who hugged his son back and sent him on his way.

Chapter 13

Oya's forbidden music screamed in Ferdinan's ear while words glowed from the screen in his hand. Even before finding the article he felt cold...empty... Gut wrenchingly painful words magnified those sensations. Clean up crews worldwide flooded into Azuté. But the devastation... They hadn't made a dent. The western-most countries – Oueshi's countries – had their own death and destruction to clean up. As did Kidico and Mundan. Most of Chūzo was ok. There were infected persons, just not as many – and only in the western countries.

Offering help to the hardest hit was a privilege few could afford. The damage plaguing Oueshi was impossible to see from the Artimus's magnificent property. But then, both Father Artimus and Samuel could heal simply by touching a person – unlike normal healers. They'd never let those who worked and lived on these grounds suffer.

The tune changed from harsh to comforting. Skipping to the next song, Ferdinan put the screen down. It hadn't finished turning off when Evelyn appeared and dragged him outside. The sun was blinding. Aside from time spent by the window listening to Evelyn, he hadn't seen sunlight in days.

Ferdinan was back in the unmarried boy's room. Keeping up with the younger Artimuses' energy was exhausting. Worse was their irrational need to hug him. It put his nerves on end figuratively and literally. Now Evelyn was done hearing "No" to playing. Outside, she showed off the playhouse Xingho built for her.

It was less of a playhouse and more of a cottage. Inside were piles of stuffed toys and a giant round table perfectly suited to her.

A dozen child sized chairs surrounded it, each with a plush animal. She removed two of them and offered a chair to Ferdinan.

Can her uncles play in here even without the chairs? Considering the barely six-foot tall Rigel was the smallest, it was unlikely. They started with a tea party and played the rest of the day. The sun was setting when Xingho called them inside for dinner.

Evelyn insisted on sitting next to Ferdinan, which turned into sitting on his lap. She tried eating off his plate but found his special meal didn't suit her tastes. This was unfortunate. He'd happily share. Focusing on anything but the constant lightning coursing through him was difficult but helped by the music screaming in his ear.

After dinner, they went to the common room. Evelyn taught them a new game called "butterfly collectors." They were to collect one of every butterfly in the world so they could cast the spell giving everyone wings. This way they could fly everywhere – even to the moon!

Her parents allowed the game to go on for an hour before announcing bedtime. Though Evelyn wasn't happy about this, no longer needing to dodge the family of giants thrilled Ferdinan. It was annoying. And painful.

After some pleading, Xingho and Raonie agreed she could have her bedtime story with everyone. Which was when she ran up to Ferdinan.

"Can you tell me a story? Please? Please? Please?!" Evelyn pleaded as lightning climbed on Ferdinan's lap. That ring of green around the black of her irises was exactly like Grandmother's... It didn't matter how many times he saw it...

^^^

"I love you, my child, my baby. But papa's getting tired. Thank you for letting me know you made it safe and sound." Evelyn's father's voice was weak and shaky.

"Oh...I'm sorry, papa. You should take a nap and feel better. I'll talk to you again! And when I come home, I'll make you all better!"

"I know, my child. I know."

Ferdinan ended the call. Not only was Liramarc crying, but he was fighting to stay composed, as well.

VVV

"Of course." Closing his eyes, Ferdinan banished the pain of that memory to the back of his mind.

"Everyone! My big brother's telling me a story he's created just for me!"

A small smile tugged at his lips. Then nearly a dozen burly men, the older brothers' wives, and various servants filed into the massive room... Red blanketed the skeleton and he couldn't stop shaking. *Focus on Evelyn...* "W-what do you want your story to be about?"

"I want a story about a bunny!"

A short pause in the music froze his heart. Only when a new song started was Ferdinan able to breathe again. "What does the bunny do?"

"Ooo! The bunny travels the world!"

"Ok. There was once a bunny who was smaller than the other bunnies... Is the bunny a boy or a girl?" Moroseness ended, but drums quickly replaced it. This was a strange soundtrack to a child's story.

"Um...a boy!"

"Well, he was smaller than all his bunny brothers and sisters, and all his bunny neighbors, and all his bunny friends. But he had a giant, fluffy tail and soft sleek fur. He also had the longest ears of any bunny in all of bunny history! His ears were so long he could wrap them around himself like a scarf and cover himself like a blanket. They were useful for that. But they were floppy and dragged the ground when he hopped around.

"His friends always tripped and slipped on his ears when they played. This hurt his ears. But seeing them fall hurt his heart. One day, he decided he'd had enough. He'd fix his long ears so he could play and have fun with everyone. The other bunnies didn't know how to fix his problem, so he left to find someone who did.

"Waving goodbye, he hopped off. He hopped and hopped and hopped. For miles did he hop! Miles upon miles, 'til he came to a large pond with a huge frog. His heart leapt for joy! The frog had no ears at all!

"'Oh, great frog!' he said. 'Please. How did you get rid of your ears?' The frog laughed and said, 'What a stupid question, foolish bunny. Frogs don't have ears.' The bunny told him about his problem and his quest and asked the frog for help. The frog thought. 'You see that bug, way out in the middle of the pond?' The bunny nodded and the frog whipped out his tongue. It stretched twenty feet to snatch up the bug. After the frog finished om-nom-nomming it," Evelyn squealed as Ferdinan tickled her belly, "he said, 'Foolish bunny, my tongue is the longest any frog has ever had. With it, I can reach food other frogs can't. It's a good thing and so are your ears. It'd be foolish to get rid of them.'

"The bunny didn't like this answer. A long tongue may be useful to a frog, but these ears weren't helping him. He bowed to the frog and continued on. Next, the bunny came to a huge lake. It was so big going around wasn't possible. So, he jumped in! He swam and swam and swam 'til his little bunny feet couldn't swim any more. But the shore was nowhere in sight. He tried staying aloft but eventually sank."

"Oh, no!" Evelyn cried, interrupting him.

Ferdinan smiled at her, ignoring all the intensely staring eyes and unceasing lightning. "A giant fish searching for a midday snack saw the sinking bunny. It swam fast! Catching the bunny on his back and lifting him to the surface... The fish took the bunny to the other side of the lake. 'What's a bunny doing so far out in the water?' The bunny told him of his quest, then asked the fish for help. 'I'm the biggest fish in this lake. If I wasn't this big, I couldn't have caught you and brought you safely to shore. Find what your ears are good for instead of trying to rid yourself of them.'

"As before, the bunny wasn't happy with this answer. He bowed politely to the fish and thanked him for his help." Ferdinan studied Evelyn – determining how long the story should be. Her eyes were wide and focused. He continued until the bunny met a bird, a monkey, a zebra, and a platypus. The latter made her laugh when it explained how being the strangest of creatures was a good thing. When Raonie – Evelyn's new mom – signaled for him to wrap it up, Ferdinan had the bunny return home. Two years had passed.

"When the bunny saw his friends, he was happy and sad. He missed them. But he still couldn't play with them. 'We never cared about your long ears.' They insisted and invited him to hop around with them. They hopped and played for hours in celebration of his return. It wasn't 'til the sun set and everyone went home that he realized his ears didn't hurt. Neither had anyone fallen on them. But why? Unsure, he asked his parents. Do you know what they said?"

"No! Tell me!"

"'Your ears are still long and beautiful, but you're no longer the smallest bunny. You've grown into your ears."

Evelyn laughed and gave him a hug – hitting one of the partially healed gashes with her lightning touch. "Yay! Can I have another one? About an ogre this time?"

Ferdinan chuckled. "I'm sorry, My Lady, but it's past your bedtime."

"Then, can I have one tomorrow night? Please? Please? Please!?"

"If you're good and your parents agree."

Loose, black curls bounced as she leapt off of his lap and ran to Xingho and Raonie. Sitting next to Evelyn's new parents were three people obviously not of the Artimus household. Seeing them stole what little color he had.

A lean, perfectly manicured woman sat, a five-year-old girl on her left and a nine-year-old girl on her right. She looked thoughtful for a moment before speaking. "The story is unfinished. You never said how the bunny's ears could be useful."

"I'm sorry, Duchess..." Ferdinan looked down – though he should be kneeling... "Sometimes we never learn what our traits are good for."

"And some traits are completely useless." Harshness filled her tone.

Ferdinan walked over to his mother and knelt down low in front of her.

"Who's she?" Everyone heard Evelyn's loud whisper to her dad.

This made Duchess Samultz scowl. Ferdinan didn't see the expression, but he felt it – along with an oppressive increase in tension. The room emptied of all but the Samultz' family. He stayed on one knee; head bent low in a proper show of respect. This was how they stayed. No one made a sound. Even the two small girls – his little sisters – didn't move.

"You've gained weight." Disdain filled her words.

"I apologize, Duchess. It became necessary." *I failed again.* Ferdinan almost reached up to turn off the music, but fear held his hand.

"Is this another rebellion of yours?"

"No, Duchess. I'm sorry."

They sat in silence a while more.

"What've you been doing?" No matter how you interpreted it, her voice was ice cold.

"To what are you referring, Duchess?"

Displeased, she backhanded him. Hard. Not as hard as his cousin, but enough that familiar dull steel knocked him back. "You know perfectly well."

"My apologies, Duchess. I don't." Ferdinan returned to his proper position – kneeling at her feet.

"Our Prince! Do you have any idea the condition he was in upon arriving?"

Ferdinan clenched his jaw and closed his eyes in time for that dull steel to backhand him again.

"How dare you leave him like that." She stood and continued – her son groveling at her feet, as he should. "It's your responsibility to care for him – to protect him. Instead of staying by his side, you came here to play make believe and tell pointless stories to a stranger?"

The Duchess grabbed hold of his hair, lifting him by it, pulling him high enough for another strike to land. He'd stay on his butt, but it wasn't an option. Back to his knees Ferdinan went. His back and cheek screamed. "I chose to follow my orders to greet our allies..."

"You dare talk back to me? The needs of your Prince *always* come before playing with some child."

"Yes, Duchess." When his lip quivered, he bit it, keeping his head down.

Chapter 14

The fourth batch of music had the perfect song. It was exactly how Xhou felt – overflowing with moroseness. *How many more like this does he have? How much music can I ask for, before he turns me down?* Xhou laid on his bed, hugging a silly jellyfish pillow his oldest sister gave him. It was a joke at the time...

Tears fell, but he didn't do anything to stop them.

This was his therapy. It calmed him – releasing the demons so he could be happy and supportive for those around him. How could he help others get better if they worried about him?

Listening to this bizarre music... He felt connected with whoever made it – certain songs, anyway. Other people felt this way. It was ok. Someone else knew the pain of loss and failure. Someone else struggled under the crushing weight of a responsibility they'd never considered. Someone else was so conflicted inside, they screamed and cried.

Then, they took all that and put it to music to connect with others.

This music shouldn't exist.

But he was glad it did.

Envy filled Xhou. He could feel this way, so long as he fulfilled his responsibilities. But he couldn't share these emotions – couldn't reach out and seek support. It was fine if he screamed and cried and tantrummed. But only if he wasn't caught. He was the example. And others were counting on him. The job was his – regardless of his desires.

His screen chimed. Drying his eyes and putting on a happy face, Xhou accepted the call. "Mama! How are you?"

"Xhou, my darling! I'll be doing magnificently, if you can confirm the claims of the medicine I've received."

"Medicine?" He removed the near-invisible earpiece, and turned off the music.

"Complications of that accursed virus takes more lives every day."

"I know..."

"'Anonymous' sent me a medicine with instructions for producing more. Also...compelling evidence for its ability to reverse the damage caused by the plague."

Is this the medicine Herrard told me about? "Is it real?"

"No recompense was requested, and assistance was offered for making it. The accompanying report was quite detailed."

Xhou nodded. "I'll look into it."

"I've sent samples your way. They should arrive soon. The included documentation was messaged to you."

As she spoke, Xhou checked. "I have it."

"We've started testing. I've included our results so far."

"I understand. I'll start right away." If this was the same thing that made Herrard better... But how did it get to her so quickly?

Tears welled up in his mother's eyes. She wanted this to be real. Xhou wanted the same. More than this, they wanted family to hold. Comfort. Love. But there was no bridging the distance between them. So, he talked to her about everything and nothing until she had to go.

"I love you."

With a final goodbye, Xhou pulled up the files and scoured them. The instructions for making more were odd. As long as they kept some of the medicine aside and fed it properly, it'd replicate itself. Like...some sort of bread starter... Pulling up the images, he studied them carefully. There was something eerie... Something recognizable... Something...he couldn't quite put his finger on. Taking the recording of the replicating medicine, he played it in a loop, watching over and over, trying to figure out what bothered him about it.

* * *

"Ferdinan? Your mother's asking to speak with you."

Somehow, those soft words broke past the screaming in his ear. Startled, he turned. Ozar stood looking inordinately worried. *Why are you delivering this message instead of a servant?* "Where is she?"

"Your family's usual room."

Buttoning up his last shirt, Ferdinan bowed to the man and hurried out. The room his family stayed in was remote. The Artimuses didn't like putting anyone in such distant rooms, but it was a long-standing request. Once there, he ended the music – allowing that cruel voice rein again. Knocking, he waited.

He was called in much later.

"You're slow."

ΛΛΛ

Weeping. Yelling. Pleading. Curses and accusations...they stung bitterly.

But...she volunteered. Now she was dead. And there was no cure. Those who cared about her...they mourned her loss. But it was their own eventual demise fueling their fury. Ferdinan couldn't blame them. It's my fault. I'm the one responsible.

The skeleton took their anger and sorrow – refusing to flinch away. His frozen insides...the numbness...it was uncomfortable and disconcerting. But it was this or feel everything else.

Everything he buried. Everything he hid. He didn't want to feel that... He didn't want to feel anything. So, he wrapped that numbness around himself and soaked up everything they threw at him.

VVV

Ferdinan knelt, head low – killing what was inside him. "I apologize, Duchess."

"Remove your shirts." Duchess Samultz stood, arms crossed, looking down at him.

You are a horrible son.

Crystal blue eyes darted around the room. His sisters sat dutifully at a little table in the corner. They looked sleepy. *I woke them. I'm sorry Minnora, Trannie. I'm a horrible brother. Don't be like me.*

No one's as terrible as you.

One by one, he laid each shirt beside him on the floor, then he unwrapped the bandages holding the medical pad in place. His back was truly gruesome. Black and green from bruising, gnarled and oozing from wounds struggling to heal... His little sisters shouldn't see this. They would, though. And they'd know why.

Down on one knee, Ferdinan waited, shirtless, shivering while his mother examined his bare skin.

"Do you delight in torturing our Prince?"

"No, Duchess."

You delight in torturing everyone.

"Do *not* lie to me. Your responsibility is to protect him. And you do this."

Guilt – that bitter iron – tried contorting his face.

"You know what'd happen to him? He'd be punished for *your* failings. *Your* misdeeds. Do you want him to hang?"

"He's my Prince." Desperation leaked into his voice. He'd done this to Zephyr... Everything...it was all his fault. He'd never have to *try* sabotaging his Prince. Just existing was enough-

"Stand." The Duchess interrupted his spiraling thoughts.

How will you kill her?

Silent, he did as commanded. The back of her hand crashed against his cheek. "You protect and support our Prince. First and foremost."

"Yes, Duchess." Ferdinan blinked quickly - keeping his face expressionless while the voice sniggered.

Her hand - that dull steel - came again, assaulting the same spot. "Our Prince comes first. Always."

"Yes, Duchess."

Another slap landed, "Stop tormenting our Prince. He shouldn't have to keep you in line every moment."

"Yes, Duchess."

One strike after another hit with instruction and rebuke until his nerves were too raw to feel.

You've done worse than kill her already.

"When you cause our Prince to do these things, you're not the one who'll be hurt." *Smack.* "You aren't the one who'll suffer." *Smack.* "You aren't the one to clean up your mess." *Smack.*

"Yes, Duchess."

Anger and frustration - disappointment - made her upper lip twitch. "What's the point of having a defective son? A freak. You're selfish - just as our Prince says. Get out. You sicken me."

Waiting long enough to give the Duchess one last chance to smack him, Ferdinan gathered his bandages and shirts and headed outside before redressing.

In the gardens, he hid in shadows and drowned in angry music.

~

Unforgivable failure bound him. But Ferdinan's eyes stayed focused on bright orange and yellow. Drums and grinding metal filled the world. And Failure. He failed his Prince - his country - yet again. *Why am I alive? I can't do anything right. I hurt everyone...*

"There you-" Jon put a hand on his ally's shoulder, only to have his ribcage rammed through. Gasping, clutching at his side, the Thinker staggered back.

Ferdinan's eyes doubled and his jaw dropped. *I saw him...why didn't I stop myself...?* He shrunk back into the flower laden bushes. Nearly transparent blue crystals couldn't tear away from the child doubled over and gasping. *No... Why did I give in to Oya? I never should've fought. I never should've allowed myself such indulgence!*

"*Ugh...* How can you be so strong while that tiny? *Ow!*" Growling out, Jon forced himself to straighten. He gathered a breath to yell, only to stop - eyes focused on the red mark marring Ferdinan's stark white face. "What happened to your cheek?"

A boney hand covered the numb spot as a low base reverberated. "Nothing."

Jon was about to argue when the skeleton turned away – facing the flowering bush. "Ferdinan?"

Wrapping an arm around his stomach, Ferdinan turned back and bowed low. "I'm sorry. I was startled."

Sighing, Jon's shoulders slumped. "It's fine."

I'm useless. Why did I allow myself to be so weak? I can't fight her anymore...I have to disappoint her...

It was troubling how long Ferdinan stayed bowed. Jon stood awkwardly, until words spilled out of his mouth. "Time for breakfast. We're waiting on you to start."

Clutching harder at his stomach, Ferdinan turned back to the plant and forced himself to straighten. "I don't feel well."

"I can get Samuel," Jon offered. A violent gag from the skeleton startled him. "Ferdinan?"

Soft leaves brushed Ferdinan's face as he gulped down air. *My mint tin's in the room...* "I'm tired."

"I can get your mom," Jon gave another offer.

Turning, Ferdinan shook his head slowly. "Don't trouble her. I just need to rest."

A strange kind of horror twisted Jon's face.

Pushing himself away, Ferdinan staggered deeper into the garden maze. He couldn't deal with anyone right now.

* * *

"Xhou?" Elbie peeked through the door.

"Elbie!" Xhou turned and shouted – lively as always. "Come in! Are you bored too?"

Elbie accepted the invitation and took a seat. "Not bored. Frustrated."

"Frustrated? Over break? Why?"

He held up the partially disassembled disk.

"Hmmm? That's one of Ferdinan's contraptions?"

"It's one of his medical disks."

"Why's it broken?"

"It isn't broken! I just removed the cover," Elbie mumbled.

"*Ok.* Why?" Xhou never knew what to expect concerning Ferdinan, so he didn't bother guessing.

"I want to learn how to make them."

"Taking one apart is a good starting point." *For a Tinkerer anyway.* "Learn anything yet?"

"No! He finally agreed to teach me! ...if I can figure out where he started with the circuit boards. It took me two weeks to decipher how he layered the case together! I've been trying all break. But it's so complicated! Why would anyone make something like this?"

In all honesty, Xhou never asked. Ferdinan's inventions didn't interest him. This worked well since Ferdinan never talked about them. Not sure what to say, he asked Elbie to show him the disk. The young boy placed it carefully on the table. Pulling some pneumatic compression tweezers from his pocket, Elbie went to work removing the circuit boards.

Wait...these aren't regular circuit boards... They were some kind of delicate micro board and unlike anything he'd seen before. *What are they made of?* They were thinner than paper and the circuitry was so fine it looked printed on. Once Elbie finished, he counted the micro boards. *Thirty-eight!*

"Thirty-eight boards! Is he insane?! Who'd put this much effort into something people find useless?"

"Why *are* there so many?" Elbie asked hopefully.

"Watching you remove them...looks like they were interconnected. Like a mini brain...maybe so many are needed to fit all the information and programming?"

Mismatched eyes drooped and Elbie sighed. "So...you can't help me?"

"I'd only make it harder for you to figure out."

"Who can I ask?"

"Ferdinan." Xhou picked up a micro board, studying at it closely.

"He said I can't ask him. Said his lab doesn't exist 'til I figure this out."

"You can try Master Ludwick. He approved this as an evaluation project."

Frustrated, Elbie dropped his head in despair.

Xhou smirked. Patting Elbie's shoulder was meant to comfort him, but the boy flinched instead. "Can you get it back together?"

"Yes." Elbie pointed to the corner as he started reassembling it. "What're you doing with a scanner in here?"

"Ha! A little research my mama asked me to do."

"Can I see?"

"Of course. A Tinkerer would have fun with this. Though I think..." Something clicked in his mind. *My search for the scientist who discovered the cure was useless, but there's one person I know who'd make something like this.*

"Think what?"

"Ha! Completely slipped my mind! Sorry about that," Xhou smiled big and turned the scanner for Elbie to access.

Once the samples arrived, Xhou discovered what bothered him about the recordings his mom sent. The medicine wasn't really medicine. It was tiny, artificial cells. *But why?* From what Herrard told him about the medicine Healer Bær offered... *I'll have to talk to the Head Healer...* There was another person he could ask too. Herrard was his suitemate. It was infinitely easier to nab a few minutes from an island brother than from someone of such high responsibility.

Chapter 15

Come morning, the Duchess was gone.

Ferdinan needed to stop wasting time.

Every day he sat with Evelyn and Mother in the little play cottage. He shared the stories Master Minjing – Grandmother – told him, recording them as he spoke. Having them in Grandmother's voice would be better. But...weak and pained, fighting for breath...

Ferdinan pushed those memories away before they could take over.

Every session he fixed his eyes on a distant point outside the window. Looking at Mother Artimus or Evelyn was impossible. It hurt the young girl. But her hair was the best he could focus on. Screeching metal distracted part of his mind. It was rude. But...it was better than that voice.

When he finished all of Minjing's stories, he recounted everything he'd heard and seen her do during his visits...until he'd said everything.

"I'm sorry, but that's all I have, Lady Evelyn. I wish I could tell you more."

^^^

"What kind of tea would you like today?" Holding up her hands, Evelyn pretended to write down an order.

"Ginger tea with orange."

"Perfect! That's exactly what I made. It's Bunny's favorite, and since we had Juju's favorite yesterday, I made Bunny's favorite today!" the five-year-old girl bubbled. "How's papa and ma-mama?"

Ferdinan held his pretend cup to the glass wall separating them and she pretended to pour him tea. "They miss you. They wanted me to tell you they love you."

"I love them too, very much. Will you tell them that? Tell them I'm helping people get better, but I want to see them when I'm done." Innocence radiated from her.

Those words made his chest ache.

VVV

Ferdinan closed his eyes against the memory.

"Thank you." Sadness dripped in Evelyn's voice.

Mother Artimus stood. Her head grazed the ceiling of Evelyn's play cottage. "My child, is there anything you need before you leave?"

There was one thing he had to set right. "May I talk to you privately?"

The inquisitive look she gave was wasted as Ferdinan kept his eyes averted. "Let's talk in my study. Evelyn, it's time to go inside."

The young girl's protests ceased when her new grandmother picked her up. Rushing to the door, he held it open for them, then made his way to her study to wait. This was his biggest threat – what she could do. He had to fix everything he broke. Somehow. This failure...it was unforgivable.

~

"What's troubling you, my son?" Mother Artimus spoke when her office door closed.

"Please don't say anything." It was presumptuous, but...the least Ferdinan could do was make his request in Yemeri, her native language – considering how greedy it was.

She sat facing his bowed head. When she tried hugging him, he shrank away. "I can't ignore this. What's happening to you at school needs to stop."

Slipping off the chair, he knelt before her, maintaining Yemeri though Mother Artimus spoke in Common. "Please."

Kneeling down next to him, Mother asked him to look at her. He raised his head but kept his eyes averted. The thought of her seeing how evil he was...he couldn't bear it.

"Ferdinan. Please talk to me."

"Please," he dropped his head, "I'm begging you."

Silence consumed the room, but metallic notes pounded against the skeleton's ear.

"Ferdinan, how long has your mother been hitting you?"

His insides turned to ice. *I've never heard her so angry before...*

"Jon told me you looked like you'd been hit."

No! It was me! Ferdinan's mind raced uselessly in utter panic.

"Your mother was the only one you saw before breakfast. She's the only one who could've done that."

"It's my fault!" he blurted out – heart racing and fighting to think.

"What?"

"All of it's my fault." *I'm bad, they have to do these things...* "I'm obstinate, and headstrong. I did it to myself."

"Ferdinan, that's not true. You're a wonderful child. You've never caused any trouble here."

Long fingers tried lifting his chin. The endless fall of her touch made him shudder. *No! Don't look at me!* He covered his eyes so she couldn't see his sins. "I neglect my duty. I hurt people. I'm a burden to those I'm supposed to support. It's my fault!"

Her next words were soft and soothing. "Ferdinan, you've done nothing wrong. Even if you had...your back – being hit – it's wrong. Nothing you could ever do would warrant such abuse."

Abuse... His frozen insides shattered. Abuse of a child in any form was met with capital punishment in North Oueshi. If he cost his country their most important ally because he let her think this... "Everything's my fault. My doing. No one else is to blame."

"Samuel told me what he found in his scan. Did the Duchess do that to you?"

"No!" That accusation...it made him furious! *I did it! Why aren't you listening to me?* "She hasn't done anything to me!"

"Then who did? My son, this has been happening all of your life."

"I did. It's my fault!" The sound of Mother taking a breath to speak spurred him on. "I don't want to hurt anyone else. Mother Artimus, you know the political situation of my country. If you mention either of these facts..."

"You haven't hurt anyone. As a child it's not your responsibility to worry about civil unrest."

Removing his hands from his eyes, Ferdinan placed both palms flat on the ground. "Age isn't a qualifying condition *for what'll affect me or my little sisters. They aren't old enough to understand what's going on. There's no abuse. Everything's my own fault. Everything's the consequence of my actions."*

"Whoever told you that is lying. No one deserves this."

Ferdinan winced, squeezing his eyes shut. The world wouldn't understand. It all looked horrible from an outsider's view.

Even if making them understand was possible...no one would listen to him. No one remembered what his job was as the fifth child of a powerful family. His duty... The fifth child...he only had to protect and defend his family.

I don't want to hurt anyone else...I don't want to cause more death... Ferdinan's voice cracked when he spoke – much to his embarrassment. *"Nothing's happening. Nothing needs to be fixed."*

* * *

"What do you think about this one?" A gangly ten-year-old asked about the hard, steady pounding as he danced around the lab.

"I don't know. I'm having a hard time enjoying this 'music.' I mean... It goes against everything we're taught." A girl one year his senior answered, grimacing as the beat pounded on her nerves.

"You mean like how drums are for war? It's so weird hearing this as music." A third, even older child smirked as he leaned back, toes bobbing up and down. "Don't know if I like it...but there's something about it I can't ignore."

Little hands joined those toes, clapping in time. "I like it!"

The three turned to the youngest of the group. Yuyu was absolutely adorable. Curly, black hair framed her heart shaped face. And stunning, pink eyes glowed against her dark skin – magnifying her cuteness.

"Thank you, Yuyu. I think I'll pick this one." The first boy clapped along with her. "It'll represent the Fighters perfectly."

"How so?" The older boy laughed, stomping on the offbeat.

"Oh! I like that too!" Yuyu giggled, joining him in switching between clapping and stomping.

The first girl stood, intrigued. Watching intently, she eventually joined in, alternating rhythms and patterns of stomping and clapping. "I'm stealing this for the Athletes!"

Everyone laughed and mimicked her. Soon they'd choreographed a nice series of moves which smoothly transitioned back to the beginning – repeating in a continuous dance until the song ended.

* * *

"*FERDINAN*!!" Oya cheered playfully, spinning around as if dancing with the glowing orbs in her peripheral. It didn't matter how fast she turned, she could never get a direct look at them.

Thin lips turned up in a hesitant smile. Perfect Oŭndo rolled off his tongue. "*How've you been?*"

"Every time I count the carpet fibers people show up. Afterward I can't remember which one I was on… Oh! There's a nearby island with magnificent cliff faces to climb," she grinned maniacally – tugging at the chain around her neck. *His smile...*

"Please don't break your neck." His alarm didn't faze her.

"It isn't difficult. You find a spot, grab, and lift yourself." She grinned at her friend's image. Everything about his smiling face was bright, save his eyes. They were dim – darkness hiding inside.

"I know the mechanics."

"Heehee."

"I have a surprise for you." He teased, covering his ears.

"Oooo! What is it!?!"

His face jumped a bit before settling. A video of him appeared in the corner of her screen. The recorded Ferdinan held his violin and commenced playing. The real boy lifted a different instrument – a mandolin – and joined in.

After a nice intro, he began singing. His recording joined in for back up and harmony. *Amazing!* It didn't suit him in the least. The music was peppy and upbeat. But both the recording and his own hands had a melancholy running through them.

Good, I can hear his heart. The song gave her hope. She praised and applauded him, but he just reddened and grit his teeth – forcefully rejecting her admiration. But she insisted her awe was fully won. Then she asked for another song.

"Another? That one wasn't good enough?" he asked, bright red and unable to look at her.

"I already said how amazing it was. But I want to see you play your violin, not a recording of it."

"…there's one I'm working on… but I only know the violin part, and I'm not proficient…" he admitted.

"*Perfect*!" She wanted to see him play before he learned to mask the important elements.

"Only for you." He switched out instruments.

The first note was smooth and graceful. But his body...every movement he made radiated pain. Longing. The song itself wasn't sad, but she heard Ferdinan's heart cry out each note. The instrument wept – tears he couldn't express. She grinned, pleased by the unspoken sorrow and his new voice. Maybe once he was comfortable expressing himself in this fashion, he'd use words.

"*That was ASTOUNDING!*" she clapped, hiding the truth he'd given away. "*You learned that in two months!? incredible!*"

"*Please... I'm neither astounding nor incredible,*" he refuted – eyes averted.

"*Yes, you are.*" A gentle grin lit her wild eyes. "*You'll see it one day. But for today, I'll forgive you for saying I'm wrong. I'm a magnanimous friend after all.*"

Flinching, Ferdinan nodded. "*Yes, ma'am.*"

"*That first song's a wonderful example of owning the music. Show it to the Scientists as one way to present it. I guess you'd have to record yourself a second time and combine the two.*"

"It really *isn't* good. But if you think it'll help them..." He cleared his throat and batted at his ear. "Anyway, I wanted to give you that before I move on to the next part of my journey."

"*Oh?*" Wasn't he supposed to stay at Jon's home?

"I'm leaving for home in the morning. I'll spend the next week at a gala honoring many wonderful people."

"*The big party for those who helped with Azuté?*" Oya masked her disappointment.

"You've heard of it?"

"*Yah, people are excited. I hope you have fun.*"

"I'll do my best. My aunt and Lady Evelyn are among the honored guests...so I'll probably not talk to you 'til I return."

"*I'll let you make it up to me when you get back.*" Oya winked, sticking her tongue out at him.

Much to her amusement, he returned the gesture. "Now, say all that in Common!"

"Meanie head!" She shouted, wiggling her fingers at him.

In accordance with "meanie-headedness," he made her practice Common for a good hour. At random moments he'd flinch and cover his ears. *What haunts you, dear friend?*

During this time, Ferdinan informed her the next block started a new academic year. She scrunched her face at him and asked if it made a difference. His answer? It didn't beyond what year you were called as classes rotated every block.

Amusingly, Jon, the older of the two, was starting his eleventh year while Ferdinan was to begin his thirteenth. *Just how amazing are you, my friend?* A knock rudely interrupted them but gave Oya an excuse to switch back to Oŭndo.

"Who could that be? Give me a minute."

Boney hands flew up to stop her. "*Actually, I need to pack.*"

"Ah, then I'll see you in a couple of weeks! Safe journeys!"

Ferdinan bowed and thanked Oya before turning off the screen. Her silliness...it was strangely refreshing. And her voice filled him with warmth. Despite himself, his lips twitched upward. Seeing her... He couldn't explain it. It just felt nice.

You don't deserve her.

A tap on the earpiece banished the voice. *I know I don't.* He didn't need that voice reminding him to know how greedy he was being. The first colors of sunset painted themselves over the water. It perfectly reflected Oya's joyful energy...

Ice settled in his belly. Now to gather his things – he only needed to ready himself.

I just have to sneak in and leave before I trouble them. Turning, Ferdinan fell backwards. He had an audience! *How long have they been there!?!* He scurried, gathering the fallen items, and forming a plan of escape...but they surrounded him.

Cringing, he covered his head and scrunched into a ball when the giants moved closer. It didn't stop them. Fire scorched his skin as Xingho hoisted him to an impossibly broad shoulder. The other brothers grabbed his stuff. Like a sack of potatoes, he was hauled inside. All attempts at squirming his way down proved futile. It was humiliating. His nerves screamed and his back flared in irritation. *What are they going to do to me?!*

Roughhousing was an Artimus way of life. So, Ferdinan was surprised when they placed him gently on the couch in their main common room. *How much trouble am I in?* Blue crystals locked onto the floor. *How bad was I?*

A warm little body forced its way onto his lap – zapping him with lightning. Evelyn's midnight hair tickled his nose. It took her wiggling into a comfortable position to force Ferdinan to look up or risk being head-butted. Having his nose broken by a five-year-old wouldn't help the situation. But the sea of faces made him wish it would. The bundle of lightning twisted around. Grabbing his face, she pulled it toward hers.

"It's time to be happy now, big brother." She scrunched her nose in the sternest look a little girl could muster.

"...um..." *I've hurt her again...*

"I know you don't want to. I know it goes against how you were raised, but we're going to talk because it's all we know to do to help you," Mother Artimus informed him, stepping forward hand in hand with her husband.

That night was the most painfully embarrassing experience he ever suffered through.

Chapter 16

Glass in one hand and a small plate in the other, Jon walked down to the gardens. Ferdinan always hid away in one of the mazes...for some reason. His heart stopped and he nearly dropped the food. On the ground lay the skeleton.

Jon lost count of how many times he found Ferdinan passed out at the hospital. Running feet slowed as he got closer. *Did Ferdinan not faint?* Studying his ally...the scene was actually sort of cute. The pleasant expression on Ferdinan's face was unusual. One boney arm was used as a pillow. The other draped across his violin case as if it were a rigid stuffed animal.

Setting the food down a safe distance away, Jon gently woke up Ferdinan. And it was hard. *I didn't know he could sleep peacefully.* But...he had a job to do. Since his ally was leaving, he needed to make sure he was on the right track.

◊

Ferdinan stretched. A complaint was on his tongue...until he remembered where he was. Between seeing Jon and not remembering laying down – he was bright red. Cackling filled his mind. *Why is Jon out here? Doesn't he have better things to do – like being coddled by his family?*

He shouldn't waste his time with you.

Ferdinan turned his back to his ally and tapped the earpiece, but all that sounded was a *beep.* Cruel laughter bombarded him. The air around him vanished. His heart beat out of control.

Now what are you going to do?

"I brought lunch," Jon tried, and was ignored.

Since arriving, Father Artimus prepared Ferdinan's food. It was easier to stomach than Jon's - though he ate little. The portions were huge. *How do they eat so much?* But they were giants... Maybe their food needs increased exponentially.

Death by food – you haven't tried that one yet.

"Stop ignoring me." Jon grabbed the skeleton and forced Ferdinan to face him. "You haven't eaten today, so you're eating now. I made it myself this time."

Ferdinan cringed. Between the needles and those words... But he didn't say anything. Being sick after meals...he deserved worse punishment.

Yes. Much worse.

^^^

After the months he'd been there...Ferdinan was sick of many things.

He was sick of the admiration.

He was sick of their constant praise.

He was sick of all the death...

But in this moment, he was sick of Jon pestering him about food. So, he turned his ally's intentions into another kind of punishment. Jaw set, he ate until his stomach rebelled.

VVV

That memory lingered as Ferdinan studied the plate shoved into his hands.

"That'll be easy for you to eat. And it's not much."

He must've hated making this.

Jon's tone unleashed a flood of guilt. Making such a bland dish must've irritated the Dinta. Still, it turned his stomach.

There was one part of the meal, however…

Steamed milk smelled faintly of mint and honey. There was something familiar about it. Something comforting. And warm. Bowing his head deeply, Ferdinan took the cup. *I've caused enough trouble.* The least he could do was cooperate when Jon was being reasonable. Taking a sip, the mint's bitterness coated his tongue – making the light sweetness of honey unobtrusive. As he sipped it, he felt his stomach ease.

"Milk tea."

Those two words barely made the distance to the Thinker's ears. Confusion twisted Jon's face. "Milk tea?"

* * *

Song one of batch five was…lively. That was the best word to describe it. It was playful and upbeat! If Xhou were in any other mood it'd be his favorite. But the second song appealed to him more.

Failure and remorse. Sorrow and shame. These words fit the song well. And it, in turn, fit his mood perfectly. This was the eighth time he'd listened to it. He hadn't bothered reading the translated lyrics. The notes said it all. Everything inside him flowed with the music. Even trying to focus on his assignment and move onto the next song, he was drawn back to this one.

This song… The singer knew some level of devastation… *Hopefully he's never lost a country's worth of people…*

Where did *Ferdinan find this?* Xhou knew the music didn't exist. He'd been searching. Songs that elicited these feelings were improper. And it had lyrics… He couldn't find a single religion with music like this. Only songs used for worship were allowed lyrics, all else was banned by the Council. Which was too bad. He could use a gospel that accepted these kinds of emotions.

Xhou wasn't the most devout member of his parish. And that stupid plague all but destroyed his belief in a god, just or otherwise. But this song, Ferdinan's music...his soul cried out the tunes and gave him the release he needed. Refreshing his mind enough to focus on something. Even if it wasn't the most important thing.

Pulling his resources to find the scientist responsible for the cure - and possibly the plague - Xhou listened. As he listened, he started thinking that maybe...just maybe...a god did exist somewhere and was using this to comfort him.

* * *

The boat ride didn't take long. Neither did the drive to North Chūzo's capital city. It wasn't that the trip was short - it took the better part of two days. Worry eroded the time, making it fly by. Music was his constant companion. Only, he learned his lesson. He kept two earpieces - one to use while the other charged. Now that he was home... His lungs refused to work. Closing his eyes, Ferdinan focused on the din in his ear and the warmth it gave. It reminded him of Oya...her joy and childlike energy...

Stop it. I don't deserve her.

He escorted Evelyn and her new family to the room prepared for them. Come morning they'd leave for the Main Capital without him as his plans were changed.

Ferdinan was ordered to attend his cousin.

Seeing Zephyr like that was terrifying. According to his Prince's healer, Zephyr wasn't sleeping on his own. When the Prince did sleep, his mind became inordinately active - stealing the rest he should be getting. No one had seen this before, so they didn't know what to do.

I did this to him. How do I fix it? Will I kill him next?

Chapter 17

"Whoever" was back. *Let's have some fun.* There was no particular place Oya was going, but it was important she get there swiftly – anything to attract its attention, to force it to follow. She'd stop randomly and start off in another direction, then seemingly change her mind again. *Come to me.*

Oya continued like this for hours. Even the orbs in her peripheral had trouble keeping up. She'd catch "Whoever" this time. At the very least, she wanted to see what'd been watching her.

Hahaha! There! Looking above the horizon she grinned. "*Caught you.*"

Winking at "Whoever," she stopped and returned to her room. Scaling the side of the building, she climbed through her window. A few jumps on her bed then she plopped down. Her unseen guest hovered in the corner. Giving a wink, she rolled to her side and closed her eyes.

* * *

Ah! Berago's! Shopping there was Jon's favorite activity. Second only to this. Falling back on his bed, the Thinker took in a deep breath. The joy and energy and brightness of Leoniel Kyo was paradise after the last few months. But home...the comfort of his room and family...nothing compared to that. *One whole week of* nothing *to do! How I've needed this!*

Things were never simple or calm around his ally. He didn't understand how someone who couldn't stand attention caused so much trouble. *But...was it really his fault...?*

Shaking his head, Jon allowed it to empty. The skeleton wasn't going home – Ferdinan went straight to the palace and was with his oldest brother. By now, the gent should be at the Main Capital enjoying the gala. There was nothing to worry about. Not for a *whole* week. All his work from the past block was done and turned in. Even the song he'd chosen was submitted with a tentative plan for representing the Artists.

This was freedom.

Weight shifted the bed to one side before his skin soaked up a comfortable warmth. Opening his eyes, he found Rigel, the third youngest of the Artimus boys. Giving his big brother a giant smile, he closed his eyes again and snuggled up close. It didn't matter how warm it was in the house, nothing beat this kind of comfort.

"I know you just got back from playing dress up with dad and Samuel, but Naizu and I are going for a boat ride. Want to join us?" Unlike the other Artimus boys, Rigel's voice wasn't deep. But it felt softer - more comfortable - somehow.

"Do I have to do anything?" Jon grinned despite himself.

"Nope. Is that your plan for the rest of break?" Straight black hair waved as he shook his head. Contrary to what Evelyn said, Rigel's hair was straight - not loosely curled like hers.

"Yes." Balling himself up, Jon scooted until he was half-laying on his brother. "I'd love relaxing on the water - but only if I don't have to put in any effort."

"I'm sure we can arrange something."

The next thing Jon knew, his nerves were screaming. He couldn't stop laughing and squirming as his brother found every ticklish spot he had. Though he yelled for Rigel to stop, it wasn't until he was panting and twitching uncontrollably that his brother listened.

"Come on." Rigel pulled his baby brother off the bed.

Once he was standing solidly on his feet, Jon realized they were almost the same height. A couple more inches and he'd no longer be the smallest...

It was a depressing thought.

* * *

"Finally decided to chat?" Oya's voice flowed across the sky.

"How did you do this, little one?"

She laughed. "Call me Oya."

"How did you do this, Oya?"

"Dreams are a fun playground, aren't they?" Leaning back, she smirked at the middle-aged man who's features were a little too perfect to be human. "I take it Kumi sent you to keep an eye on me."

The man smiled and offered his hand. "I'm the Fisherman."

Grinning, she took it. "Nice to meet you, Fisherman."

"Can you actually see me when you're awake?"

"How can I see what's not there?"

"Then why do you keep looking at me? You were even toying with me."

Giggles filled the air as soft grass cradled her. "You have a strong presence. Ah! If you're a fisherman, then you might prefer this."

The surroundings changed. A river flowed through a mountain pass. The Fisherman was waist deep with a long rod he obviously wasn't used to. On a giant rock splitting the water, Oya sat.

"Fly fishing, hmm? Why this kind?"

"Regular fishing's easily available; so here's a change of pace. Don't stop swinging that rod or you'll never catch anything."

"That's why I choose common fishing. I can catch a nap more easily."

She laughed, "You sound like an old man I met once. He was an interesting fellow."

"Am I interesting?"

"I don't know, but that nap comment suited him perfectly." She laid back on the rock, crossing her legs. "What brings you here?"

"The same as you."

"Oh?"

"I'm being held in reserve 'til I'm needed. Just as you are." The Fisherman lowered the fishing rod. "You've projected the most interesting persona."

Oya smirked. "Thank you."

"Was that a compliment?"

"Thank you for talking some sense into my friend. Even if only a little."

"You knew I would."

A perfectly knowing look bore into him. "You really are like the others."

"We're one in the same, yes." Sorrow dimmed his eyes. "I'm sorry I couldn't make the boy better."

"There's only so much you can do for a person who doesn't want help – who doesn't think they deserve it." A delicate finger tapped the rock. "Too bad you couldn't clean those self-destructive feelings eating away at his heart."

"He wouldn't let me. Can you?"

"Maybe. I'm trying. Every time we speak, I try."

A thoughtful expression bloomed on his face. "What makes this boy so important to you, Oya?"

The river disappeared into the horizon before her. "We aren't so different. I'm looking for redemption too."

"If you can help him, you might pay for some of your sins?"

"There's always the hope," she winked and held out her hand. Evening light glinted off the silver strand wrapped around her palm. "I have the she-devil. But…I'll need help reaching all those connected to her."

"You already know how to do that."

"No." Wild green eyes scanned the scene – turning it from an evening mountain brook to a twilight ocean beach. "I've never searched out those connected to someone I held. Mom didn't have time to teach me."

Putting down the rod, the Fisherman lounged deeper in the beach chair looking unduly troubled. "I'll have to talk to Kumi…"

"We don't have much time…"

"Trust me," the Fisherman pointed to the glowing orbs hovering around her, "we know that better than you."

"You know what these are?"

Amusement filled the man's face. "Yes, I know who they are. As do you."

Instead of arguing, Oya smirked. "You really do have watchers keeping me in line."

"Is that what they are?" The Fisherman sounded like a teacher who'd answered the same question one too many times.

That tone told her exactly what she hoped to confirm. Nodding, Oya changed topics. "On a positive note – I found the Mwã-tonô. It's only fitting...I nabbed that woman months ago..."

"You mean you found Tonō."

Oya looked away. "If I admit that, I'm admitting who I am."

The Fisherman nodded then glanced at the silver, web-like string Oya brandished. "You'll be holding that for a while."

"That's fine."

"Oya..." Once again, the Fisherman became completely serious. "Considering your age and the limited time, finding guardians for the rest is your only option."

"I know. What do you think I've been doing?" Puffing out a breath, she continued, "I placed three before running into *her*. Only six more to go."

"Generations have been spent finding guardians. What makes you think you can place six before confronting her?"

"I know who one of them needs to go to...have a pretty good idea for another..."

"That leaves four."

Fire shot across those alien green eyes. "That...that she-devil, that Kōjomầ!"

"Oya."

Ignoring his disapproving tone, she pressed on. "There're only three tribes left. And one camp. She's destroyed the rest. Four groups can't handle six charges plus the ones they already have."

Silently the Fisherman sat and waited for her to calm down.

"But...even among the original descendants, finding a proper guardian wasn't easy...now I'm in a place with almost no one."

"You'll have to leave the islands then."

"Yah...but...there's something I want to do first." A wicked grin took over her lips. "Besides, the resources here are invaluable."

* * *

Rage bellowed through the door and down the hall along with a deep *crash.* Yet no one heard it. Not in a palace this large. Pain blinded Ferdinan as ungiving oak proved itself harder than his bones. His arm breaking instead of his skull should've been considered a good thing. But after the last year...

Regardless, no one could know Zephyr broke him. Sleep deprived insanity or not...keeping his Prince from killing him was top priority. His cousin was exhausted and incoherent. Sloppy movements were slowed from a taxed mind. This gave Ferdinan the upper hand. Pushing himself away with his uninjured arm, Ferdinan reached for the neural blocker.

Dodging left, then right and right again, Ferdinan herded Zephyr between him and the bed. Only then did the skeleton dash forward. Not giving his Prince time to react, the Tinkerer slapped the neural blocker on his cousin's forehead and activated it. By the time it kicked in, Zephyr was falling onto the bed. Neural blockers put his cousin's body to sleep, but did little for Zephyr's brain. It made no sense...

Silence filled the room while screaming filled his ear. *This is my fault. I did this to him...*

Ferdinan staggered out of his cousin's room panting from pain and adrenaline. He knew what to do. Ten minutes later he sat at the bottom of some stairs, smashing a vase that'd been at the top. He let out a cry and waited. *Why wasn't I born a Healer?* Half a dozen feet came toward him. Considering the location of this staircase, the maid and kitchen hand were expected. His aunt, the Queen, however...

"Ferdinan! What happened?!" Zephyr's mother knelt beside him, strait black hair falling forward. Yuchio flowed flawlessly off her tongue. Only Grassland natives ever mastered that language. It was complex and beautiful. More so even than Oya's Oŭndo.

Clutching at his arm, Ferdinan gasped in passable Yuchio. "I fell. I'm sorry. I think I broke it."

Chewing her lip, she apologized, then called out to the maid. "Call Aguilla!"

"Right away, your Majesty."

Turning back to her nephew she watched him pale considerably. "I'm sorry, I know you don't like healers, but if it's broken..."

"No...I..." Of all people he had the least right to say anything.

^^^

My place? My *place?! I know exactly where* my place *is. My place is in my lab making things to improve human life!" Ferdinan shouted - composure completely lost. Everything inside and out and all around! He couldn't control it. He couldn't contain it. It was all he could do to not throw up. "If you're saying that pampering a functioning individual is more important than thousands suffering a most heinous form of torture...suffering for weeks before death! If that's what you think! Then it's not my priorities that are twisted!"*

Face hard and fuming, the General stood to speak, but Ferdinan didn't allow him a word.

" The disease is *spreading! Are you going to hide away in a corner and wait for it to come to you? If you're too scared to look death in the eye and challenge it, then you don't deserve the position you were* given. *" The skeleton shook uncontrollably. For pure insult and to drive his point home, Ferdinan added, "If a*

scientist…a mere child is braver than you – more resolute in decisions and willing to take the consequences – then what's the point of a military leader?"

VVV

I've said many things I had no right to… Shaking his head, Ferdinan thanked her and apologized for the trouble he caused.

Aguilla was a servant the Queen brought with her when she married his uncle. She was a healer…just not a traditional one. More accurately, she was a medicine woman from Oueshi's Grasslands. A lifelong servant to royalty, her loyalty was well proven. And she didn't ask questions. Like him, she'd never harm Zephyr.

"Let's get you to your room." The Queen slipped an arm around his waist. Sharp steel sliced deep and helped him stand.

It was uncanny… Zephyr looked exactly like his mother. Tiny, she was easily a head shorter than Ferdinan. Golden skin only emphasized the perfection of her face. She always had a glow about her which amplified her beauty. It wasn't just looks. She and her son's touch both felt like perfectly sharpened blades. There was only one difference. She was an actual Fighter whereas Zephyr was an Athlete.

"I'm sorry I failed you." Shame forced his eyes to the floor.

"You've done everything I've asked. That isn't failure." The loving smile she gave was one he never saw.

* * *

Jon walked down the gangplank. Two cases swung at his sides – neither of them his. That night… They tried. They really did.

After dragging the gent inside, Jon's family opened up to Ferdinan. They told the skeleton how much they loved him. How worried they were. It made Jon jealous...and yet Ferdinan couldn't even look at them! And the gent refused to speak.

It wasn't until hours later, when it was just Jon and him, that the Tinkerer finally opened his mouth. And what did he say? "Please take these back to school for me." That's all. Neither could Jon get him to utter a single word more.

As annoying as that was, Jon couldn't turn down the one request his ally made. If he did, who knew if Ferdinan would ever speak around them again. Lost in thought, the Thinker walked under a tree and nearly collided with a head. Blood red hair spiked out in all directions and wild green eyes made him shiver.

"Oya? What happened to your hair?!" It was short and devoid of any black. Neither did it compliment her golden-brown skin. *It was more beautiful dark.*

She grinned and flipped off of the branch. Those crazed eyes shot him an accusatory look when she saw the familiar box in his hands.

"He asked me to bring his instruments back."

Satisfied, she headed toward the boy's dormitory. The confidence surrounding her expected him to follow without question. By the time he got there, however, she was nowhere in sight.

It was strange walking into an empty suite. Lonely...

Sighing, he unpacked. There was something about hanging up new clothes that made Jon smile. One shirt in particular he was excited about. It was handsome and the material exquisite. He'd been annoyed when Samuel insisted Leoniel make it larger. But his big brother said he was in the middle of a massive growth spurt... *I'm not ready to be a giant yet.* He loved being small.

Walking to the mirror, he held it up to his neck. "Guess it'll fit soon."

Those words hadn't fully left his mouth when Oya's reflection appeared next to his.

Heart three feet from his chest, Jon yelped and spun. "Oya! Don't barge into people's rooms uninvited! How did you get in here anyway? I...I'm sorry..." *I didn't hear the door...*

With a grin she held out her personal translator. *"Three stories isn't a difficult climb."*

"···times I wonder if your death wish isn't stronger than Ferdinan's."

"It's enjoyable and relaxing. And it keeps my hands busy. Creative people with idle hands are dangerous," she sneered.

"You're creative?" *Isn't she simply obnoxious?* That thought was one he mentally scolded himself for. Oya was a girl. Even if she didn't act like it.

"*You've no idea."* She spun about the room. "*Consider the imagination Ferdinan has for all his inventions. I have just as much...except not focused on scientific pursuits."*

That thought made Jon squirm.

"Tell me about your vacation. Starting at the beginning." Lunacy tinged her forceful grin.

Chapter 18

The screen filled with Mother Artimus's commanding presence, elegance, and concern. Black eyes glistened with something between sorrow and rage.

"I apologize for the wait, Queen Mother."

"Thank you for responding quickly." She nodded to the man, not entirely sure where his loyalties lay. Regardless of her youngest son's wishes, she couldn't do nothing.

"How may I help you?"

"Do you know what's happening at your school?" No matter what those tattoos claimed, this man had some serious explaining to do.

"Excuse me?" The tone of her voice told him he was being inexcusably neglectful.

"When my sons returned home, the youngest was seriously wounded. He'd been beaten."

"Jon?! Is he ok?! What happened?!"

"No. My youngest." Mother eyed the man – warning him to rethink his opinion of her claim.

"Ferdinan…?" Dæya's lips tighten. The shock from a moment before morphed into something entirely different. "What happened?"

"I was hoping you'd tell me." Mother made herself comfortable, preparing for a nice long talk.

* * *

Oya sat on the pier waiting and considering everything Jon told her. The difference between herself and Ferdinan was unexpectedly stark. *Amazing how much family impacts your life...* Delicate fingers tugged at the chain around her neck and those glowing orbs danced. Hard soles clicked on the wooden dock - stopping next to her. Jon looked down. She gave her signature chesire grin, stifling a giggle when he shivered.

Next thing she knew, he was sitting beside her - slumped low. They enjoyed silence while last night's conversation ran through her head. It wasn't a long talk, but it told her just how little Jon understood about her friend. How little *she* understood. It wasn't until he posed a strange question about frozen treats that it clicked. This was something Ferdinan asked Jon back at the hospital, but he didn't get it. She doubted the growing giant ever would.

The boat docked. An eternity passed before people shuffled off. Excited chattering about the gala filled the air. Ferdinan was the last straggler to appear - moving slowly and holding his right arm awkwardly.

Wordlessly Oya stormed the plank. A black eye and purple jaw stood starkly against pale skin... Ferdinan averted his eyes as if he couldn't bare looking at them. Or maybe he couldn't bare them looking at him.

"What happened to you?" She demanded in Oŭndo.

Jon slid to a stop beside her. Not knowing what she said, he ended up repeating the same thing, only more passionately and in Common.

A dishonest smile curled thin lips and blue crystals avoided making contact. "I fell."

Taking his hand, she pushed back the sleeve. A hard brace wrapped down to his wrist. She felt up his arm and continued on to his shoulder. "*What's this?*"

"What's she doing?" The oddity of her actions distracted Jon. "What's that?"

Every time they poked and prodded him, he winced – paling at the unwanted attention they were gathering. "Please, I'm fine. Leave that alone. Ah! Don't–"

I'll teach that mutt a lesson he won't soon forget. Jon had lousy aim, but Oya found every tender spot on her friend. Squatting down and jabbing his thigh must've taken things too far.

"Don't touch me!" This grabbed the attention of the few who weren't already watching them. Ferdinan purpled and bolted away.

"Wait!" Jon called after him.

"I'm tired." Speeding up, Ferdinan limped toward the dormitories.

"What was that about?" Jon wondered.

Alien green eyes rolled at him. Oya's screen was still in his room from the last time they talked. And that's where she headed. At the dormitory's entrance Oya winked at him and disappeared. However she got into places, taking the stairs wasn't it.

A little welcome back party had started in his suite. Tuel hovered above the table and made the announcement. With the last of the now eleventh-years back, stories of the gala could begin.

Oya's spiky red hair poked out from his bedroom door.

"I can't wait...but I need to talk to someone first. Um...if you'll excuse me." Jon rushed to his room. There she laid on the floor, twirling her screen high above her head.

"You're slow."

"I'm sorry. I don't know how to disappear and reappear at will." Despite his irritation, Jon stopped himself. "I apologize."

"Why? I'm the master of snark." She waved her hand before sitting up. *"I have a question."*

"Yes?" Jon asked, slouching down beside her.

"Where was his cousin?"

"Zephyr? I didn't see him get off..." He moved to his desk and searched the boat's passenger list. "Odd...he wasn't on board."

"*Really*?" Her grin filled with satisfaction. *"I wonder how the gala went for Ferdinan."*

"Huh?" What a huge jump in topics. *Did it translate correctly?*

"Hmm? Oh, sorry... I look forward to talking to him tomorrow. I bet it was exhausting."

"Aren't you concerned about-?"

She interrupted him with a wink and a wave of her hand. *"If you see a problem, then look for the source."*

"What do you know?"

"It's up to you to find out." She gave him another wink before disappearing again.

◊

The moment Ferdinan fell asleep, Oya slid open the window. The hole in his chest festered magnificently. Those clouds covering his mind were solidified and cracks had formed. What sleep Ferdinan got was fitful – it was only a matter of time before he awoke from whatever haunted his dreams. *What alternative can I give you to nightmares?*

Dreams were her playground. And…this was a perfect opportunity…

Wicked green eyes closed. *What sort of dream does my friend deserve?* A pleasant surprise awaited her when she searched his mind. His priorities were changing. What was once most important was being replaced by truly important things. She grinned. *Now to see what Evelyn's doing.*

◊

Something chased him…something which wasn't there anymore. Instead, a toothy grin under a ridiculous floppy hat beamed at him.

"Fisherman?"

"Have you reconsidered, son?"

"Reconsidered what?"

The Fisherman pointed to his ear. "You drown yourself in angry music instead of letting me clean your wound."

"This is a dream." Once again, Ferdinan voiced his disbelief from the first time.

"Then what can it hurt?"

Ferdinan looked at the ground. Except, it wasn't ground. It looked like clouds from Evelyn's paintings, the ones she'd been so excited to show him. The atmosphere was completely different here. *Where am I?*

"If you're not ready now–"

"I'm not hurt." Brushing a hand across his chest, Ferdinan grit his teeth. "There's nothing wrong with me."

"You honestly believe that?" When the skeleton looked down, he offered again. "I'll clean the infection if you'll let me."

"And you'll keep bothering me if I say 'no?'"

"I'll keep offering."

"Why? You know what I am. What I did..."

"That's exactly why."

Shoulders slouching, Ferdinan shook his head. He couldn't keep dealing with this. "If you'll leave me alone, then yes."

The man's hand glowed inches from his chest. Slowly...ever so slowly, he felt... *What is this?* His very being lightened. For the first time he could breathe in deep without restraint. A weight lifted from his heart. It wasn't until pain and agony ebbed out of him that he realized it'd been there the entire time. *How is this possible?*

"Someone's waiting for you."

"Huh?" Ferdinan looked around. The sun was bright and warm and colors abounded incoherently. Above him was the Pegasus Evelyn drew coming over a rainbow. And she was riding it. *But...she hadn't been in her picture...*

"Enjoy your reunion." The Fisherman smiled and walked out of existence.

"What's going on?" He'd never had a dream like this. It was too bright and colorful. And happy. This dream radiated happiness.

"Big brother!" Evelyn called to him. "How did you get here?"

"I don't know! Do you?!" Morbid curiosity wondered what horror this would morph into.

The flying horse landed and she leapt off right into his arms. "My fairy god-dragon!"

"Your what?" he chuckled. *...she doesn't feel like lightning...* He pushed the thought away. Of course, she wouldn't. This was a dream.

"My fairy god-dragon! She said I was a good girl and earned a wish! Whatever I wanted! Isn't that great?!"

"It is. What did you wish for?"

"I wished we could play whenever I wanted!" She squeezed him tight. "It worked! She said there were conditions though."

"What conditions?"

"The fairy god-dragon said I could play with you as long as we were asleep at the same time."

"Really? And why's that?"

"She said it's easier to travel this way, and that it's more fun playing in dreams! She said I could make anything happen here if I tried hard enough."

Ferdinan stood flabbergasted. *Would I really dream a story like this?*

"There she is!!" Evelyn half stood in his arms pointing as high as she could.

A giant, scaly beast soared above them – wings twice as long as its body and wearing a ruffled skirt and a gaudy, silver crown. *I'm going mad...*

As far as madness went, it could be worse.

"I want to fly with you!" Evelyn squirmed out of his arms and pulled him off the cloud.

Hand in hand they flew.

◊

Oya took back her hand and grinned. "*Sleep well, my friend.*"

Slipping down to the floor as if meditating, she didn't move until sunlight hit her.

Chapter 19

"Attention!" Xhou shouted from the stage – voice harsh and gravelly. "I'm glad you've returned with exciting stories, but break's over! Time to get back to work."

That caught everyone's attention.

Immediately his face and voice lightened. "I hope everyone's worked on their assignment."

Around of grumbles and the Science Lead passed their attention to Ferdinan. Their attitudes were something the Tinkerer could've done without. Though it didn't compare to that voice... *Where is it...?*

For months it'd haunted him. But...after his dream with Evelyn...it was gone... It wasn't possible... And Ferdinan didn't want to be hopeful. Letting his heart believe he was free only to have it come back... He couldn't handle that.

"Many complained the instructions weren't specific enough." Ferdinan gave a warning look. He wasn't putting up with such nonsense. "I've made an example. Our benefactor also put something together...actually, she's put together a mini show of her own. Pay attention."

Seeing everything Oya did this break... *I won't leave her to her own devices again.* He never met someone so ill prepared for boredom. *Why didn't I think of arranging activities for her? Why didn't I think about her at all before leaving?* It was rude expecting Oya to fill a month in a strange place with no one she knew. Maybe he should've stayed? But...he'd only have made her sick of him... *Still...I would've rather spent break with her...* "This song...this is what I pictured. It'd easily represent the sciences or the arts."

Connecting his screen to the audio-visual system, a laser projection of himself appeared on the stage. The projection raised its violin to its chin and played. Another projection appeared with a mandolin and joined. Lastly was one of just him singing – supported by the voices of the first two.

Projections or not, this was humiliating.

Words swam above them – translating the powerful lyrics. Projected orbs ebbed and waned – dying off and combining together. Building and growing. Just like thought. Like an idea that must be experienced – expressed. As the song reached its climax those orbs ruptured into an explosion of light. They painted the stage in gears and bonded shapes. Again, they formed something new. The song ended zooming in on the creation until everything disappeared.

The Scientist's faces nearly made Ferdinan laugh. This was the reaction he expected. No one moved. They didn't even blink. Even Xhou was speechless. Then someone clapped. A laugh the skeleton knew all too well followed. Looking back, he smiled at her but didn't get up. His leg and back didn't like him moving around, and his arm was generally useless. But...he felt better than he should.

"That was absolutely amazing! You're an extraordinary child." She said in Oŭndo, knowing he wouldn't refute her here.

Jumping off the stage, she dragged Jon up against his will. A wink signaled Ferdinan to start her show. The first song was new and obviously manipulated. Not only was it sped up, it was given an extra beat – making it a fast four step waltz. With some effort, she signaled Jon to lead her around the stage until the music changed. The new song was even more upbeat with strong drums. Soon she had the Dinta moving with her as if locked in a one-sided battle – and painfully in her favor.

The music continued changing and with it, her presentation. Some songs they sat out while an intricate light show overstimulated the audience. Some she performed by herself. Ferdinan was impressed. *Is there anything she can't do?* For the last song she took the screen from him and manipulated it as it played, adding butterflies and random effects. The crowd of faces contorted all the more when she distorted the sounds.

Once finished, she returned the screen and sat next to him on the edge of the stage, grinning playfully.

"Thank you, Jon Dinta, you may take your seat." Ferdinan didn't bother looking behind him as his ally grumbled - out of breath from the exertion. "This young lady is our benefactor. Now that you've seen what a Scientist came up with and a number of examples from...an entirely different kind of genius, I'll introduce you. This is Oya."

She gave a silly half bow - twirling her arm around before waving to everyone.

"Her Common...is pretty lousy." She gave him a small push and a mock stern look. "But she understands it well... Just don't speak too quickly." This was a lie. She could actually understand the fastest of talkers now. Her talent for language amazed him.

"How do we address her?" Xhou asked uncertainly.

"By her name - Oya. She doesn't care for titles."

"How's she going to teach us if she can't talk to us?" a girl from below asked.

"She can talk, though not very well." Ferdinan smirked at his own "meanie head" thought, as Oya would call it. *Why is sitting next to her so...warm?* "This'll be good for you. It'll teach you creativity. If there's a problem you can't figure out, she'll get me. Any other questions?"

Silence fell.

"Who knows how they'd like to present their song?"

A few timid hands poked up, trying to stay low.

^^^

A number of questions filled his mind as Ferdinan stood outside the lab door rubbing his belly.

Are they sabotaging my efforts?

Did Dæya tell them to not get any samples, just to do enough to appease me?

They know I won't stand for that...but...

If real samples were taken from infected persons, why is the blood clean?

The images sent along with the samples showed the virus. So why not the blood?

VVV

Frustration wrinkled his forehead both at the unbidden memory and the lack of raised hands. "You six stay there. Everyone else, gather around Oya."

No one moved. Instead they watched Oya help Ferdinan to his feet. Once he was standing, she shouted, "MOVE!"

This got them going. Ferdinan joined the six, discussed their ideas, and helped flush them out.

"Master Ferdinan! Look at this!"

A smile spread across the skeleton's face as his first pupil clapped and stomped in an unusual rhythm. It looked fun. The beat made his own feet want to move – despite his injuries. "Wonderful! Yuyu, what are you wanting to use that for?"

"Winrad's using it for the Fighters!" Pink eyes turned to the boy next to her – adorable smile on her face.

Turning his attention to the suddenly bashful ten-year-old, Ferdinan nodded. "How would you make this for the Fighters?"

"It was more the song...but..." The gangly boy looked away uncertainly. "Maybe with two groups doing this back and forth, it could look like fighting."

"Possibly. It'll *sound* like a fight to the audience. Think about it for a moment." Ferdinan turned to the next person. "Dedar Lumick, how about you?"

◊

It was excruciatingly fun watching the Scientists squirm as Oya tested them on various entertainment skills – starting with vocal abilities. Dancing, however, was even more amusing. Dozens of styles were tried to see which each student moved most easily to.

Not everything she demanded pertained to performing. Outside she made them run an...*interesting*...obstacle course. Wild green eyes watched greedily as they neared the end. One Scientist after another was knocked off their feet by large, weighted bags – making her laugh uncontrollably.

There was no grace, style, or reflexes she could see. That was ok. Oya enjoyed a challenge. Two younger children – one with mismatched eyes and the other with pink – stepped up to her trial. As strange as it was seeing two different colored eyes on one face, the pink held her attention.

First the pink-eyed girl dashed forward. Long, black curls bobbed playfully through the first trap. Her agile feet easily glided past the second and third. It wasn't until the wobbly balance beam that she hesitated. It took a bit – and she nearly fell thrice – but the young girl overcame and continued on. Then the boy with mismatched eyes started.

One obstacle at a time they conquered. Unlike the other Scientists, these two had some athletic ability. Or maybe they were better at predicting what was coming. All the Scientists watched the traps and each other, but they didn't spend that time figuring it out. When the girl came to the swinging bags trap, Oya held her breath. *Can you do it, little one?*

Taking her time, the girl stood. Pink eyes watched until she found the rhythm. Readying herself, she jumped the moment the bag passed in front of her, stopping dead on the step stone for a breath before jumping again. Each bag moved at different speeds. Cautious, the girl would stand for a bag to swing a few times before moving past. By the time she finished, the little boy was waiting to start.

And he did as good a job as the girl. He was less cautious, though, making it through significantly faster. At the end, the young boy jumped down and celebrated with the girl.

Ok, not everyone's helpless. Oya turned to her friend. Bold as brass, Ferdinan smirked at a flustered Xhou.

"Think we can do it again?" The girl bubbled with adrenaline and excitement.

"I hope so!"

Grinning, Oya waved at them with a nod. Delight brightened their faces and they bolted back to the start.

The only person excused from her "assessment" was Ferdinan. She already knew what he was capable of. Still, seeing the jealous looks everyone gave him was amusing.

When the sun kissed the horizon, she was forced to stop torturing them. This was fine. She'd been making things up for a while just to see what they'd do.

◊

"Luyou'll be mad at you for stealing her island sister." Xhou spoke as fast as he could while smiling at Oya. "She already doesn't like you."

"Her and the rest of the school." Ferdinan answered with indifference. *I know how everyone feels about me... Neither are you fooling Oya.*

"I like you. I know Elbie and Yuyu do too." Xhou stretched out sore muscles while grinning at the red skeleton. To make a point, he nodded to the course where a laughing Elbie was running through yet again.

That wild grin turned on him. Red turned to purple – forcing Ferdinan to look away from her. "Lord Elbarrat and Yuyu Inoa... It's wrong burdening apprentices with social pressures."

Xhou looked long and hard at the Tinkerer, deciding it wasn't worth responding to that. "Why didn't you join the rest of us for calisthenics?"

"The perk of being in charge." Ferdinan turned away – waiting for his face to return to normal.

"You have to ask?" Jon butted in looking wearily at Oya. "He wouldn't survive running around like that. Oya didn't make him because she knew I'd tell her 'no.'"

Turning farther away from them, Ferdinan nearly melted from humiliation. *I'm not an invalid!*

"You? Tell a girl 'no?' Though, it looks like she's the one in charge. Ah! She's mean!" Xhou rubbed out a knot in his shoulder. "What was the point of half of that anyway?!"

Ferdinan burst out laughing. *They didn't realize Oya was having fun with them?* Even toying with them, Ferdinan respected everything she'd done for them today. *She really is amazing...*

"What's so funny, Mr. Lazyman?"

"I'm curious as well." Surprise painted Jon's face - and confusion.

Oya circled around behind Xhou - sniggering with Ferdinan.

Laughing hurt. For some reason, their words made him laugh harder. Maybe he *was* going mad. He couldn't complain. This was a more enjoyable madness than before the Fisherman... This thought stopped him cold. *What right have I to feel happy?*

"What's wrong?" Jon asked at the sudden change in mood.

"Nothing."

Oya's bare toes raised her high enough to pat him playfully on the head, *"It's good hearing you laugh. Thank you."*

"What does she want?" Xhou asked suspiciously.

"You need to run another twenty laps around the island, you were slacking off too much," Ferdinan sneered to hide his embarrassment.

"She didn't say that!"

"How could I know? She isn't speaking any of the languages I know," *officially*. "You'd better get going before nightfall."

"*Bah*! We'll discuss this more tomorrow." Xhou left reluctantly.

"I'm sure we will."

"I thought he'd never leave!" Jon griped. "I'm hungry, just as you two should be. I'll be back."

"You where going are?" Oya tried.

"Where am I going?" Jon asked, "I'm going to prepare dinner."

~

"What are you thinking?" Ferdinan asked once they found a nice spot for stargazing.

She grinned, searching the sparkling dots. *"They need regular exercise or they won't last two hours. I'm happy to come up with something."*

"I'll do that. You might kill them. Most of their time is spent in classrooms and labs. You can't expect them to do half of what we can."

"Fine. You design the program. I'll lead. Heeheehee."

"You're enjoying this." The skeleton commented on her far too joyful grin.

"I like seeing people expand their horizons. It makes me feel all warm and fuzzy."

"I don't know how much of that is sarcasm." A chime interrupted them. A call request from the Artimuses flashed on his screen. But he was in no mood to talk to them.

"You're not answering?"

"No."

"What if it's important?"

"There's nothing important they could possibly have for me."

"What if they're trying to get a hold of Jon. We've kept him busy all day."

"You're the real meanie head." Ferdinan turned her own favorite accusation back on her.

"Pah! You're wrong."

"Excuse me?"

"There's a huge difference between a 'meanie head 'and a 'villain.'" Eyes extra wide – she gave him an evil grin.

Ferdinan sighed and smiled softly. A pleasant warmth glowed in his chest. *It really is nice being with her... "You're too silly..."*

A wink was her answer.

Hesitantly, he accepted the waiting call. The box opened and Evelyn's excited face appeared. Those green rings and her joyful energy reminded him of the meanie head beside him.

"You answered me, big brother! I knew you would. Everyone said you wouldn't, but I knew better!" She turned to the side and wiggled a finger at whoever was out of view.

"Lady Evelyn, what do you need?" Ferdinan wasn't sure what to expect anymore.

"I wanted to see you! I wanted to talk to you!"

"I've been wanting to talk to you too." He smiled warmly at her. Words spilled unbidden out of his mouth. "I had the strangest dream last night. You were in it."

Jon placed a tray in front of them. Knowing he'd never pull Ferdinan away from Evelyn, he started eating and motioned for Oya to do the same.

"REALLY! I DREAMED ABOUT YOU, TOO!!!" She shouted at the top of her lungs, bouncing on her chair. "I found you while riding Diniea and I finally got to show her to you. You saw my fairy god-dragon too! It was so much fun! We flew through the clouds and played all sorts of games! It was so much fun!!!"

"That was your dream?" Concern and confusion leaked into his voice.

"Yah! Doesn't it sound great? What was your dream? What did we do?"

"Um...mostly we talked," he lied. "We talked about silly things, like green pudding and why lizards have seven feet."

Her giggle was his favorite sound in the world.

"Do you feel ok? Are you happy now?"

A light chuckle escaped him. "I'm ok. Tell me about the party? Did you have fun?"

Her eyes lit up. "YES!! Everyone was so nice! The food was yummy too!"

This began an hour of ramblings. Ferdinan smiled gently the entire time. "Oh! I met your aunt lady! She's really nice! She asked about you. I told her about all the fun we had! Did you know she commands thousands of people? She told them to clean up my home, and they did! She said she helped too. Wasn't that nice of her?"

Ferdinan nodded. *Just like the Duchess said...someone else is cleaning up after me...* "Yes. It was hard work. Did you thank her?"

"Yes!" Pride emanated from Evelyn. "And you know what she said?"

"What?"

"She said she should thank me! I don't know why though..."

"She's a nice lady."

Xingho's face appeared above his daughter's. "I'm sorry to interrupt, but it's bedtime."

"I understand." Ferdinan looked down.

"Wait! Big brother, don't forget to sleep so we can play tonight!"

"That's what your fairy god-dragon said?"

"Yes!"

"Ok." He watched Evelyn be lifted and carried away.

This was when he handed the screen to Jon. The Dinta could have them now. Objections sounded through the speaker. But one intervention per lifetime was more than enough. Jon stumbled - pointing out it'd been a long day and Ferdinan hadn't eaten yet. The Thinker then spent a good hour saying goodbye.

~

While Jon talked and Oya stared at the stars, Ferdinan grabbed another screen. There were countless designs for the various electric stringed instruments. Now to decide the elements he liked best to design his own. *How hard will this be to build?* Searching. Studying. Just having this ancient knowledge open in his hands was...it was calming... He should be fascinated and curious. But it wasn't like that. It was like sitting and talking to Oya. Only more personal and less embarrassing.

Melancholy entered his heart. *Her common's improved. How much longer 'til she finds someone better?*

Once Jon ended the call, he put down the screen. A strange look came over his face as he watched Ferdinan - eyes glued on one screen and hand scribbling notes on another. "You weren't at the gala?"

"No," Ferdinan admitted - catching Oya's attention.

Narrowed brown eyes studied Ferdinan more intently. Then Jon looked down at his own hands and mimicked writing something in the air. "Why not? They made a fuss about you being there."

Ferdinan turned away from Oya's sharp look. "Zephyr wasn't well. My sisters went and I tended to him."

"What kind of 'not well?'"

"You know how he wasn't sleeping before break?"

"Ya." Putting his hands in his lap, Jon pursed his lips. Whatever his mind was focused on, it wasn't the subject of this conversation.

"He didn't improve."

"What happened?"

Oya sat up silently, morbidly curious.

"I don't know. Too much stress maybe? Nothing helped. They couldn't get his brain to stop. Before I returned, he was placed in a coma...even that didn't stop his mind." Crystal blue eyes drifted to the diamonds overhead. *This is my fault, but I don't understand why. How do I fix it?*

"Wow."

Once again, Ferdinan focused on the screen – drawing Jon's fascinated attention. "I hope he gets better. It'd be bad if he doesn't."

"How so?" Those words sounded distant – as if Jon responded automatically without any thought.

"He's the King's only child," Ferdinan sighed. *Put two and two together, Thinker.*

"No one wants their future ruler to be broken."

The look Ferdinan shot Jon warned how rude and unappreciated that comment was.

"I apologize, but–"

"Good."

"What happens if his mind breaks?" Oya asked, devoid of compassion.

Ferdinan didn't expect the same courtesy from Oya, but her question annoyed him anyway. *"It'd be disastrous for everyone."*

A delicate hand tugged at the chain around her neck. *"Yourself included?"*

"Myself especially."

Reaching over, she tapped Ferdinan's chest, stood up, and left. The void of her touch lingered.

"What was that about?" Jon asked, not sure what they said.

"I've no idea..."

The two watched her walk away, hand held aloft as if holding onto something. *Why didn't she disappear?* It was odd seeing her leave. Once she was out of sight, Ferdinan went back to work and Jon returned to gawking – that strange look still marred his face.

"Why are you staring at me?"

A light pink tinged Jon's cheeks – embarrassed at his own rudeness. "I thought you were right-handed..."

Crystal blue eyes looked up – appraising his ally. After a moment, Ferdinan shrugged and went back to work.

◊

I only meant for him to have nightmares... I wonder what I did wrong. Hand aloft, she held onto the strand connecting Ferdinan and his cousin. Unlike the sad blue one connecting him to Jon, the one that bound him to that mutt was a dark purple-gray until it turned red and black. *Will this work...? If not, he might die from sleep deprivation.*

Oya sneered. It didn't matter to her...but it did to her friend. She'd end this lesson and give it a chance to sink in. If this didn't work, she'd do something more hands-on until the dog understood its place. Her entourage of glowing orbs followed her to a hidden clearing.

Lying down, she held onto that string and closed her eyes – picturing it firmly in her mind. It appeared in the black abyss of pre-dreams. She'd succeeded. Connecting directly to someone's dream was easy enough. However, that mutt wouldn't return to the islands for her to fix this – not in the condition he was in. But…if she could use Ferdinan's connection with Evelyn to set up dream playdates, she could do this – maybe. Signature Cheshire grin on her face, she followed it through that black abyss to Zephyr without leaving the spot where she lay.

◊

Whatever hovered threateningly disappeared into blackness. Everything stayed this way for some time.

"Stand up."

Leaping, Zephyr spun. A tall, elegant elf woman towered over him. Hair the color of starlight framed a sharp smirk and incredible sapphire eyes. His hands danced. "Who are you?"

"It's not important." A mad grin stretched across her face. Tilting her head reflected light off the silver leaf circlet above her brow.

"Why are you here then?" Zephyr gave her an odd look as he pointed to his palm then to her. This dream was new.

Stepping forward, she looked down upon him. "Why're you so angry?"

"Excuse me?" Zephyr was taken aback. "I'm not angry."

"All I see in your face is anger. Why?"

Zephyr stepped away. *What is this?*

"Why do you hate him?" The elf stepped forward, maintaining their distance.

A golden ring finger tapped at his temple. "Who?"

"Your cousin."

His usual arguments wouldn't leave his tongue.

"You don't know...? How can you hate family and not know why? You don't understand why you're angry either..." She looked hard at him – searching the depths of his soul. "You've noticed. It's the very thing inside you. You hate that too... It's why you hate him."

Chapter 20

Ferdinan's first attempt ended in disappointment. But an in-depth study of the violin strings taught him something interesting. The basic construction for an electric stringed instrument was simple – wire coiled around a magnet. But getting the proper sounds for the lower tones, regular stretched wire wasn't good enough. Eventually he found a detailed picture of the lower strings. They weren't only thicker, but textured. A fine wire wrapped around the stretched one. After finagling a lathe from storage, he managed a number of various wrapped strings. Now he was searching for the right tone.

Stringing them, he plucked and tuned before taking up the bow. This batch was close. Spot on with all but one. *Who thought of metal for strings?* But traditional gut couldn't induce current...

Building his electric violin and the amplifying device was wonderful, though its body looked about as far from a violin as you could get. Twisted plexiglass was bent into a swirling fog with strings laid on top. It played beautifully. And...he liked the oddity of its appearance.

So did Oya. Her excited eyes and unfounded praise turned him red but boosted his confidence. She insisted it needed a tiny, green flower on the bridge. But that spot was only easily visible to the player... The next day, she arrived with a flower carved from a shell. He stained it green.

Ferdinan smiled softly. When was the last time he smiled because he felt like it? *I don't deserve to feel this good...* But neither did he want to stop...which made guilt intensify...

Tweaking and tinkering, Ferdinan soaked in the silence. For months that voice haunted him. For weeks he drowned it out with music. And now...it'd vanished... But how? The Fisherman wasn't real - couldn't be real...but... Did a Psych realize he was broken? Were they capable of healing a mind? Why invade his dreams to do so?

An alarm chimed. Ferdinan put down his new toy with a sigh. Making the last string and attaching the flower would have to wait. Now for a meeting with the Superintendent. *Why isn't Xhou doing this?* The Sciences needed more time. But how did one convince an administrator to let an entire group of students out of classes for two weeks? And why send the least charismatic among them to try?

Packing up, he headed to the main island and on to the administration building. He stepped into the reception area as the Superintendent's office door opened. Dæya escorted out a Science student. A boy three years younger than Ferdinan and normally well behaved. But from the look on the man's face, the child was in trouble.

"Rupert Nauo? What are you doing here?" Asking was rude and out of line, but he hadn't put this much work into the stupid show for its players to get into trouble.

Arms folded, the boy scrunched his face and grumbled, "The instructor was being unreasonable..."

The rumbling sound of Dæya clearing his voice stopped the rest of the young Thinker's words. Even without that deep, intimidating voice, everyone knew those tattoos weren't just for show. "Lord Ferdinan, feel free to escort Rupert out then report back."

That wasn't a generous offer. The look on the Superintendent's face... This was Ferdinan's fault. Turning, the skeleton scolded the younger boy. "You know where you're supposed to be and what you're supposed to be doing, Rupert Nauo. Get there and do it."

"Who put you in charge!?"

"You did. Along with every other Scientist." Nodding to the Superintendent, Ferdinan walked the boy out into the hall. "I know you're in pain. But...getting in trouble is only hurting yourself more."

"And what do *you* know? Have you ever lost anyone?"

ΛΛΛ

Self-loathing. Fear. Desperation. It all refused to be buried with the rest. It burned and punched at his chest. It constricted his lungs and stole his strength.

I'm failing her again… I let her die, then her son. *Wrapping a stick-thin arm around his middle, Ferdinan tried stilling his trembling.* Now her granddaughter. I'm killing an innocent child! Why is she sick? I should be the one in there!

"Please don't die." His voiced cracked, forcing him to whisper. "Please. Please don't die…"

VVV

"No." Ferdinan hid squarely behind his mask of stone, lying. "No, I haven't. But how would your parents feel about you expressing your sorrow like this?"

Clenching his jaw shut, the boy looked down.

"You've never acted this way." It wasn't just Rupert. Others Scientists were particularly moody since the end of break and it intensified the longer they prepared for the show. *Is the stress too much?* "What can I do for you?"

"Um…" Rupert hesitated. "There're a few musicians...can I get more of their music?"

Huh? What does that have to do with anything? "If you stay out of trouble."

"Yes, sir."

Excusing the child, Ferdinan went back in. *Hopefully Master Dæya isn't too unhappy with us...*

* * *

Timid and uncertain, Ferdinan's apprentice approached. "Jon Dinta, may I ask for your expertise?"

"Ah! Um... Lord Elbarrat, right?"

"Call me 'Elbie.'"

"Elbie. Of course. Please sit down." Jon lowered his voice. Everyone was working silently, figuring out the details of their assignments. "What can I help you with?"

Elbie held out a medical disk and removed the cover. "Do you know *anything* at all about these?"

"Uh...I didn't know they came apart." Jon's comment was less than helpful. "I'm sorry, but I don't. Not really."

"'Not really?'"

Jon gave Elbie his full attention. "Two years ago, my brother requested a hundred of these. Thinking I'd be useful, I offered to help make them. Replicating things is easy for me... But he turned me down."

"Why reject help with such a big order?"

"I didn't ask. Guess I didn't really care. Between classes and earning my evaluation..." Looking at the disk, Jon said more to himself than Elbie, "I should've been more insistent."

"You think this looks complicated; I'll take it apart for you."

"It comes further apart?" The question dripped with skepticism. *Aren't the insides too delicate for removal?*

Elbie disassembled it for Jon as he had for a dozen others. "See?"

...whoa... Ferdinan made this? No, not just made...thought it up, designed it, and figured it all out? From scratch...?

"I understand you don't know much about them, but do you know where he would've started? Or what he was thinking? Anything?"

Jon shook his head. *Who would think of something like this?* The circuit boards were custom made. He'd never seen any so thin. They were smaller than standard micro boards, and there were a number of them. *Why?* "Mind if I keep this for a little bit? I'd like to take some time thinking it over."

Elbie's mismatched eyes lit up. "Of course! I'll show you how to reassemble it."

* * *

Nothing's more painful than doing nothing.

Sitting still, being useless...this wasn't what Athletes did. Athletes were active. Leaders were always doing something – not nothing. Being still hurt physically. Not even calisthenics could ease Zephyr's aching muscles. Not within the confines of his room.

After that odd dream with the elf woman, the Prince slept properly...for two solid days. Or that's what his healer told him before leaving him in this isolation.

"You've slept two days but are in good physical health."

Those were the last words he'd heard. The last thing anyone said to him. *How long have I been in here? A week? Feels like a year...* Each passing moment he wished harder for his mom, aunt, anyone he trusted to come.

The longer he sat, the tighter his chest became. That tightness spread to the rest of his body. His insides shook. If he didn't run, work, do something...! *Why won't they let me out?*

Stay calm. Onyx eyes stared at the ceiling, praying for someone - *anyone* - to come. A week of solitude... Food and clothing were delivered...but he never saw by whom. It felt like he wasn't here. Like he didn't exist.

"Why?" his voice broke.

* * *

Their request was granted.

Starting tomorrow the Scientists would all but live on this island until the show. Jon watched the Tinkerer drag in a work board with a detailed schedule. Ferdinan announced when they'd arrive, how hard they'd work, and how much complaining the gent would listen to.

Completed assignments were gathered up then Ferdinan let Oya at them. He was walking easier and the metal arm brace was replaced with a lightweight skeletal one. Even if the gent broke it at Jon's home, it'd need the solid brace until the show. Maybe Ferdinan did something less serious? There was no way the skeleton saw a Healer for it. And assuming he was healthy enough to undergo healing, one session and he'd be fixed. *I'll never understand him...*

Later that evening, Jon sat in the common room of his suite deciphering the disk. *No wonder he didn't accept my help...* These were inordinately complicated. The detail... *When did Ferdinan learn this level of programming?*

The skill, knowledge, and genius this took blew his mind. Jon fought with all his power to catch up to Ferdinan in their science classes, so he knew the skeleton hadn't been taught anything like this. *How did Ferdinan dream up something this complex at twelve?*

No wonder he received a lab so early.

But...he's started everything early, huh? Ferdinan wasn't yet three when starting his first year – normally students began at five. He completed his apprenticeship by the time he was four – in half the time it normally took – and before most actually started classes.

It just continued on. *Is there such a thing as a genius among geniuses? I'm smart, but I can't replicate these.* For the first time, Jon kicked himself. He should've paid attention to his ally's work. But Ferdinan's inventions were silly or pointless... *What've I missed out on thinking that?*

Taptap. Taptap. Fingernails drumming on glass interrupted his thoughts. Jon looked around. *Wait...* The only glass was the common room window. And he was on the third floor! Yet eerie green eyes stared in mischievously. Shoving his heart back into his chest, he ran to open the window.

Making his voice a whisper took great effort. "Are you insane?!"

"Come," Oya commanded in a cheery tone.

"You *are* insane, I'm not jumping out a window." Not wanting anyone to fall from this height, he braced himself and offered a hand.

Green eyes rolled. She took it and swung inside. A giant grin curled her lips when she offered a long screen. "Sheet music this is for you."

"You're making deliveries? Past curfew? Don't you have anything better to do?"

"Hmmm...No."

Jon shook his head. *Oya's a girl, stop being rude to her.*

A small stack of papers was plopped on top of the screen. "A secret between you and me."

"Why?" *Her Common...she's getting better.*

"It's...ah...surprise," she winked.

"For whom?" he asked, though he already knew.

"Our friend."

"Our?"

Oya pointed at Jon then herself. "My friend and your friend is *our* friend."

Ferdinan? A friend? It was an odd thought and felt wrong.

"Friends are more important than allies." Her pose spoke to generations of wisdom concerning such things.

"Um..." The moment he blinked, she disappeared. *Am I dreaming?*

* * *

Ferdinan sat in his lab fiddling with everything submitted to him. There was so much... Even delegating...

Some things *he* had to do simply because he was the only one with the skillset. Like these cuffs. Oya wanted to fly. It was an odd request...but he had an idea.

Energy conversion.

At its most basic level, all Energists did was convert energy into something they could manipulate. Whether healing the body or moving objects around – it was basically the same. From there, energy converting cuffs came to mind.

Working was difficult without full dexterity of his arm. But every time he started, Oya materialized and took his tools. Thanks to her two sets were completed. It wasn't a bad arrangement. She followed directions perfectly and had steady hands. But...burdening her was unacceptable. *I'll make the next set before she arrives...*

No sooner had he thought this than she was there an inch from his face.

"Hi!" It was her last word in Common for the night. *"You're ready to work?"*

Seeing her there, sitting across from him...the warmth she brought... Ferdinan smiled only to look away. *I don't deserve this... Why am I troubling her? It's wrong. I'm horrible...she's already done so much for us...*

But...this was fun... "Yes, I've started them."

"May I help?"

Permission or not, she'd help. It was nice of her making it sound like saying "yes" was generous. "Thank you, please."

"Your arm's healing quickly." Bare toes danced on the floor as delicate fingers placed one piece after another.

"Yeah..."

"You developed a regeneration potion or some such?"

"That'd make me a popular child." *Hmm... How would I make such a thing? I have that powder. Turning it into an oral medicine...*

As he considered, he turned cold. He was healing fast. Too fast. Then there were his dreams. Every time he slept...nightmares started but never lasted long. Evelyn would appear and take him to her fantasy world. When he talked to her, she described the same dream every time.

Is she a Psych? He needed to talk to Mother Artimus about it. If he could bring himself to... Whenever they took Evelyn away from the screen, he'd give it to Jon or turn it off. After *that*...he couldn't face them.

"What's wrong? Isn't healing quickly a good thing?"

"Yes. But no..."

"Anything you'd like to share?"

He wanted to, but he wasn't sure. *What does she know about dreams?*

"I love listening and I've no one I'd tell, unless you want me to."

"I've been..."

"Hmmm?"

"I've been wondering about Evelyn."

"How so?"

"She keeps appearing in my dreams."

Oya grinned. *"Those must be wild!"*

"Yeah...but when I talk to her...she describes the same dream I had."

"That's a bad thing?"

"I don't think so. But...they only found you recently. Maybe she also has abilities we didn't realize. If this is the case, how many of us are roaming around unawares?"

Oya laughed. *"I think you worry too much. Or maybe you think too much. How's sharing a dream something of concern?"*

"It isn't possible. Once, for coincidence...but it's happened almost every night this week."

"Does it scare her?"

"I haven't told her."

"Does it scare you?"

"No…I look forward to sleeping… What worries me is it shouldn't be possible."

"Hmmm…" Oya put down the nearly completed cuff and looked at him. *"This girl loves you very much, doesn't she?"*

Red flushed his face. *"I don't know why."*

"Doesn't matter. Stories my grandfather told… When he traveled for work – during those times his son, my dad, appeared in his dreams. Dad had the same dreams. Grandpa said it was because his son needed him, and he desperately wanted to be there for his son. So, they found each other in the dreamlands." For as outlandish as that story was, her face said it was both normal and completely true. *"Maybe she needs her big brother. I know how much you care for her."*

"I don't think I can believe that level of superstition."

"You don't have to. Just enjoy this precious treasure for what it is." She grinned playfully and went back to the cuff. *"Besides, people've walked the dreamlands since before humans started making records. You can find a number of stories and legends on that cube."*

The cube...he'd spent countless hours listening to music and learning about forgotten instruments. It...it filled him with a strange kind of peace... Exactly how much could he learn from it? But that had nothing to do with this. *"You don't think it's an ability?"*

"Jon's family knows about the mutation. Two of them are Healers. Don't you think they'd have noticed? Besides, she's open and cooperative," Oya laughed.

"Speaking of which," Ferdinan grinned at her Cheshire smirk, "has Healer Ilu caught you yet?"

Mischievousness filled her face and her exotic green eyes doubled in size. "*No.*"

"Classifying you is required for passing his evaluation."

"His what?"

"*Before starting advanced studies, students have to pass an evaluation to determine if they are capable and ready. When you take it too young, they give you an extra project to see how badly you want to pass.*"

"*And I'm his project?*"

"Unfortunately for him."

"I see," she shrugged. *"His luck will turn soon. You can only hide for so long…"*

"Yeah." Ferdinan felt the same. After twelve years, everything was falling apart. If things continued like this, others would find out...he'd fail irreparably. Just like he did with Grandmother... Rubbing at his arm, he found it didn't hurt at all.

"Are they doing better split into groups?"

"Hmm? Oh! Yes. It was a good idea grouping them together. Those representing the Psychs and Healers are having some trouble still."

"Haha! Oh, ye of little imagination! It's not that hard. Watch."

Grabbing a cuff set, Oya attached them to her wrists and ankles and jumped out a window. Ferdinan hurried after her. He'd only gotten to his feet when she shot straight up into the sky until she was barely visible. Then she was falling. Fast. His insides froze. His heart struggled to beat. Cold sweat broke across his skin. *Did I make a mistake? She's going to die.*

"Pull up!" Ferdinan screamed as soon as she was close enough to hear. But she didn't. She nosedived. Alien green eyes glowed with crazed excitement. Her mouth was a perfect Cheshire grin.

The world froze.

Only Oya moved.

The only one who called him "friend."

The only one who talked to him for fun.

The only one left who was kind to him because she wanted to be.

He was going to watch her die.

Just like Grandmother.

Just like Liramarc and Yewaru.

Just like the millions he didn't know.

I'm going to watch her die... "This isn't funny! Pull up!! Oya!!!"

Oya loathed losing her game of chicken with the ground. Activating the cuffs last second, she flew forward - circling wide. Slowing, she landed next to her friend. Ferdinan stood – rigid as a statue. His eyes were completely dilated. No color was left in his skin. She didn't have a chance to tease him before those blackened crystals rolled back in his head and he dropped to the ground.

"Guess I went too far. I didn't mean to stop his heart..."

Chapter 21

Time was running out. Two days. People arrived in two days. Pathways were constructed. Costumes arrived yesterday. Everyone memorized their parts.

For the first time in months nothing occupied Ferdinan's mind.

Oya disappeared – most likely finding new and interesting ways of cheating death with the cuffs.

Everyone else was dismissed for the evening.

It was hours too early for bed. His course work was completed. Everything that could be done with one person was finished. Scouring the cube was appealing...but he couldn't afford being tempted by a new project right now. And that cube held so much inspiration...

So, the skeleton sat on the edge of the stage looking out over the seating.

An odd sound floated in. It was faint – sounding far away. Standing, he searched for the source. Louder it grew as he wandered down the hall.

Crying? Someone's crying? But why?

One classroom door was open... He reached it and the crying became wails.

Groans and screams of agony!

They assaulted his ears. He tried leaving but sank instead. Fighting! Struggling against blood-soaked quicksand! Hands grabbed him. Countless hands. They pulled – dragging him below.

And above... Ferdinan's face contorted. *Master Minjing...* She was frail. Exactly as the last time they'd talked – a matter of hours before...

But her voice... When Grandmother spoke, it wasn't weak and raspy. It was hard and angry.

"Enjoying my granddaughter? Are you happy having taken her away from me as well? My granddaughter, my son, and my life..."

"I'm sorry!" Ferdinan pleaded. But it didn't matter. He couldn't change any of it. Not then. Definitely not now.

"Will nothing satisfy you?" Those green rings glowed against dark irises. "I gave you everything I had. How could you take so much and still demand more?"

An endless chorus of voices and death masks joined her – all demanded the same thing. Why weren't their lives...their deaths...enough? Why did he take their children, their spouses, their parents, their friends...? Why was he taking more still?

"I'm sorry! I'm so sorry!" Ferdinan cried. "I'd trade my life to bring them back! I want to bring you back!"

"How great do you consider yourself?" Grandmother sneered. "How could something as pathetic and useless as you be worth all of us? How could one as worthless as you pay the price for even one of us?"

He pleaded out an apology but was dragged under.

Rancid, gritty blood filled his mouth and belly. He couldn't see. Couldn't scream. Skeletal hands shook him, wrenched him, jerked him – forcing the life from him.

◊

"Wake up!" Xhou shook Ferdinan violently – panicked from the inhuman shriek. Those blue-black eyes were scared witless.

Jon yelled too – trying to pull the Zi away from his ally, only to be shrugged off.

Dilated blue crystals burst open, startling Xhou further. Pulling away from the Science Lead, Ferdinan nearly fell off the chair, but the table caught him. The skeleton went transparent. Sweat beaded on see-through skin. In the next heartbeat he dashed away.

"Wait!" Xhou grabbed Ferdinan and turned his younger peer to face him.

"Xhou, don't-!" Jon warned.

"No!" Ferdinan struggled – teeth clenched, skin taking on a green hue.

Adrenaline hijacked Xhou's brain. "Calm down! It's me!"

They struggled until both regretted it.

Jon jumped out of the way in time, but Xhou stood stunned, not releasing the boy in his grasp.

Renewing his efforts, Ferdinan broke free from the vice grip.

Xhou watched helplessly as Ferdinan dashed to the storage area at the back of his lab. "Am I really covered in vomit?"

"Didn't you see how pale and clammy he was?"

"I was focused on the screaming." Xhou's face twisted. "This is disgusting."

"Guess I can trust him to eat when I can't babysit..." Jon tried lightening the situation. "There's a shower in my lab. You can rinse off."

"Thanks...I'll do that. Then burn these clothes. You have any clean scouring sponges?"

"A bit melodramatic?" Jon folded his arms, eyebrow raised. There wasn't much to scrub off.

"Has this happened before?"

"Why do you ask?" The sounds of painful retching made Jon flinch. "I guess he wasn't finished."

"We'll talk later."

While Xhou left to scald off a few layers of skin, Jon headed to the bathroom at the back of the closet. The door was locked. Heaving a sigh, he leaned his back against it – sliding to the ground. There he sat, waiting for silence to fall.

"It isn't your fault," he started. How many times had this happened at the hospital? Nightmares of the dead... Jon didn't understand. "Those people...you couldn't have saved them. Please believe me."

No response came.

"Ferdinan, speak to me," Jon demanded, only to be answered by silence. "Ferdinan? I'll break down this door."

Nothing.

In the end, Jon didn't break the door down. He removed the hinge pins.

~

With his ally taken care of, Jon returned to his lab. Xhou sat waiting for him in nothing but a towel. Looking the Lead over... Like most students with a lab, Jon kept clothes here for when he spent the night. However, there wasn't much hope of the older, broader child fitting into anything he owned. Ferdinan's clothes were out of the question entirely.

"Don't worry about it. I'll head to my lab in a bit." He spoke as if reading Jon's mind. "Is he ok? You came pretty fast."

"Oya showed up."

"Ah... What was that about?" Xhou gave one of the few serious looks he ever managed. "You know what's going on."

"He has nightmares. Sometimes they're intense."

"For how long?"

Jon shook his head. He couldn't say too much, but if he didn't offer enough, the lead would keep pestering them. "I don't know. I learned about them when we were gone."

"What're they about?"

Xhou was a good gent but too nosy. When dealing with anyone other than Ferdinan this was fine. *I'm tired of dodging questions for him. Why do I have to be the one dealing with Ferdinan all the time?* "You think he'd tell me?"

"Yah...he's pretty secretive. How can I help?"

"Don't tell anyone. Looking at you tomorrow will be hard enough for him. If he thinks you've said anything...I doubt he'll come to practice. Or the show." *Will I be able to get him to eat? He won't look at me either.*

"What causes the bad dreams?"

"I don't know..." Jon lied. *Was he dwelling on* that *again?* "He gets worse when he isn't busy..."

"Let's keep him on his toes then."

Chapter 22

"Please! Look at me! Talk to me!" Zephyr yelled when the delivery box opened. Lunch was slipped inside, but the servant stayed out of sight. Still, he caught a glimpse of Captain Rutoric. The few times he escaped, the Captain caught him and brought him back. This felt like a betrayal from his lifelong tutor and previously loyal manservant. The man wasn't one for words. But nothing... Even his unspoken pleas... Rutoric didn't offer a single gesture of the Grassland's hand language. The language this man taught him personally.

Why wasn't his family here?

Why was he treated like he didn't exist?

"What's going on?!!!"

Pounding on the solid oak doors made him feel better. He could break them...oak wasn't hard to an Athlete. But there was no point. Even if he broke it...Rutoric would catch him and they'd bring another door.

This hurt. But it didn't compare to the tightness in his chest.

I'm a caged animal...

Only no one looked at him. Even the beasts in zoos and shows were acknowledged. People looked at them, talked to them, let them know they existed.

Zephyr reached a hand high, tapped his chest and threw it forward. "Why are you doing this to me?"

Leaning a shoulder against the door, he slid down, breathing erratically.

"What's happening to me...?"

* * *

"Let's get this over with." Jon cornered Ferdinan in his lab. "The extension I asked for ends today. I have to give them something before everyone arrives."

"I-!" Skin splotched from paling and blushing simultaneously, Ferdinan searched for an escape. The room swam. Sharp, erratic breaths intensified his trembling. "You're so close!"

"Then cooperate." Jon offered breakfast to his ally. "I'll even let you eat first."

Swallowing hard, Ferdinan looked at the cup and plate. Every meal came with milk tea now. The portions started out reasonable, but...

"You're getting too ambitious." Ferdinan complained.

"I know you can do it."

ΛΛΛ

The bots did well on the tissue and blood samples...but not the airborne samples. And not inside the body... What am I missing? I can see it. It's right there in front of me. Why am I not recognizing it?!

Ferdinan's eyes drifted back to the man's lifeless body.

VVV

Swallowing hard, Ferdinan banished the rest of that memory. To get Jon off his back and give himself a little more weight, Ferdinan stuffed most of the meal inside him. Burning red head to toe, he approached the scale...how he loathed this. *What right have they?!*

While he grumbled internally, Jon looked pleased. "You did it."

"Huh?" Ice crawled across his skin and ran up his spine.

"You did it!" Jon laughed. "Fourteen and a half pounds! That's wonderful! I thought you'd digress at home. I guess I didn't need to worry."

I gained how much!!?

"The school's going to love this! You beat your goal by half again."

"It wasn't my goal..."

"Ya...that's fair." Grabbing his screen, Jon opened up a box to send his report.

How do I drop five pounds without him pestering me?

"Wait..."

Ferdinan looked up. Chocolate brown eyes stared at him intensely.

"We're still the same height?"

"Looks like it..."

Stinging needles seized Ferdinan's wrist and dragged him to the wall. *Why is he so grabby? Stop touching me!* But he couldn't handle another fight, so the Tinkerer grit his teeth and stood still while Jon marked the top of both their heads. They were exactly the same. Like always. A troubled expression filled the Dinta's face.

He's realized... But height wouldn't matter when he returned home.

* * *

Oya grinned.

An onslaught of people flooded the islands. There was plenty of room to host such numbers, far more than she'd ever seen here. For weeks now everyone hustled, preparing for what lay ahead.

It'd been fun torturing the Science students but right now... The islands held their breath in anticipation for everything to begin. Everyone was on their toes, poised on a knife's edge.

Excitement and anxiety filled the air waiting for the fun of this week. Before her, rooms and arms opened, offering love and joy and bliss aplenty. All for those rushing to the islands.

Oya grinned.

* * *

"Gather around!" Ferdinan hovered high above the ground. Once they coalesced, he lowered himself to the grass and deactivated his cuffs. "Go greet your families after you've finished! If you can't keep your mouth shut, stay here. Understood?"

Cheers followed the unexpected announcement. This was fair. He forgot to give them meal breaks most days... But he knew how excited they were for family visits. It didn't take long for everyone to bolt – starting with Xhou. Jon hesitated, but a nudge sent him off. Soon it was only him and Oya. Even the few who didn't have family here ran off to join friends.

Blood red hair and a mischievous grin moved closer – bringing that pleasant warmth and making him smile. *I need to leave her alone. She'd have dozens of friends by now if not for me.* But being around her. Spending time with her... Giving that up...how did he do that? *I've always been alone. It's easier. It's safer. I just have to go back...* But he didn't want to. He didn't deserve her. But he wished he did. *A little longer? Is it wrong to be selfish a little longer?*

"You aren't greeting your family?" Oya asked in Oŭndo, smirking.

"No one's coming."

Delicate fingers played with the chain around her neck. *"I'm sorry. You're staying here to keep yourself busy?"*

"No. I'm avoiding Jon's brothers."

Oya's grin curled up higher. *"Are they so bad?"*

"They aren't bad people…just overbearing. I had my fill of 'togetherness' during break."

"Ah." She gave him a strange look but changed topics. *"We have a whole island to ourselves…what should we do?"*

"You aren't greeting your family?" Ferdinan offered her an opportunity to leave. *Don't waste your time with me when you can be with people who love you.*

"It isn't possible for them to see these islands."

Ferdinan tried reading her face, but there wasn't anything there. If her parents couldn't see the islands, then it was too dangerous for them to travel. *Is she a forbidden student?*

Usually students from such places weren't allowed off the islands until after starting advanced studies. Elbie was one. He arrived as an infant and hadn't left. The child wasn't a lord either. He didn't know any of this yet – Elbie wasn't old enough.

As the young boy's mentor, there was limited information Ferdinan was privy to so he could adjust his mentorship accordingly. He was one of a handful who knew such students existed. The others were also mentors who held the possibility of traveling with advisees for training.

But she was old enough to know...and she arrived recently. *Is this why she's so secretive?* *"Ah, they are busy too?"*

She grinned knowingly. *"Precisely. Wanna race?"*

"Bah, like I would–" He dashed off, giving himself a good head start.

"Cheater!!!!" She laughed, running after him.

* * *

"Jon, wait!" Xhou came running up from the direction of the administration building.

"Do you need something?" Jon raised an eyebrow. "I'm kind of excited to see my brothers."

"No! I understand completely. They have my sister!"

"Rura? She's here?" Jon smiled.

"Yah! Your family brought her. Ferdinan was killing me keeping us so long!"

"Me too." Jon grinned all the wider.

Grabbing his younger peer's arm, Xhou bolted. "Come on!"

The two laughed as they stormed across the bridge to the guest quarters. Never before could they run so far or so fast. Oya was a miracle worker...and a mean drill sergeant.

"Jon...Ferdinan'll be on his toes 'til the show's over...I made sure of that... But what about afterward?"

Breathing as heavy as Xhou, but not as much as he expected, Jon answered easily with a grin. "Don't worry...my brothers and I'll take care of that."

"I knew I could count on you... We'll plan long term...once the excitement dies down."

"As if you could think...of anything other than your sister...once you see her!" Jon's smile widened.

Xhou gave the younger boy a push – making his underling stagger. "You'd know better than anyone...now wouldn't you? It's impossible to...pull you away from family!"

Both laughed as they approached the guest quarters. Two of Jon's brothers stood waiting with a tiny girl...or maybe she just looked tiny next to the giants.

"It's about time, baby brother!" the men laughed. "We're starving!"

"XHOU!" Rura screamed, running for him. Joy filled her face and leaked out her eyes.

Not missing a beat, Xhou lifted the six-year-old and spun her around. His own tears came and he squeezed her tight. "Rura! I've missed you so much! I've missed you! Thank the heavens you're alright!"

The Artimuses were used to giving affection, but they didn't see as much given outside Oueshi. The three brothers stood smiling at the scene. Jon didn't watch for long though. While Xhou and his sister enjoyed their reunion, he went inside and started cooking. People wanting to eat his food was a pleasure he missed lately.

~

"Baby brother, you need to come home more often to cook for me!" Ozar boomed.

"What? Dad taught you how to cook too!" Jon teased. "And you need to practice for when you have your own children."

"Ya, but dad *can* cook." Samuel nudged his older brother. "You got a lot of training ahead of you."

"I've heard tales of the King's astounding food," Xhou smiled and squeezed his little sister. "What did you think, Rura?"

"Yummy! Thank you very much!"

Jon beamed... *When did I last smile like this?* "Thank you!"

"Why so emotional?" Xhou raised an eyebrow at the response.

"For months I've only heard complaining."

"Oh... Ferdinan, right?" Xhou looked at his little sister. "If my super picky sister loves it, then you're nothing less than amazing."

The older brothers laughed and agreed.

"It's getting late. Time to get Rura ready for bed. I can bring her here in the morning, right?"

"Of course. Samuel's an early riser, so don't worry about waking us." Ozar grinned and the three waved Xhou and his sister off.

"Now that your bellies are full, any messages from the rest of the family?"

His older brothers grinned and yelled "WE LOVE YOU" in unison as they grabbed him and pulled him in for a bear hug. Jon laughed. They were probably told to deliver it just like this.

"How's Ferdinan?" Samuel asked more seriously, letting his baby brother sit up. "He talks to Evelyn whenever she calls, but the moment she's away from the screen, so is he."

"He's doing better. He's acting happier and more sociable. I've even put fifteen pounds on him. The brace is off too."

Ozar jumped in, "What brace?"

"His arm was in a brace when he returned, but it was off a couple weeks later. He uses it without any problems now."

"That's odd." Ozar sat in thought.

"Fifteen pounds is good," Samuel offered – focusing on the positive.

"He still has over forty to go before he's at a healthy weight…" Jon shrugged. "Healer Bær and I are trying to figure out when to bring up his next goals…"

"Hmm. That'll be difficult. Are you sure he's up for so much?" Worry knit Samuel's eyebrows.

"Over fifty pounds underweight!?" Ozar was aghast.

"Ya…kind of. He's grown nearly four inches since I started feeding him back at the hospital, so the amount of weight he needs to gain keeps increasing." Irritated, Jon continued on. "Fifteen pounds seemed like a success. But I did the math. Taking into account his height, he hasn't accomplished anything."

"Really?" Surprise painted Ozar's question.

"He was forty-five pounds underweight at the hospital and still is now. It's frustrating."

"You didn't invite him to dinner tonight?" Samuel interrupted.

"I tried…he doesn't know how to face us. It was hard, what we made him do before he left."

"Sitting him down and telling him we love him, care about him, and want to help him was important." Ozar looked toward the water. "He needed to hear that."

"It was still hard…" Jon responded.

"As long as he's talking to you." Samuel gave Jon a squeeze and mussed his hair.

Ya…but Ferdinan doesn't do anything without a reason. His ally had as much reason to talk to him as the rest of his family. There was something going on Jon couldn't figure out. "Samuel, do you know how those medical disks are made?"

The abrupt change in topics made the Healer pause. "No. Why?"

"Ferdinan's apprentice asked for help figuring them out. I've tried, but it's beyond me."

"Why's Ferdinan's apprentice asking you for help?"

"It's one of his lessons. Only...I don't know what Elbie's supposed to learn."

Samuel nodded. "I looked at the blueprints once. They gave me a headache."

Chapter 23

The little patch of grass cushioned his back. Taking in one slow breath after another, Ferdinan focused on the rise and fall of his abdomen. Oya won the race. But he won the fight. *I need to stop. This isn't good. I know better.* But... It *felt* good. Only running brought him any semblance of joy...then Oya appeared. Running by her side. Fighting hand to hand. And her cube – searching through that treasure...! *I need to forget this. I need to give this up... Put her first!*

"Ready for this evening?" Her native Oŭndo danced joyfully in his ears.

Don't remind me... Am I really doing that *this evening?* Making himself sick wouldn't be hard... A drawn-out sigh escaped as he rejected the idea. He'd failed enough the last many months – another failure might break him.

Smooth breaths turned shaky. His mouth tightened. Air shifted to the side of him and a pleasant warmth materialized in the space between his head and shoulder. Daring a glance, Ferdinan found inhuman green eyes and blood red hair grinning at him. If she'd laid any closer their ears would touch. Something about her presence melted away the tension held in every muscle.

"Only a few more hours."

^^^

"If this doesn't work, I can't think of anything else to do," Ferdinan answered Jon honestly. Saying this to his sheltered, coddled ally was terrible...but he couldn't protect the boy anymore. Swallowing hard, he stepped toward the door, keeping his eyes averted from Jon and Oya. I'm sorry, Mother Artimus. I can't do anymore...

Taking the samples collected from Evelyn, Ferdinan headed to the biohazard area. There he waited.

Ferdinan couldn't be still.

He needed to do something.

But until morning, there was nothing more he could do...

This didn't feel like enough.

VVV

That memory made him tense up. *I've never done enough, have I?* "*No. But it's coming anyway.*"

"*Indeed.*" That grin turned Cheshire and emerald eyes drifted to the diamonds above.

Awkward silence fell. She didn't move – laying beside him still and calm. He wasn't sure what to do... Then his unease faded. There wasn't a time Ferdinan remembered being comfortable around someone. This alone should trouble him. But it didn't. He loved it. And he hated himself for loving it – for wanting something he didn't deserve.

Still... He laid there, praying she wouldn't move.

* * *

Boats brought hundreds of people. Guests were ushered to chairs while they waited. Xhou fiddled with a near invisible microphone wrapped around his ear. Then a cylinder of light hit him – drawing everyone's attention in the darkening evening. Dramatically, the Lead swept his shiny blue cloak around.

"Hello! Hello! Honored guests! Fellow students! Most generous staff! Before we start, I'd like to draw your attention to my right-hand man for instructions. Lord Samultz! Take it away."

The light swiveled to Ferdinan as he jumped upon a tree stump. Bowing, he swept his oversized green top hat past the tails of his matching coat. "Greetings from the islands! We are grateful to each of you for coming. And we are excited to show you something new! That being said, this *is* new. We understand if you don't like it but beg you to see it to the end. If you're wondering why you're sitting in less than comfortable chairs on the beach listening to me talk... It's simple. The show starts here. Follow. I'll lead you through the appetizer and on to the main course."

Ferdinan jumped down. The stars shone brightly. Now was the time. He projected as much whimsy and energy as Oya showed him, even though it was outright humiliating. But she insisted it'd make the show perfect. *I'm glad my family isn't here...*

Snapping his fingers, tiny lights appeared on the ground – dancing around like willow-the-wisps. Playfully he led the audience down the lit path, setting the mood. Fireworks shot off as he passed the first checkpoint. There he stopped – allowing the crowd to enjoy them. Soon "Psychs" came out and "read" the audience's minds.

"You're wondering what we're doing, aren't you, sir?"

"Wow! Those fireworks are beautiful! No wonder they chose to have this at night!"

"Why's this child staring at me?"

Some of those "thoughts" made Ferdinan smirk. With a click of his heels and a magnanimous sweep of his hand, he led them to the next clearing – just as Oya demanded he do.

Crazed green eyes free fell from the highest branch of the tree behind the skeleton. Inches from hitting him, Oya stopped and circled his head a few times. Giving the audience her playful grin, she snatched his oversized hat and soared away.

Four other students shot out of the bushes and joined her in an aerial acrobatics' performance. They looked like mischievous pixies. A confetti cannon exploded over the audience - covering everyone in two tons of teal glitter. It'd be months before they got it out of their hair. Good thing it was biodegradable because it'd never come out of the sand.

Moving on, they passed a number of students who took the hands of those closest to them. Diagnosing made up diseases and conditions, they offered ridiculous remedies to cure what "ailed" them. It was silly, but it made the audience laugh. At the auditorium's entrance two students stopped everyone. They were dressed in obnoxiously colorful military garb. Painfully obnoxious.

"I'm sorry, sir, but you're forbidden from entering this place. Such silliness cannot be tolerated here!" A third student – dressed suspiciously similar to one of the more serious instructors stepped up.

"But, sir! Our honored guests! They are hot and miserable and have traveled such a long distance. Can't you let *them* in?" Ferdinan grimaced speaking such ridiculous words. *Who wrote this?*

"Come, come now!" Replied an older student representing the Superintendent...with added monocle and crazy hair. "We mustn't let down the guests! Especially honored ones. We must keep our alumni happy after all!"

If the script wasn't bad enough, the random squiggles painted on the "Superintendent's" skin was cringe worthy. *This was the best they could do...?* Everyone on the islands knew what those tattoos meant. Not representing the accomplishments Superintendent Dæya achieved would've been wrong. Neither could they in good conscious paint real symbols on someone who hadn't earned them. But this...? It looked like Evelyn scribbled on the boy's face.

"But, sir! Look at him! He isn't properly dressed!"

The "Superintendent" walked circles around Ferdinan. He fought laughter as hard as Ferdinan fought utter humiliation.

"Quite right!" The boy grabbed Ferdinan's arm, sending razor blades across his skin, and slung him aside. "I don't know what you're thinking, child! You don't even have a hat!"

The completely hatless monocled boy approached the crowd and bowed. "Honored guests! Please! Come! Refresh yourselves with the nice cool air we've saved for you! Don't mind the riff raff! They won't be allowed in!"

The "guards" and "instructor" led the audience in and ushered them to their seats, while the "Superintendent" greeted them. When Dæya reached the entrance, the "Superintendent" made a fuss over the man mocking him. This encouraged a number of laughs. Though, Dæya didn't get the joke at first.

With everyone distracted, Ferdinan ran to the side door. Oya flew behind him – catching his shimmery green jacket and bright orange, poufy shirt as he threw them off. She dropped his tuxedo shirt to him. Boney fingers latched the last button and opened the back door. On the other side, Elbie waited with a bow tie in one hand and a screen in the other. On the rack beside him was Ferdinan's immaculately tailored tails and cummerbund. Oya held his violin box patiently while he tied his tie.

Straightening his jacket, Ferdinan grumbled to himself. He detested fitted clothing. This was only the first of a dozen such costume changes. He wasn't sure whose idea it was, but he'd been outvoted in the end.

Violin and bow in hand, Oya closed the case and tipped the oversized hat to him. It fell to her shoulders. Trying not to giggle too loudly, she pulled it off. *My hat!* The appropriately sized top hat was a classic black with a blue band matching his bowtie and cummerbund. While he put it on, Oya fiddled with an opal rose and his buttonhole.

The "Superintendent" ran backstage and up to them - wiping the paint from his face. "Sixty seconds to cue."

"Thanks." Ferdinan dashed to his spot - front stage right.

It was dark. And the hum of the audience was deafening. *I feel sick...* A cold finger brushed against his neck - leaving behind a line of perfect emptiness. Crazed green eyes flitted past his peripheral, giving him a wink.

The door closed.

All light vanished.

And Ferdinan struck the first note.

It was long and he kept it going until the crowd settled down. Only then did he start the song. Stage lights slowly brightened, and all eyes drifted up to him. A laser projection joined him in a duet. Then a second for a trio. A third and fourth and fifth. One projection after another until the audience was overwhelmed with an orchestra of strings, each playing different parts.

This song didn't exist, but it pulled at their hearts. It lifted them high and dropped them low - spinning them around. Thwarting all expectations. Then came a dramatic climax before winding down. One by one the projections faded. And at the end, it was back to a duet. Then Ferdinan was alone. He drew out the last note - loathed to let it end. Bowing his head, he lowered both arms to his sides. And the lights died once more.

Silence.

No one knew if they should applaud or not. So, they waited. Wondering.

Lights jumped on with full vigor and energy. A new song started. Dancers swarmed from both sides of the stage stopping in the middle - holding their ground against the opposite group. And when the drums kicked in hard and heavy, they moved again.

Stomping. Clapping. Colorfully clad dancers moved aggressively – weaving in and out. Thunderous rolls and passionate cries warred back and forth. Everything escalated with the drums! Everything. A projection of a younger boy playing the xylophone appeared. Each line of notes played influenced the battle. All according to the whim of the xylophone player… Oya twirled in the wings. But he stepped forward with an older girl and they sang their parts back and forth – cheering on their team to overcome the fate of those manipulative notes.

When it ended, the room went black a third time and everyone scattered from the stage.

Magnificent colored lasers stunned eyes while distorted music beat against their ears. The show progressed from the choreographed battle to art and the magnificence of the human mind. It highlighted wonders of energy and life and the universe. All to music which hadn't been heard in countless centuries.

One song was of particular pride to Elbie. He'd seen it as a painting. Designing the images himself, the Tinkerer programmed the planetary evolution to the ebb and flow of the music.

All singing was divided between six students, three boys and three girls. Twenty dancers took turns on stage. The instruments were more difficult. Aside from Jon and Ferdinan, only three others showed any proficiency. Pre-programmed projections were used heavily to pick up the slack.

Multi-colored lights flashed on and off in a seemingly random fashion when Xhou sang and danced to an obnoxious, lively, happy song. He told a story of a group at a dance in his attempt to represent the one Weaver on the islands. There was no matching a Weaver, but between the music and his boundless energy, he got the audience swaying and bobbing. Some were even clapping. Seeing them sucked into the show…

It felt wonderful.

* * *

The music oscillated between lively, soothing, and outright grating. Dæya soaked in the audience's reactions. None knew how to take this. *How did the Scientists get ahold of forbidden music?* Music that'd been long since destroyed. Every part of him wanted to search it out – to stop it. But... He knew his place. And his place was to wait.

Foot tapping and head bobbing... *This is impressive...using forbidden things to represent each classification...*

It was fitting. If the world knew about them – what they could do... They'd be declared improper, hunted down, and destroyed. Yes. This was most fitting. But how would the "improper" residents of these islands and their families respond to an equally "improper" performance?

An elbow nudged his arm, stopping Dæya's thoughts and dance. Leaning in close, Bær whispered. "We should stop this. It's pretty intense. I'm not sure the audience can handle it."

"No." Dæya bobbed his head a few times in beat with the current, rather angry sounding music. "No. Unless things get out of hand, we'll let the Sciences show us what they've prepared."

"Are you sure? The backlash..." Bær frowned.

The last few months, Dæya had more meetings with students figuring out how to help their countries than in his entire career. Good or bad, this performance offered his students something different to focus on. He'd let it continue. "That's a concern. But this is the best performance they've ever given, brother. Ferdinan wasn't lying when he promised to make every extra minute count. How long has it been since someone did the show right?"

"Right?" Bær was confused.

"Read the description. You'll understand."

Chapter 24

The end was nearing...

It was...

Ferdinan couldn't describe it. There just weren't words.

Darkness engulfed the room and he walked to center stage. Taking in a slow breath, he waited for the blue spotlight to hit him.

This was the second song he chose. After coming up twenty minutes short, Oya made him choose an additional one but volunteered to fill the rest herself. *Why did I pick this one? What was I thinking? It's too personal...*

But it was too late.

Instead of the violin Oya gave him, he held the one he'd made. The swirling plexiglass fog was light. *Blow them away with its unique sound and all your energy...maybe then they won't notice...*

Soft, beautiful music pulled the audience in despite unnatural tones. Metallic notes danced out so gracefully it was easy to miss the sorrow they held.

Breathing in deep... All his frustrations bubbled up!

^^^

Gray clouds hung over Ferdinan's head. It didn't matter how many times he went over what little information he had. All it was, was ink on paper. The virus didn't stay together long enough...

Frustrated, he racked his brain for why. Its instability was a key point. If he could figure that out... But the plains had little research equipment...

Turning to her data... She's so weak... No. Not this. Anything but this. *All that came to mind were the observations Huzhi offered during their last conversation. He didn't want to think about this either.*

He didn't want to think about anything.

Everything was painful.

VVV

Time to sing... Pulling back a step, he let the ancient words waltz off his tongue. Would anyone understand their meaning? Anyone but him...?

The song pleaded for retribution, for the opportunity to set right his wrongs.

How fitting!

The first time he heard it felt like daggers – spot on and with deadly accuracy. He'd been alone... If not... The repercussions of crying in front of someone made him blush as his words turned rough.

The chorus came. Coarseness tightened his throat. *Please listen! Please believe me! It was my fault!!* He screamed at them. At everyone. He screamed the song writer's confession. What Ferdinan wouldn't give to have these as his own sins. His only sins...

ΛΛΛ

"Doesn't it hurt? Aren't you sad in the least?!" Jon yelled – frustrated.

"Being sad won't change the past. It won't stop this plague."

Jon batted away tears. "A dying woman – a grandmother – means nothing to you!? The one you *called 'Grandmother!' The one you asked for stories from! This means nothing?! Not a part of you cares at all?! You feel nothing at all?!"*

Stone mask in place, Ferdinan chose his words to end this conversation quickly. "There's a reason Master Minjing asked me to do this. She knows the kind of person I am. Feelings won't stop this plague. Caring about the individual will do nothing *to understand it. I was given this challenge because* being challenged *is all that matters to me. Don't get mad at me for doing what needs to be done. Feelings. Emotions have nothing to do with what's happening."*

∨∨∨

The violin's metal voice screamed alongside him. Showing no mercy. Together the pair let everyone know they were wrong. They were wrong denying him the punishment he deserved. They were wrong telling him he succeeded. They were wrong ignoring atrocities and waving away his responsibility. They were wrong about everything!

∧∧∧

"You missed a minor flaw in the painting. Circle it...draw an arrow to the spot...! They still can't see it! I've gone over the data! I don't see it! I have no idea what you found!" Jon stopped there, not sure where to go. They were both frustrated. And neither knew how to fix it.

"It's ok if you don't. It's ok if the world never does. I was hired to see it. An honorable woman died waiting for me to figure it out. You want me to look at you, fine." Ferdinan faced his ally head on but couldn't keep his cheeks from burning. "Other's incompetence doesn't excuse my own, Jon. It makes mine unforgivable."

∨∨∨

They didn't understand...

...not at all...

There was something cathartic about this. His voice and violin trailed off until he stood perfectly still. Arms at his side. Head lowered.

But the lights didn't go out...

Instead, Jon's piano rolled on stage playing a song Ferdinan didn't recognize. *What's he doing?*

Oya spun around him - taking his violin of swirling fog and placing it atop the piano. One more spin and she froze in a classic dancer's stance at the edge of the stage. Then Jon's voice joined the music. *I know this song. Oya loves it...* Only there were no distortions. Just the piano.

The song invited listeners to live extraordinarily. It was graceful and lovely with a message she lived. Two words in, Oya raised an eyebrow to cue him.

Not knowing anything better to do, he reached his hand out - inviting her over.

The dance began. A dance with the perfect emptiness of a total void. Ferdinan followed her cues. It was brilliant. She led without showing she was leading. If only he could see them as the audience did. For as stunning and graceful as the dance felt, it must be magnificent to see.

Their movements slowed. Oya leaned in, shifting to a waltz, and whispered, "*This song is for you.*"

Words floated in - hitting him hard. "Fight for something better. Don't become discouraged anymore," it said. It was beautiful. The music was soft and smooth. It felt like waves washing over the beach. It felt like a warm sun tempered by a cool breeze. It felt like hope.

And the words perfectly reflected this feeling. *These are her words…she's pleading them to me…* A lead weight dropped on his heart. Intense green eyes told how strongly she wanted him to believe those words. *How long did she search for this?*

But she's wrong…

A nod signaled him to lift her.

This was all a surprise for him. *But why?* A wasted effort… *I'm sorry. She can't possibly want such things for me. I don't deserve it.*

~

The lights went out and the last two songs continued as practiced. Deciding it was best to end the show how they started, the last song was a calm duet between the piano and violin. This seemed prudent after Ferdinan screamed at them for a good two minutes. Hopefully it was enough to bring the audience's bombarded senses to rest.

This time the lights didn't go out – they grew brighter.

The audience sat in awe. Or maybe confusion. Possibly horror.

Laughter bubbled up but Ferdinan managed to contain it. Barely.

Regardless of what happened, it was worth it. Vastly different emotions fought for dominance inside him. *Is this the feeling Oya has when she's toying with people?*

No one moved. The audience processed what had been thrown in their faces. And the Science students looked for Xhou to end the show.

Left with no other choice, Ferdinan sighed and approached the crowd.

"On behalf of the Sciences, thank you for coming tonight and for seeing us through to the end. We worked hard bringing you something new. It was fun. We hope you enjoyed experiencing this as much as we enjoyed creating it."

Xhou ran on stage and winked at him. "Wasn't that something folks!? Bring your hands together for everyone's hard work! I can't tell you how much we had to learn to do this!"

Ferdinan edged his way to the wings while Xhou talked.

"Before we end, I want to introduce you to the one who made it all happen!"

He wouldn't! Ferdinan glared at him.

"He put more time and effort planning and organizing these last two months than the rest of us combined!"

Ferdinan mouthed "I will hurt you," so he couldn't be mistaken.

But Xhou grinned. "Lord Ferdinan! Come out and take a bow!"

A murmur rose from the audience.

Ferdinan considered leaving. He also considered beating Xhou senseless. But he chose to walk out and set everyone straight.

"Thank you, Xhou Zi. I'm afraid you've given me more credit than I deserve. Would our actors please take a bow?"

Slowly, everyone who started the show on the beach shuffled forward and bowed. Ferdinan clapped, spurring the audience into action. Applause filled the air, bringing relief to the performers. He announced each group and each group bowed to the tremendous applause.

"There's one last person I'd like to announce. She did everything – provided us with everything... She brought us together and gave us what we needed, from the ideas to the confidence. Please show your appreciation to our inspiration and our teacher. Oya!" *And our meanie head...* Ferdinan smiled at that thought.

From amidst the dancers, unnatural red hair skipped forward – a giant smirk on her face and eyes unnervingly bright. Ferdinan removed his earpiece and handed it to her. *Why did she want me to do this?*

Delicate hands took the microphone. Winking, she leaned in and whispered, *"Thank you. Good luck."*

What...? He didn't know why, but his chest felt as warm as his face. Her soft expression was replaced by her usual crazed grin and she stepped forward. Why did this feel like self-sacrifice?

"Greetings everybody! Call me Oya! Hi Luyou!" She waved to her suitemate with all the might of an excited three-year-old. "This show was so much fun! I taught them what I know and they helped me improve my Common so I can stand here and tell you 'hello'! Haha! I forward meeting to look...wait..."

Ferdinan whispered to her.

"I look forward to meeting you! I think that's all! Thank you for coming! Enjoy your time with your families! Bye-bye!!" She returned the microphone to him then waved and pranced back to the dancers.

ΛΛΛ

There it was.

Confirming the language with the written and oral samples collected from her, he grabbed everything. Soon the screen beeped *again – this time with the translation results:*

"Hello, you can call me Oya. I hope to learn your name one day. Feel better soon." Why would she write that?

He didn't understand the "Feel better soon," but he'd tell her his name. He just needed to learn her language.

VVV

Ice formed in his gut. The stress...it'd kept him from realizing... *She distracted the spotlight from me... Why? Why would she do that? She values her privacy too...* In that moment he loved her completely and made a note to properly thank her.

"Lights!" Ferdinan shouted.

Darkness fell with the curtain. The backstage lights rose. Ferdinan cut the mics and called everyone over. "I know you've worked hard and all you want is to spend time with your families. So, those who have people to be with may leave. Anyone who doesn't have someone to visit can stay and help clean up. As a reminder, the beach needs cleaning too."

This last comment did the trick. Even those who didn't have family here were nudging friends to invite them along.

"Dismissed!"

They didn't have to be told twice. Everyone bolted – still in full costume. Everyone but Oya and his second shadow. Watching them run from another day of work...it was funny. Mad giggles rang out. Oya's laugh – it was pure. Perfect. Every embarrassing thing he did this evening – everything she insisted on...it was worth it to hear that laugh.

Her laughter was all it took to release his own.

Poor Jon stood confused, staring at the two of them. Oya rolled back and forth on the floor. Ferdinan was just as amusing. He'd dropped to sit, hugging his middle and gasping in air between laughs.

"Did I miss something?"

Lying back – still chuckling – Ferdinan calmed himself. "If you aren't laughing, you've missed it."

Oya rolled until her head stopped next to her friend's, her shoulder grazing the top of his head.

Why is laying like this so relaxing? He didn't like being touched...being too close...but for some reason, this was extremely comforting. *"You're an evil genius."*

"Evil? I thought what I did was kind."

"What?" Jon was lost beyond the help of a translation.

"Find your brothers. I'm sure they are dying to shower you with more affection than the world has hitherto seen." Ferdinan rubbed his eyes. With the show done, he felt drained. *Did I really do so much? No. Acting like Oya takes too much energy.*

Giggles filled his ear... Peace washed over him. *I don't deserve this...so why can't I leave her alone?*

"How about you?" Jon asked.

Ferdinan yawned, "I'll hide here 'til everyone leaves. Then crawl into a hole and stay 'til I'm twenty."

"Is that appropriate for a general's nephew?" A woman's voice floated onto the stage.

Immediately, Ferdinan rolled to his knees, forehead on the floor.

He didn't say a word, but his demeanor was completely changed.

Chapter 25

"General Samultz," Jon straitened from a deep bow, "it's an honor."

A small woman with salted black hair smiled warmly. That smile accented her age with light lines around her dark brown eyes. "Ah! Jon! How's your family? Are any of them here?"

"They're well. Samuel and Ozar are visiting. They'd be happy to greet you."

"I haven't seen little Samuel in years." She stopped, "Though if you're here, they'll arrive soon."

Turning to her nephew, the General continued, "Ferdinan, you're family, not a servant."

"Every citizen is your servant, General."

"Please stand. I'm your aunt first. There's no need to call me 'General.'"

Despite her command, Ferdinan didn't move right away. How did he choose between what he'd been taught and what was expected of him at the moment?

"Nephew."

"As you wish, Lady General." Ferdinan's knees didn't want to straighten. Neither was his head happy being elevated so quickly. Suddenly Oya was beside him, that complete void steadying him. *Why is Oya here...?* That question stuck in his brain and opened the floodgate of all the thoughts he'd been avoiding. Why was she helping him? Why was she by his side? She could now speak Common well. There was no reason to stay with him... There was nothing else he could do for her. She had no more need of him. So why was she here?

"Aunt Tenalia," the General corrected. "I've told you, I'm your aunt before your General."

"Yes...ma'am." Was this respectful enough?

Tenalia sighed and walked up to her nephew. "Wow. You've certainly grown. Weren't you yea high?" She held her hand below waist level while looking up to his face.

"It's been some time."

At this comment, Oya studied him – surprise loosened her jaw. Ferdinan hadn't noticed either. They'd been nearly the same height when they met, but now he had a good four inches on her and was a head taller than his aunt.

"It's been, what, five years?"

"Eight, Lady General. My apologies for not honoring you at the gala."

"I'm aware of your mother's command. Eight years? Really?"

"Yes, Lady General. It was at Prince Zephyr's Right of Ascension ceremony."

"Wow." Disbelief coated her face. When she moved toward her nephew, Ferdinan stepped away. "Is something wrong?"

"No, Lady General."

"Aunt Tenalia." She corrected then gave him a hug.

White hot fire melted his skin. It was pathetic, but he turned his grimace into a smile.

"My!" She held him at arm's length. "You're skin and bones, child. Don't you eat?"

"Yes, ma'am. I've even acquired my own personal chef of late." Ferdinan shot a nervous glance at Jon, begging to be released. That fire! It was spreading, consuming him!

"Jon? Interesting." Releasing Ferdinan, she stepped over to her ally's son. "Thank you for your generosity toward my nephew. I met your niece at the gala. Your family's lucky to have her."

"We're grateful Evelyn Oza chose to live with us."

"She chose? I was unaware a five-year-old had a choice."

Glancing at Ferdinan, Jon clarified, "She was nervous, but Ferdinan spoke up for us."

Tenalia turned back to her nephew, "You've met her? Do you know who her big brother is? She rambled on about him to everyone who talked to her."

Ferdinan blushed and looked away. "She started calling me that soon after we met."

"Odd. Why?"

Why…?

Ferdinan hadn't realized Oya was missing until she materialized in front of his aunt – startling all of them. "Because your nephew's the one who played with her while she was sick."

Why didn't I think of that?

"May I ask your name, Miss?" The General smiled, intrigued and uncertain. And impressed.

"Call me Oya." Holding out her hand, Oya ignored the boys clearing their throats.

"And your title?"

"I have none. Call me Oya. That's all."

Tenalia looked the girl up and down – her curious expression directed toward the delicate handheld aloft. "My name's Tenalia. It's nice to meet you, Oya."

"Likewise, Tenalia." Oya gasped when Ferdinan's razor sharp elbow nudged her. "What?"

I didn't mean to hurt her! But neither could he let her be ignorantly disrespectful. "She's General over North Chūzo's military forces."

"Remarkable! An impressive rank to reach at such a young age."

"Thank you, Oya. That's sweet."

"She didn't work up from a foot soldier. She was groomed for the position from birth."

Blood red eyebrows knit in confusion.

I should've explained better when we talked... "'General' is a royal position. It outranks the monarchs in my country."

"Ah. How powerful is a king if his military doesn't support him?"

Dark brown eyes appraised the girl. "I know Jon, but I've never heard of you. Are you also a Scientist?"

Hearty laughter rang out – making both boys sweat. "I try understanding, but the things they do are beyond me."

"Then how did you come to know my nephew? You're not a twelfth-year... No, Ferdinan, you've started your thirteenth year now?"

While Ferdinan nodded, Oya answered, "I met him when Evelyn did. He taught me Common."

This answer confused her. Tenalia turned back to her nephew, "What exactly did you do in South Chūzo?"

What did I do? I tortured our ally and failed everyone...

ΛΛΛ

"Why do you care, Jon? You don't know her. You've never met her. You haven't even seen the world she lives in." Ferdinan's tone hinted heavily for his ally to leave this alone. He needs to back away. It's just the beginning. She's going to get a whole lot worse.

"How can I not care!? Sorrowing at another's suffering is natural! How cold are you? Feeling nothing after listening to her day in and day out!?"

Considering his options, Ferdinan decided he'd force the warning. Painting on an amused smile, he answered. "You're right. She's getting weaker. I let her keep going today to see just how much. But this is nothing. Yes, she's tired, but she isn't in constant pain. She isn't suffering yet. And since there's no suffering, there's no reason for you to cry. Oueshian or not."

VVV

"Ferdinan?"

That memory made him cringe. "I apologize, Lady General."

"Aunt Tenalia."

"Tenalia? I didn't know you were here!" Samuel strolled up to his baby brother. "Jon...that performance was...different."

Picking his baby brother up like a rag doll, Ozar squeezed him. "Why're you still back here? Everyone else is gone!"

"You kept us waiting, baby brother." Samuel scolded playfully before smiling at Tenalia. "But...I'm glad you did."

And thus began a second reunion. The adults reverted to children – reliving old memories and catching up on current lives. Ferdinan and Jon found themselves staring in awe as they witnessed the phenomenon.

But Oya... Her entire being was fixed solidly on Ozar. And not just those intense green eyes - but a knowing grin... Whatever she saw in the giant...it had her full attention. No. That wasn't quite right. It was as if Oya found something she'd been looking for in a completely unexpected place. Coyness curled her shapely lips. Whatever it was, she approved.

Strangely...it seemed Ozar had trouble looking at her. Whenever he glanced at her, a strange look took over his face - almost as if she was the only thing in the world he couldn't bring into focus.

This was odd, but Ferdinan had other worries commanding his attention.

Eventually they made their way to the boats. All the night worthy crafts were gone. Of course. Luckily, there was shelter and plenty of food. It didn't take long to build a fire on the sand or for Jon to concoct a meal. The beach glittered but couldn't outshine the beauty of the stars. Conversation, food, and laughter filled the remainder of the evening.

~

There was only so much togetherness Ferdinan could take. Vaguely excusing himself, he headed into the auditorium and out the other side. A cool breeze accompanied him...until Oya was there beside him. *When did she...?*

"Please teach me how you do that."

"Do what?" Exotic green eyes glinted madly before turning toward the stars.

"Go completely unnoticed. No one sees you when you don't want to be seen."

She only grinned. *"I don't know if it can be taught."*

They walked – enjoying the silence. Or…Oya was. Ferdinan's mind agonized. *What does she want…? There's nothing else I can offer, so…what?* Being beside her was wonderful. Just seeing her…it made him smile. It felt amazing… There weren't words to describe it, simply because he'd never felt this way before.

At the same time, not knowing what she wanted – what she expected…it was disconcerting. No one "just spent time" with him. No one bothered with him unless he was the only one who could provide what they needed. Even this stupid show. The moment it was over, everyone bolted. Except her… And Jon. But his ally didn't have a choice with Healer Samuel and Ozar Hei-O here. Oya though… She was smart and talented and amazing! She didn't need him anymore. *I should ask her…but…would that offend her?* He didn't want that. And…he didn't want this to end…But… *What do I do? Is it wrong to pretend?*

Bare feet bolted toward a line of old trees. Oya climbed one – playfully leaping from branch to branch.

"I don't understand." Ferdinan called from below. "What's your fascination with this?"

"With what?"

"Is there anything on these islands you haven't climbed?"

Spikey red hair leaned down. *"Nope. Not that I've found anyway. Climbing's fun and relaxing."*

"Breaking your neck is relaxing?"

"See for yourself."

Ferdinan shook his head. But he grabbed the lowest branch and hoisted himself up. It'd been a decade since he climbed a tree… It *was* fun.

"Look," she pointed.

The view was magnificent. Water reflected the stars perfectly. A sweet breeze mussed at his hair. *"You're right. This is relaxing."*

"Are you happy seeing your aunt?" Oya tugged absentmindedly at the chain around her neck.

"Why wouldn't I be?"

"You looked uncomfortable when she hugged you."

"I don't like being touched. My family…we aren't the Artimuses. Physical affection…" Ferdinan shook his head. *"I wasn't expecting it…"*

"You didn't have a problem with Evelyn."

"Evelyn needed it. She was always surrounded by love and–" Ferdinan choked and his lip quavered. *"Then she didn't have any."*

"You're incredible, Ferdinan. Getting close to someone who could've easily died…But you weren't going to let that happen."

Ferdinan sighed. *"There's nothing incredible about not wanting to watch a little child die."*

"True. But you were the one who stopped it."

His chest tightened, flooding him with a dull aching pain. *Please stop... "Why do you always do this?"*

"Do what?"

"You're always saying I'm amazing for doing things anyone could. There's nothing praiseworthy about me. Please stop." It hurts.

She hugged him with one arm - wrapping him in nothingness. *"You can't even fathom how wrong you are?"*

Her words made some place deep inside him ache.

Chapter 26

"Is Elbie in?" Xhou towered over the six-year-old who answered the door.

"Um..." The boy craned his head up. "Let me get him."

"Thanks."

High giggles floated from behind Xhou while they waited.

"See, there's no reason to hide, Rura. We're weird, but we're mostly the same as you." They'd passed some Energists flying around – moving heavy rocks. It'd scared her. So, Xhou thought he'd introduce her to some of the younger children. The second-year girls were excited to meet her. Now for the boys. Most classifications were represented between the second-year boys and girls. He'd show her they were fun – and not scary at all.

"Xhou? You're the giant at the door." A grin and mismatched eyes greeted the Lead.

"If you want giants, go see Jon's brothers," Xhou chuckled.

"Is that your sister?" Elbie pointed to the half-hidden girl.

"Yah. This is Rura. Rura, this is Elbie. He's also one of mine." Xhou spoke proudly – pushing his sister forward. "The second-year girls are meeting us for games to show my sister what being us is like. I was hoping you boys would join."

Elbie bowed to the girl and smiled. "Sounds like fun. I'll ask my suitemates. But...I'm helping Yuyu with an experiment before dinner."

"That's fine. I'll get Jon to cook so you have an incentive to come back."

"You're so mean!" Elbie pouted, making Rura giggle again.

"We're meeting at the cliff jumping spot along the southern beach in thirty minutes. I've got snacks and lunch taken care of." Xhou winked, picked up his sister, and swung her around. The hall filled with high giggles and deep laughter. "See you there!"

* * *

"There's no winning..." Ferdinan whispered to his reflection.

The skeleton scrutinized every inch of his body. The Duchess would notice how much weight he'd gained and accuse him of being willful and selfish. But...his aunt - his General...she'd take one look at him and...

He wasn't sure what to expect. Lectures he could take. But if she ended up being like Jon... He couldn't handle that much food.

The last time... *What happened then?* It was shortly after his little sister's birth... *I was seven...* He'd finally gotten where he didn't crave fighting. *It was at the beach after Zephyr's Right of Ascension Ceremony...* The General wanted to play with her nieces and nephews before returning to work.

I remember...she had a fit... That was the first time he'd seen adults openly argue. And it was grand.

Proportionally, he looked the same now. *I don't want to repeat that...* But she refused to let him out of today's activities. Playing on the beach was the adults' decision. Water was something Ferdinan generally avoided. His swimsuit hung loosely at his waist - cinched as tight as it would go.

I don't want anyone to see me. There was more than his protruding bones. Various pink and white streaks marred his skin. They looked ghastly stretched against his ribs. Ferdinan's back was worse... All the knobs of his spine disgusted him and emphasized the last batch of gashes he'd earned. Though healed, the scars were still new...still fresh.

Sighing, the skeleton pinned his suit – finishing right before the Dinta barged in.

^^^

"Whoa! Whoa! It's me! Stop!"

Panting erratically, Ferdinan scrambled away from whatever was in front of him. Slowly, his ally came into focus. Along with the welts on Jon's arms and a swelling eye.

"See...it's ok..." Jon spoke again once Ferdinan started calming down.

This wasn't the first time... Violent nightmares plagued him for over a month. Two days ago, Bær had to heal a rib he'd cracked. Pushing himself to his feet, Ferdinan gasped out an "I'm sorry," and dashed for the hallway.

vvv

Jon's silent disappointment sparked Ferdinan to pull on his shirts while the Dinta preened in the mirror. "Do you usually do that?"

Ferdinan shook his head and grabbed a screen. "Do what?"

"Wear multiple layers of clothes?"

"Does it matter?" Shame forced those blue crystals down.

"I was just curious. You're old enough to decide what you wear."

"What're you doing?" Enthusiastic giggles burst forth. Oya watched Jon leap and her friend fall backward in panic at her sudden appearance.

◊

"That was mean." Ferdinan rubbed at his hip.

"Aren't you supposed to dress appropriately for the water?"

"I am. I'm also dressed appropriately for outside the water," he said, pulling another shirt on and eyeing a fifth. *"How did you get in here? The door locks automatically."*

Oya opened her mouth, then noticed Jon's annoyed stance, so she switched to Common. "Figure it I'll let you out on your own. I know you love a good challenge."

"I've had it up to here with challenges," Ferdinan didn't correct her, just raised his hand as high as he could.

"Warning: they're on their way. Should be knocking any minute now." Approaching her friend, Oya ran a finger along a new string attached to his chest. This one was different. The others were dull or subdued. Save the one cheerful yellow. But this one... It was a bright, vibrant green. Just like the new eyes she saw every time she passed a mirror. Running her finger, she traced it...

The string stopped a foot from Oya's chest. Moving out of the way... It followed her – desperate to reach her. But it ended a foot short. *Why...?*

After a moment's consideration, it made sense. People grew attached to things that couldn't form attachments all the time. How was this any different than a soldier whose most trusted ally was his weapon? Humans were irrational this way. Her little entourage of orbs seemed to vibrate at that thought. *He isn't the only irrational one...*

"Are you here to warn me or do you want to greet them?"

Oya winked. *"Call me the scout. Your aunt's excited. She doesn't get to relax often, huh?"*

"That's the price of being one of the world's most powerful leaders." Ferdinan picked up the screen he'd dropped. *"Even here, she's high profile."*

"Better your aunt than me, I suppose." A knock came and Oya was gone.

◊

"I guess I'll see you there," Ferdinan's shoulders slumped. *Why…why am I…disappointed?* She vanished – leaving him cold, hollow… Turning, he was bombarded with an annoyed look from Jon. "What?"

Irritation increased on the Dinta's face, but Jon shook his head. "Nothing."

Moments later they were abducted by the adults and hauled away. The two boys set up while Oya distracted everyone with her usual silliness.

"What're you doing?" Jon towered over Ferdinan who lounged under an umbrella, flicking through a screen.

"Maintaining my complexion." Sarcasm dripped from his tongue.

"Please, my brain's bursting with nonsense." Jon looked at Oya, "I doubt that'll change."

"Here's hoping." Ferdinan went back to his reading. It'd taken a while, but he loaded the literature from her cube onto his screen. Now to find an interesting title. But…just having this in his hands… The kind of comfort that comes from familiarity filled him. If only people were this wonderful to be around.

While scrolling, he wondered how Oya kept people from noticing her. *I need to learn that.* It was inexplicable how adept she was at controlling people's attention. No one noticed her when she didn't want to be noticed and no one could ignore her when she wanted their attention. He envied that talent. *What's her ability? Could a Psych manipulate perceptions so perfectly?*

Hours of blissful solitude followed. It was just Ferdinan and a curious story of a mechanical man. Until the others got hungry.

Everyone rushed over. Jon prepared lunch while the adults talked. Oya sat beside him drawing pictures in the sand. *This is pleasant...* Even lunch wasn't too bad. No one pestered him about how much he ate...neither did they notice Oya pick off of his plate. He gave her a questioning look, but she only winked. *This is too good to last.* But he'd enjoy it as long as it did.

True to his luck, the peace of being generally ignored ended after lunch. Tenalia called for a swimming race. Everyone jumped up and ran for the water. Everyone except Ferdinan. He just wanted to wrap himself in the mechanical man's journey.

A shadow fell, drawing his attention. Above him, his aunt stared down, looking cross. Quickly he knelt before her.

"I was nice letting you lay around earlier. Now it's time to play. You're in desperate need of sun, child. And socializing." She pulled him to his feet – sending searing white flames through his arm. "Get out of those clothes. It's time to swim!"

"Yes, Lady General, as you wish." Ferdinan kept his head down. This was harder now that he'd grown. Whoever decided all heads should be lower than the rulers wasn't a tall person. It didn't help that Athletes – Fighters in particular – tended to be small. He waited for her to move. But she didn't.

"Don't keep your aunt waiting, dear child. Look, your friends are waiting too."

Shaking, Ferdinan stripped down to his suit and one shirt. He stumbled toward the water – tripping over his own feet multiple times. *Please be enough to appease her.*

"Maybe I should insist on some grace classes before he kills himself...?"

Chapter 27

Planned events continued for days before wrapping up. But that didn't mean he could relax...unfortunately. Everything his General asked was his responsibility to fulfill. It was exhausting. Even her visit to his lab... She asked about every little thing in it and tried prying into his experiments and inventions. But...how did he make this worth her while? It was nerve wracking. *She should be with Zephyr. I'm just wasting her time...*

The only "break" was picnicking with the Artimus brothers... Excessive time with these three wasn't any better. But the General wanted it. So, he escorted her to the meet-up spot.

Oya laid in the clearing completely absorbed in the yellow butterfly sitting on her nose. Things got noisy once the others joined. Jon served lunch. And the adults talked and laughed while the three watched – letting them enjoy their vacation. Midway through a particularly boisterous story, Oya's ears perked. She didn't respond when Ferdinan looked at her.

Sharp green eyes focused on something through the trees beyond view. Oya stood. The empty void of her touch seized his arm – dragging him behind her.

No one noticed them leave.

"What's going on?" Ferdinan asked when they broke into a full run.

"Someone's hurt."

Alarms screamed.

^^^

A beep *blared out, warning of a significant change in the patient's status. Putting the screen down, Ferdinan watched.*

Crystal blue eyes stayed fixed on her. Not once did he look away. Not until her stats vanished and alarms cried out her passing.

How long did he stand there listening to that awful sound?

VVV

Oya moved faster – so Ferdinan increased his speed. *Why is she so calm?* Neither stopped or slowed until they reached the building. That void disappeared. Bare feet dashed forward and jumped! Knees tucked high, Oya rotated so her back broke through a low window. *Wait!*

A sleeping part of his brain kicked in and his body moved. Boney hands covered his face as he passed through the falling shards.

It was *hot.*

Fire licked at the walls. But it didn't faze Oya. She'd passed through the flaming doorway and headed toward the center of the building. Only once did she stop. Pausing half a heartbeat. Debris fell and she pulled him out of the way. Then they pushed forward. Flames engulfed the center lab. The room was half-buried...

Who...?

Inside a child dug desperately. *Elbie?!* "What are you doing in here!?"

Elbie turned a tear streaked face to him, hands burnt and bloody from his efforts. "Help!"

ΛΛΛ

They are going to die because I'm useless. I can't even convince a healer to help me heal... *Pressure built in his eyes so he closed them. Boney hands covered his face – sealing away what was trying to come. His heart ached and his stomach corkscrewed. He was seconds from running...*

An odd, unsettling numbness set in.

Time stopped. That numbness killed everything inside him. All that existed was his racing mind and its futile attempts at finding an answer – a solution.

VVV

Oya jumped in, pulling away rubble. "Someone's buried under here!"

For a long breath, all Ferdinan could do was watch her dig. She didn't hesitate. Didn't flinch. Nothing. Not the flames or broken building bothered her. She just pulled away each piece of debris as she reached it. *She's amazing...*

That thought loosened his frozen muscles – allowing him to run over and help. *What kind of person runs into danger like this? Puts her life on the line? Doesn't think twice to save someone? Risks her life for someone she doesn't know?* He'd underestimated her. She was always kind and warm and amazing. But this... *I'd never deserve someone like her. I can never live up to her. I'll never be worthy of her friendship... I'll never be worthy of her.*

ΛΛΛ

"Please don't die." His voice cracked – forcing him to whisper. "Please. Please don't die..."

A gasp hit his ears. Ferdinan was on his knees, head pressed against the glass and twig arms wrapped tightly around himself. His body spasmed, jerking him farther down. And tears rolled out of his eyes. Digging sharp fingers into his sides, he fought desperately to keep everything back. But it became one more thing he failed at. Stop it! Why am I so weak?! This isn't helping anyone!

Alone or not, this was unacceptable behavior. There was no excuse to be like this.

"What am I doing wrong?"

VVV

Murderer.

Ferdinan's heart rate tripled. *No!* The voice was gone! *Go away!* Refusing to believe his reprieve had ended, he rushed in deeper – signaling Elbie to stay near the opening. Sending his pupil out would be murder. *He'll never make it alone...*

Useless.

Ferdinan wasn't sure *he'd* make it. *But Oya can.*

Weak.

Surely as he knew this building was a death trap, he knew she could save them.

A delicate hand stopped him. Placing the other on the largest part of the debris, Oya closed her eyes for an eternity. Then wild green glowed and motioned for them to dig again. One piece after another was cleared...until they reached the last obstacle. A large beam crushed the girl's legs.

Oya glanced at Elbie then turned to the Tinkerer. *"I'm lifting this. Take her and run. Run as fast as you can for three seconds then turn left."*

"*That doesn't make sense!"*

"Have I ever made sense?" she grinned, looking like she was enjoying this a bit too much.

Laughter echoed around his skull. Pulling off his shirts, Ferdinan handed two to her and one to Elbie. *"I'll get the beam. You pull her out."*

"Drop it as soon as I have her and take the girl," Oya instructed. *"I'll get Elbie!"*

Ferdinan nodded. Sense or no, they'd wasted enough time already. The beam glowed with heat. But adrenaline was a powerful force.

His flesh sizzled.

Yet, he didn't feel anything...

◊

The beam lifted. Oya threw his shirts around the half-crushed child, wrapping the tiny body tightly and quickly. When she lifted... *How did I miss you?* The orbs in her peripheral dashed forward and dimmed... *I'm glad...if he did this part...we'd all die here.*

A wild grin and nod signaled her friend to drop the beam. Ferdinan grabbed the girl and sprinted for the opening. Oya approached the boy with mismatched eyes. Smoke filled his lungs – choking out what he was desperate to say.

"It'll be ok. Don't worry."

Placing a delicate hand on his head, she eased him to sleep, picked him up, and sprinted out. Soon she was running in step alongside Ferdinan. *Trust me, dear friend!* Oya grabbed his arm and led him toward a wall. Something crashed. Again, she changed directions to kick down a door. The room was as consumed by fire as the hallway. She pushed Ferdinan sideways, pointing to one window while she ran full speed toward another.

◊

"Give me a head start!" Ferdinan ran as fast as he could. *Please be enough to delay her!*

The window loomed. *The child's covered...it'll work!* Ferdinan buried his face as best he could and turned his right shoulder to the pane. Leaping, he crashed through. Livid flames escorted them out – wrapping themselves around his unprotected back and shoulders. He didn't stop moving. Not until they were safe. The first thing he did was check the child.

Yuyu... His first apprentice. Crushed and burned...

Am I on fire...? Suddenly Ferdinan became perfectly aware of his body. He couldn't stop coughing. Every nerve screamed! But that didn't matter. *He* didn't matter. Boney fingers found her pulse. But it wasn't just Yuyu.

You killed them.

Frantically, he searched. *Oya...!* She stood holding Elbie...

We did it... Ferdinan smiled through violent coughs. Worry painted Oya's face as she moved beside him. He'd never seen that expression on her. *No...don't worry about me... It's not your fault. I'm weak...useless...*

Darkness encroached on the edge of his vision. *"El...bie..." Is he alright...? Did he get burned? Is he safe?*

Everything blurred.

Chapter 28

The handle turned. Zephyr scrambled for the door. *Please, someone talk to me. Tell me I'm here. Acknowledge me.*

Anyone!

Please!

A face peered in – looking at him sharply. Seeing her…it felt like being wrapped in a soft blanket.

And…

She was *looking* at him.

Those coal black eyes saw him, stared straight into him.

Shaky breaths escaped as he tapped five fingers against his sternum and pointed to her repeatedly. "Aguilla! What's going on?! Why…?"

She silenced him. "You're being quarantined."

Hearing her speak Yuchio surprised him. *She doesn't usually speak her tribal language. What's going on?* "Why?"

"For observation." She motioned him to the couch. "I'm going to speak. When you respond, do so as if answering a question."

There are no translators listening then? "Yes, ma'am."

"You stopped sleeping and went into a rage. You'd yell at things that weren't there and attack beasts only you could see."

His mouth dropped and his hands shook. "What are you talking about?"

"For six weeks. That's enough time to permanently break a mind. Though this stupidity is more likely to do so." Aguilla rolled her eyes and gestured to the room.

"I don't understand," he shook his head.

"Locking a man in a room. Ignoring him for weeks without explanation would break him. But a child? Stupid Chūzites." She pursed her lips. "'Til you're cleared as 'not broken,' you'll be kept here. If no one sees or talks to you, it's easier to hide something like this."

"I'm being observed?"

"Yes. Don't forget, you're the one answering questions."

"Yes, Aguilla," the Prince nodded. "You got them to let you in."

A confident smile spread across her deeply lined face. "Never underestimate the Grasslands' power. We're feeding your people, so we have a large say in your evaluation."

"Then I can leave after this." *I never want to see this room again.*

"No. A Chūzite's evaluating you as well. The woman wants to observe you for another week."

Ice stopped Zephyr's heart cold. *They think I'm broken... They wouldn't do* that *would they? Mom, Aunt Tenalia, Duchess, Aguilla, they wouldn't let that happen, right?!* "But your assessments might not agree."

"Trust me, my child, they will agree." Standing up, she looked down at the boy she'd raised alongside his three mothers. "Calm yourself and bear with it a week longer. Can you do this?"

"Yes, ma'am," he nodded. "Aguilla. Thank you for telling me. I thought I'd gone mad."

No smile danced on her lips, but it shined in her eyes. "I won't let them break you."

* * *

Darkness. An oddity. Usually Ferdinan was hunted or haunted. But it was just dark. And quiet. How long he stood there was anyone's guess.

A sliver of joyful yellow light appeared. Without hesitation, he ran toward it – not expecting to actually reach it.

A small form emerged. Joy filled his heart.

"Evelyn!" Dropping to one knee, he wrapped his arms around her.

"Big brother!" She squeezed his neck. "I didn't know I could see you during naps too! Yay!"

"I doubt it'll be a regular thing."

"Why?" A disappointed pout puffed out her lower lip.

"Some things only happen once in a while. It makes them special."

"Oh, ok." This didn't alleviate her disappointment. "Why is it always dark in here?"

"...I...don't know."

"Let's go to my dream then!" She grabbed his hand and pulled him toward inviting light – toward her silly little world.

"Where are we today?" He stood on a tiny island surrounded by purple water stretching out as far as the eye could see.

"We're at the beach! I wanted to build a sand castle. You sit here."

Delighted, he sat, resting his chin on his knees. It was beautiful. What would it take to have dreams like this whenever *he* wanted?

"Put on your swimsuit!"

As was only possible in dreams, he looked down to find he was wearing one already and smiled.

Screams brought Ferdinan to his feet. "What?! What's wrong?"

"Your back!" Tears stung Evelyn's voice. "And your front..."

Ferdinan's image reflected off the water. *Why am I hurt here? Isn't this a dream? Why am I burned...?*

Incoherent blubbering filled the air.

"No. No. It's alright. There was a fire, but I'm ok now. We got out. There was no trouble." He knelt down for her to examine his skin - willing the burns to fade.

When Evelyn poked at it, fresh pink scar tissue appeared. "Now your skin's all scarred."

"It's ok."

"Why were you in a fire?" Even here the green rings around her irises were intense.

Unbidden, the memory played across the sky. Amazed and enthralled, Evelyn watched. *No! Stop! She doesn't need to see this! Don't hurt her with this too*! But it continued playing until Oya knelt beside him, coughing. That grin never left her lips despite the worry in her eyes.

"Wow! My big brother's a hero!" A tea set and a picnic appeared. "Let's celebrate!"

* * *

"What's bothering you?"

Tenalia found herself clutching the shirt collar of a crazed looking girl with blood red hair. Approval danced in those bizarre green eyes.

"Impressive." Oya grinned, patting the woman's hand. "Good reflexes and good control."

"What are you doing here?!" she demanded, heart racing. *How did she get this close and I not notice?*

"You look troubled."

Tenalia released the girl. "Sneaking up on a Fighter is dangerous."

"Yah, I know." Oya grinned as if she knew a secret the woman would kill for.

Every troubling thought hit her with renewed force. Seeing her nephew save that little girl... She rushed to check on him and praise him for his bravery. But then she *saw* him. Saw how disgustingly thin he was. Then...the scars marring the right side of his body...they vastly outnumbered her own. *What happened to my family?*

Ferdinan's left side was melted and bubbled from horrid burns – destroying any scars that might've existed. Despite this, her nephew insisted on putting his students first. Even in dire condition, he argued for Samuel to help them until Oya took the younger children to Healer Bær. Only then did her nephew pass out.

"I'm not the best talker, but I'm a good listener. And I know how to keep my mouth shut."

"This doesn't concern you," Tenalia shot back. Green eyes flashed and...curiosity welled up unbidden. But...what was she curious about?

"I get that often enough. Ferdinan's family...are all of you scared to speak of important things? Or just the two of you?"

"We aren't scared, Oya." *What does she know?* Tenalia's heart pounded. She needed to know! But...why...? "We don't concern those not involved."

"He's my friend so I *am* involved."

"You're a stranger. How long have you even known him?"

"Not half a year. Yet I knew about his condition and you're sitting here surprised. There're other things too. He's smarter than he lets on. And he does things beyond what anyone gives him credit for. There's something he's protecting and will die for. And when he realizes you saw his body; he won't be able to look at you. Do you any of this know? It's been eight years since you've seen him? How much have you bothered knowing your own nephew before then? I'll not be called a stranger by one who *chose* to ignore my friend."

A lecture from a child wasn't something Tenalia was in the mood for. But...that curiosity...that desire - *need* - to know more. She couldn't ignore it. *What is this?* "Who are you? Speaking so rudely to me? A leader of the world's most powerful militaries?"

Tickled, Oya grinned. "For every question of mine you answer, I'll one of yours answer."

Somehow that desire grew stronger. It took over her soul and chained her in place. "Why would I play such a game?"

Oya turned her gaze to the clouds and breathed in deeply, grinning mischievously.

Unquenchable curiosity continued growing. It wasn't her own. It couldn't be. But neither could Tenalia dismiss it. "You'll answer me honestly? Tell me everything I ask?"

"I'll answer as honestly as you do. If I don't know, I'll simply say so."

"What's your first question?" *Why am I playing this game? I don't want to. I need to talk to Dæya and my sister-in-law. I should check on my nephew...* Dozens of other things she should do...yet...she couldn't step away...

"Why's my friend so submissive to...your other nephew?"

"He has trouble stepping back from his position within the government and family structure. He has no inheritance, but as long as he supports his queen and general, he's free to do whatever he wishes...though it *is* a bit excessive."

"Hmmmm." Oya considered her answer. "One who'd dare speak so rudely to such a powerful person is one who has nothing to lose and therefore nothing to fear."

"Everyone has something to lose. Holding something dear is human nature. It's what gives us hope and a reason to live."

The look Oya gave spoke more than any words could about how little Tenalia understood.

"Ah, next question." *Who is this girl? Why can't I leave?*

Oya giggled.

"What's so funny?"

"All in good time. My question first."

◊

Hours passed. Talking with Tenalia was quite enjoyable. And it gave Oya the opportunity to delved into the woman's mind. Before assessing, Oya calmed Tenalia. Ferdinan's aunt was open and honest...as much as a leader could be, with a mind that was easy to search and understand. Sharp and caring – the woman had a deep seeded sense of duty to family and country. So...

Why is she completely unaware of her family? Is this a powerful person problem or something only plaguing Ferdinan's family? "Well answered. What's your next question, Tenalia?"

"Why do I feel you don't trust me when you obviously care for my nephew?"

Oya smirked. *I don't trust anyone who raised that mutt.* But she knew where Tenalia could be depended on. "Good question. Before I can answer, there's something I have to know first. I'll allow two questions to make up for the inconvenience."

"Fair enough."

"It's a hot day. Putting aside his dislike for sweets, Ferdinan's outside eating a frozen treat. It melts faster than he can eat it, and half of it falls to the ground. What do you do when you see this?"

"What a bizarre question... I'd call someone to clean it up then have two more brought out."

"Two?"

"I'd *have* to see what it was he liked," Tenalia laughed.

"Fair. Now, what would his family do?" Oya watched as understanding dawned on the woman's face.

"That's quite the ingenious question."

"I stole it from a friend," Oya admitted. "Your turn."

"Why do you care about Ferdinan so much?"

"He's amazing. One day I'll deserve the kindness he gives."

"He is remarkable. You're the first person to say so."

Oya frowned. "That's sad."

Regret tightened Tenalia's jaw. "My second question. Is all this to keep me busy?"

A grin glowed from Oya's alien eyes. It didn't matter who this woman was, she couldn't let anyone make life harder on her friend. There in the fire... He'd been doing so well. The infection eating away at his heart was in check. Then his chest exploded.

This morning it thrived. With a vengeance. *Why? What upset him at that point? We'd already been inside for a while. He saw both children...what did I miss?* Would those odd behaviors return now? They troubled Jon – making things awkward for Ferdinan and harder for her... "When did you figure it out?"

"When your answers lead to more questions. Why?"

Standing, Oya offered her hand to help Tenalia to her feet. The two felt equal in size, though far from the same. Oya was taller but leaner with the body of a child who spent a little too much time running. Tenalia, though short, was formidable. Broad for a woman and obviously well-muscled. She wasn't one to mess with. "Why keep you busy? Because you needed help thinking straight. I don't want you causing my friend more difficulty."

"I'd never trouble Ferdinan."

"All rash decisions cause someone trouble."

Tenalia's lips tightened. "What's this he's protecting?"

"He keeps it hidden."

"Then what makes you think it exists?"

"I've spent time with him." Oya moved toward the water. "An observation?"

"Yes?"

"If you get him talking, really talking, everything'll be fine. Though he'll still have trouble looking at you."

"You've said twice he won't look at me. Why?"

"That's how he deals with embarrassment. Being seen like that when you're as shy as he is?" The desire to protect - Tenalia shared this trait with her friend. *Will you see the ugliness in Ferdinan's life? Will you make home safe for him? Do you understand now?*

When Oya started toward the dorms, the General hurried to keep up. "Thank you. I'll remember it. You're a strange child."

"I'm not the only one." Oya turned a bright, slightly crazed face to her then it turned dark. "They're digging out the building."

"Yes. There's a child unaccounted for."

"It was too late for the girl or Ferdinan would've never left her."

"Excuse me?"

Walking up close, Oya whispered in the woman's ear, "Forget what I just told you."

Tenalia froze - eyes cloudy and unfocused. And Oya grinned. *This is getting easy...* "They're digging out the building."

"Yes. There's a child unaccounted for," the General responded...slightly confused.

"Hopefully they don't find them there. I can't imagine how much that'll crush the family." Giving a sympathetic grin, Oya continued, "Do they know who's missing?"

Chapter 29

Tenalia watched her nephew grimace at the small container Jon offered. *What's Ferdinan doing?* Their conversation didn't make it past the door's window, but Jon was rather animated, and Ferdinan had turned away while Oya stood smirking at them both.

Why are they bothering my nephew when he should be resting? But did she have the right to be irritated? Ferdinan spent more time with Jon than anyone else. Looking into his travel plans from the last five years was eye opening. Only once did he go to Chūzo. But Oueshi and Azuté...just about every time. Kidico was also frequented. *He's well-traveled but traveling alone isn't safe. No wonder he's so scarred.*

"When did all this happen?"

"I can only say for the newest ones." Samuel pointed to the fresh pink scars. "The others...he never received medical attention for them."

"He couldn't possibly care for those on his own." She noticed he didn't say anything about the newer scars.

"They would've healed cleaner if a trained healer cared for them." Samuel pointed to a ragged one on his side. "That one needed stitches, but didn't get them. A competent healer could've prevented most of those scars. At least partially."

"Partially?"

"He's been malnourished most of his life."

Tenalia nodded and returned to her earlier question. "When did those new ones happen?"

"Last break."

"That happened at your home?!"

"No. He arrived injured." The Healer guided her attention to Ferdinan's weakened body. "I healed him as best I could. But..."

"Why didn't you tell me?"

"You aren't his parent."

That comment annoyed her greatly. "What happened?"

"He wouldn't say."

"Excuse me? He's a child. You *make* him say."

"We tried." Samuel's jaw tightened.

"Never mind. Shouldn't he be resting?"

Samuel checked the time. "No. It's almost dinner. Whether he agrees or not, he needs to eat. For that little bit of healing, I leached a number of nutrients from his bones and organs."

"I'll call for something to be brought."

Samuel scratched the back of his head. "I think Jon prefers cooking for him."

"Really?"

"Ya. It irritates him though." After a forced chuckle, Samuel turned to his old friend. "Don't tell him about the girl."

"Why would it matter? They determined she died before Ferdinan could reach her."

"This kind of news...he won't be able to handle it."

"Was he close to her?"

"No. If they met it was only this week. Don't mention this to Jon or Oya either. Leave that to us."

* * *

The song Ferdinan screamed out during the show shrieked loudly in Xhou's ear. It played on repeat with the other sorrowfully angry songs he'd collected.

But it wasn't cathartic today.

"Xhou?" Ozar pushed open the bedroom door. "Think you'd be up for some food?"

If I don't eat it'll make everyone worry. If they worry, I'll never get home to help mom. Still, he felt dead inside. What next? Will the ocean swallow up his country and mother too? "Yah. I'd love to eat."

"Anything in particular?"

"Surprise me...nothing spicy, but other than that."

"No problem."

Silently, the man walked away. The Artimuses agreed to care for Rura, not him. There was no reason... Tears stung his eyes but he beat them away. *No. Not now... Not now. Later. When they've left. Later. When no one can see me.*

Focus on the good. Yuyu and Elbie survived. They're fine. Will make a full recovery. ...but two of my charges could've died...

Neither did he save them.

Ferdinan did.

Ferdinan. He knew what kind of person Ferdinan was, even if the boy did everything to hide it. And true to form, the skeleton could've died rescuing them.

Looking down at his sister's picture, Xhou's face contorted. But he held back the flood. *Why...of all people...* She was so tiny, so innocent... And now this was all he had left of her.

No one rescued Rura.

He'd watched the Energists remove the debris. There'd been so much on top of her... His own calculations proved Ferdinan wouldn't have seen... According to Bær, the explosion killed his sister instantly. It wouldn't have mattered if...

Yet, Xhou was angry. Ferdinan always managed the impossible! Why didn't he turn the tables on this? Why did he leave Rura behind?

Somehow the sickly boy broke into the burning building, found Elbie and Yuyu, and got out. In those moments Ferdinan did the impossible, so why not save his sister?

It's not his fault. There was nothing he could've done. It's a miracle he saved Elbie and Yuyu...

Logically, he knew this...but his heart still cried out. Xhou was livid with the skeleton for not getting her. And because he knew he had no right to be, he told himself it wasn't Ferdinan's fault. His heart didn't believe his mind. But he'd keep repeating this until it did.

Releasing a shaky breath, he wiped away more tears. *How did he know they were in there?* The alarm sounded and Xhou arrived in time to see Ferdinan crash through a window carrying a wrapped bundle. It was amazing. *Ferdinan's tiny... Where did he find the strength?*

Massive burns bubbled the skeleton's skin... According to Ozar, Samuel had difficulty healing it. This should worry him. But his angry heart felt Ferdinan deserved it. It was the child's own fault for not taking care of himself.

Blue-black eyes turned to Rura's picture again. *Please keep mom safe. I can't lose her too.* Calling mom, telling her...he couldn't handle it. So, Ozar had. Even from his room, he heard his mother crying. He couldn't stand seeing girls cry – least of all those he loved. It killed him. Being powerless to ease her heart.

That's what awaits me at home... How many are crying...inconsolable...?

* * *

Moaning, Ferdinan pushed himself to his feet – but Jon pushed him back. He was weak. Everything ached. The inside of his head most of all. Was it possible to go deaf from a voice only he could hear? "I'm cold."

Jon nodded – pity coating every inch of him. Until the Thinker opened Ferdinan's closet. He couldn't see his ally's face, but those tense shoulders said it all. One shirt after another was pulled out and discarded. "When did you last update your wardrobe?"

Slothful even in something so simple?

Purpling on the spot, Ferdinan looked down and away. *Why's he so picky about clothing?*

"These will never fit over your shoulders. How..." Jon sighed and rolled his eyes. "I'll be back."

"You don't–" The door closed, stopping Ferdinan's argument before it started.

Hyena giggles came out of nowhere – magnifying his shame. Still...his heart leapt – excited to see her. *Why...? Is this...is this what people feel when they see their friends?*

Impertinent thinking she'd ever consider you a friend.

That voice was correct. Besides. What right did he have making anyone's life more difficult? Especially after she'd been so nice to him... *I need to put her first. I need to stop being selfish.*

"He sure loves clothes." Oya grinned. "Thank you."

Huh? "...thank you?"

Oya sat next to him – tugging at the chain she always wore. "Jumping into a burning building... You astound and amaze me."

She believes that? Pitiful girl.

Biting the inside of his cheeks kept his lip from quivering. Ferdinan opened his mouth to correct her, only to have her delicate hand block his words.

" *You* are completely amazing. I'm lucky having a friend like you bless my life."

Something sweet and light and warm filled his very core. Then bitterness replaced it – turning his stomach. *No. I'm not. I'm awful.*

You're the worst.

Ferdinan was never so grateful to see Jon in all his life. Though his eyes rolled at the giant pile of neatly folded clothing the Dinta carried.

"These'll be a little short in the sleeves, but at least you can get them on," Jon announced unfazed when Oya grabbed the top shirt.

It was huge on him.

"Guess it's better than being too small." Ferdinan rubbed his throbbing head – focused on Oya dancing around the room. *She's so silly...*

Pathetic.

A knife twisted every time that voice spoke - bringing back desires he thought he'd banished.

"Where're the blueprints for that second skin machine?" Jon replaced the shirts from the closet with the ones he'd brought – eyeing the slacks while he was at it.

"Why?" Exasperation saturated that word.

"Isn't this what you designed it for?" Jon sounded perturbed. "To protect extremely damaged skin – like those of burn victims?"

"I'm not a victim." Ferdinan turned to the window. "I chose to enter that building."

It took a while for Jon to find any words. "You chose to save two children, so you don't deserve the medical care your own device would provide?"

ΛΛΛ

"I wanted to thank you personally, son." South Chūzo's General bowed to the skeleton boy. When he stood up, his face was stern. "Make sure you learn some respect before next time. Not all leaders are as forgiving as I am."

"Yes, sir." Blushing, Ferdinan bowed.

Thanking you for murdering millions? He's quite the military leader.

"Thank you for allowing me my anonymity."

"I don't feel right about it."

"I'm a child. I don't want that kind of attention or pressure."

Weren't you taking responsibility? Or was that posturing to get what you wanted?

"I understand," the General cleared his throat. "I'm glad I know who to thank. You did a wonderful job. When you graduate, contact me. You'll always have a lab here."

"That's most generous, sir." Ferdinan bowed again.

VVV

How come no one understood how little he deserved...? "I'm tired..."

The healing Samuel forced upon him rendered his second skin useless. He'd been better off if the Healer left him alone. His powder and that skin was all he would've needed...if he hadn't been partly healed.

Samuel opened the door. "Jon, isn't it time to start dinner?"

"Thanks for reminding me." He hurried out – Oya waving him off.

"Your aunt wants to talk. Are you up for it?" Samuel asked.

"She's my General."

She's sick of you too.

How do I keep what's in my mind from her? Between that voice and Samuel healing him, it was all he could do to not be dizzy or sick.

Always a failure.

His heart tore and twisted. That voice wasn't as loquacious, but it sounded harder. And its truths felt more brutal. It no longer simply delighted in tormenting him. It hated him. As much as he hated himself.

* * *

There was no easy way to do this.

Xhou steeled himself and triggered the chime. According to Elbie's yearmates – the young Tinkerer was the only one inside.

No answer came.

This was a pain he'd become all too familiar with these past months. Not about to back down, he knocked. "Elbie. Can I talk to you?"

Dead silence. The world held its breath. What response would Elbie give? Time stood still until a soft shuffling made its way toward the door. There was a hesitation...the knob turned. Haggard, bloodshot eyes looked up at him, but Elbie's face was resolute.

"Please come in." Stepping back, Elbie showed the Lead to the couch. "Everyone's with their families. We won't be bothered for a while."

Sitting, Xhou closed his eyes. Elbie and Yuyu were playing with Rura. She wanted to see the labs. Without pause, this sweet little boy jumped up and volunteered. *If only I insisted they help with lunch. All I had to do was say I'd show her. I should've told them to play on the beach. Anything but "yes."*

Elbie took her there...but he was the last person to blame.

It was Xhou's fault...he blamed himself. And his heart blamed Ferdinan. He should've prevented this. And Ferdinan should've been a superhero when he failed to be a diligent big brother.

Unable to take the silence anymore, Elbie dropped to his knees, crying. "I'm so sorry! I didn't mean to! ...I didn't...I didn't know...! I'm sorry!"

Sliding to the floor, Xhou closed his eyes against his bleeding heart. He hugged the small boy – squeezing tighter when Elbie winced. "Thank you, Elbie. Thank you for playing with my sister. Thank you for making her happy. Thank you for being kind. You really are Ferdinan's apprentice."

"But...but! She...I-" Elbie stared at his gloved hands.

"It's not your fault. It was horrible timing."

A tear streaked face looked up. "What...?"

"There were improperly stored chemicals. You were being a good boy and a wonderful friend. I'd forgive you, but there's nothing to forgive." Squeezing the child tighter, Xhou continued on. *I can't let him become like Ferdinan.* As Lead, the health and wellbeing of his charges were top priority. "I can't express how relieved I am that you and Yuyu are safe."

"But..." Hiccups took over.

"I was terrified when I saw Ferdinan jump out with you and Yuyu." Those words shook Xhou's voice, but he forced himself on. "I was so scared. I thought the world would end. But you're ok. Everything's ok."

"No...but..."

"I'm right here. I want you to be happy. I need you to know you did *nothing* wrong. And I'll drop everything whenever either of you need anything, ok?"

"Ok..." Squeezing Xhou back, Elbie grit his teeth. "I'm sorry you lost your sister."

"Me too." Xhou released the boy and looked out the window. "Guess I'm alone now..."

Tears filled mismatched eyes. "But...all of us, we're right here. Just like you are. We're here too..."

"But I'll be leaving soon."

"You...um... I never thought a King could be alone." Elbie frowned, looking away. "Sorry...a Nu."

Reaching up, Xhou mussed Elbie's hair and gave the boy a smile. "You're right. Thank you for reminding me. You're my island family and I love you very much."

Elbie sat stunned by those last few words.

"Do you think we can go back to how we were before? I really liked how we all were then."

"I did too. Everything was happier," Elbie answered.

Somehow...there was a spark of hope in both their faces.

* * *

"Yes, Lady General?"

Annoying, useless child.

"You haven't been happy during my time here."

"I'm sorry, General. I'm not particularly comfortable right now," Ferdinan kept his eyes on the ground – sitting instead of kneeling.

She waited, but he didn't say more. "Why won't you call me 'aunt?' Please, answer me honestly."

"You're my General. Isn't that more important?"

Tenalia sighed before looking dazed a moment. "Are you happy at home?"

"Why wouldn't I be?" Ferdinan twisted his foot into the rug.

"How did you get those scars?"

"I'm clumsy." Guilt flooded over the skeleton as his improper desires grew. Sitting here, answering his aunt less than honestly...her concern told him how much he'd failed. *I've failed my Prince, my Duchess, my General, and my country. I've lied. I've killed. I've put everyone in danger. Why is she here? Why is she wasting her time on trash like me?*

Why indeed?

"I asked you to be honest."

"I *am* clumsy." Years of training and practice made this a "truth" everyone accepted.

"But the two aren't related."

Setting his jaw, Ferdinan didn't waver.

Disappointing.

White-hot flames consumed Ferdinan's hands. It was only then he realized he'd covered his ears.

"Why won't you eat? You are so malnourished Samuel couldn't heal you properly." The General brought those boney hands down to rest on Ferdinan's lap.

Once the General released his hands, truth spilled off his tongue. "I don't feel well when I eat."

Pathetic.

After all these years the sight, taste, and smell of food made him ill. The voice laughed, making him cringe and tightening his chest. But he kept his stone mask in place – hiding his crystal blue eyes from her. *What did I do with my earpiece?*

"Doesn't being hungry make you feel less well?"

"No."

That dazed look flashed across her face again. "Does it have to do with your mother?"

Ferdinan froze. *Stupid! What am I doing?*

"It does, doesn't it?"

He straightened but kept his eyes down. "She doesn't forbid me to eat."

"Then what does she do?"

Eyes closed, Ferdinan thought. Lying to his General was wrong...but neither could he answer truthfully. And she expected a real answer. "She's fulfilling her duty to her country and *all* her children to the best of her abilities."

"I can't fix something if I don't know it's broken."

"There's nothing to fix, Lady General."

Failure.

"···I really am the stranger." Sorrow filled her admission.

"I apologize for offending you." Ferdinan bowed forward until his skin screamed.

"I'm the one who should apologize." She knelt down beside him and took his hand, encasing it in white hot fire once more. "How do I become your aunt? A general's important for a country, but an aunt's important for a family. I want to be your family first."

"But...?"

Selfish.

"It's important."

"I don't know what to say." Ferdinan turned far enough away she couldn't see his face. "But if you tell me what you want, I'll fulfill it."

"I'd like to get to know you."

Her command was overwhelming. Was there anything about him important enough to tell? "What would you like to know?"

Nothing. You're insignificant.

"Tell me about your inventions."

"Ok." *She picked something benign...why?* He waited for her to sit before starting. "I don't know how interesting you'll find them..."

Chapter 30

"You ate more than that before the fire and your body's in desperate need of nutrition." Jon pushed the barely touched plate forward.

Taking it, Ferdinan slid it behind him - away from the Thinker - and rubbed his belly. He'd already eaten one of his bars. There were more nutrients in one of those than in a week's worth of what Jon punished him with. *Why should I have food when countless thousands are starving?* Fewer people should mean more food to go around, but there was no one to pick and distribute. Having a personal chef was obscene and selfish. "I don't feel well."

Evil child.

"You'd feel better if you'd eat. You were doing well before the fire."

"I'd prove you wrong, but I'm tired of being sick." Ferdinan looked down - preparing himself for one last duty before he could rest.

Destroy the one passion your ally has.

"Then..." Jon hesitated.

"Then what?" The exasperation in Ferdinan's voice said quite plainly he wasn't up for nagging.

"Then...are you ready to talk about what happened?"

"'What happened?'" Ferdinan parroted back.

"At the beginning of break." Jon didn't appreciate Ferdinan rolling his eyes. "You were fine when you got on that boat. Ours was the first stop, so someone-"

"Nothing happened."

He doesn't care. No one cares about you.

"The same kind of nothing as when you stopped the virus?"

That ugly voice laughed cruelly. Between it and Jon, Ferdinan's face burned – only this time with anger. If he opened his mouth now, he'd prove he was uglier than the voice haunting him. Instead he made his way to the door.

"Ferdinan! We're worried about you." The skeleton paused, so Jon continued. "When Oya said you shouldn't go to the palace, I thought she was being her weird, silly self... Then I saw your back flogged and... It scared me. Scared all of us. We want to help you, but we can't fix anything if you won't talk to us."

"You – all of you – look too deeply into things." *She said that to him?* Why? It didn't make sense. Yet...his heart ached in longing...and shame. *Why would she care enough about me to...to do anything?*

Who could care about you?

"Ferdinan..."

He kept his back to Jon. "There's nothing to fix. Nothing happened. Oya is Oya, silly and nonsensical. I should think a Thinker was smarter than this."

This entire conversation...! Any more and he'd be yelling. But...she cared enough to think of him... It made him realize how cold and alone he felt when she wasn't there... His life before her...it was a long winter's night.

"Ferdinan!" Jon tried commanding his attention.

Pathetic.

Ignoring both annoyances, Ferdinan forced his body to move. Sore and stiff, his skin felt like old paper, crinkling and cracking with each step.

◊

"Where're you going?" Battle lost; Jon followed the gent outside.

"To see my General off." Ferdinan's head flinched to the side as if something flew too close to his ear...but nothing was there.

"You're unwell. Tenalia will understand you not coming," Jon insisted while the skeleton grimaced with each step. Aside from minor cooking burns, he had no idea what his ally was feeling right now. It looked far from pleasant. *Why is he always so stubborn!?*

"She's my General."

"Ya. And she'll understand. Didn't she order you to rest and eat?"

"She's not the only person I answer to." The ground was suddenly closer to Ferdinan's foot than he was expecting – shocking a gasp from him.

"Careful!" Jon reached out to steady the skeleton, but the gent jerked back – causing himself more pain. *Right...he doesn't like being touched...* Why was that so hard to remember?

Ozar rushed over when they came into view. "Why're you out here, little brother?"

Pain glowed in those blue crystals as Ferdinan backed slowly away from both brothers. "I apologize, Hei-O. I'm here to see my General."

"Ah...she's talking to Samuel," Ozar grinned despite the boy using his title. "She's trying to convince him to stay a while."

Ferdinan turned five shades of red and hid behind his overgrown hair. "My apologies."

"What for? I agree with her." The Hei-O laughed while his baby brother smirked.

"I'd be happy with him staying. As much as I love my island family, they can't replace you gents." Jon gave Ozar a squeeze - or whatever a child is capable of giving a Redwood.

Ignoring them, Ferdinan hurried off. Once the boy was out of sight, Ozar knelt - putting himself at eye level with his baby brother. "There's something I need to tell you."

"What is it?" Those serious words made Jon's heart race.

"We would've spoken sooner...but you were spending so much time with Ferdinan. I knew you couldn't keep it from him and it's important he heals."

"What?" Jon felt his heart triple in speed.

"Ferdinan and Oya saved those two from the fire, but there was a third in the building."

"...what...?" That knocked him off his feet. How hadn't he heard? But...Jon spent every hour with one of his brothers since the fire. The only ones he'd been around were them, Ferdinan, Oya, and the General.

"Ferdinan's apprentices were showing Xhou's sister the lab. The explosion killed her instantly and buried the other two. Elbie had just gotten free when Ferdinan and Oya arrived."

It wasn't often Jon was shocked beyond words. There he stood, mouth agape - unable to do more.

Ozar's face contorted - whatever he was about to say, he didn't want to say it. "Ferdinan will find out eventually. We need you to be there when he does. Can you do this?"

"...um..." How could he help anyone when he was still reeling from shock?

"Not today, of course. Oya already knows. She volunteered to be with Ferdinan 'til you're able."

Swallowing hard, Jon stepped forward and hugged his brother. "I'll...I'll do my best..."

* * *

From here it looked like his General and Samuel were haggling. *What's Xhou doing here?* The older boy approached them - stance sure and purposeful. That wasn't the Xhou Ferdinan was used to seeing.

Meddlesome.

Curiosity sparked - ignoring the voice - the skeleton's pace picked back up. He hid behind a pile of luggage within earshot. When Samuel finished, he turned to find Xhou waiting.

"I'm sorry to interrupt," Xhou bowed - voice rough. "Thank you for personally caring for my sister 'til she reaches home."

"I'm sorry we can't do more." Samuel's answer was soft...delicate.

Throwing back his shoulders with the air and dignity of a true Nu, Xhou bowed to the Healer. "Even if it's a simple thing for you, it means the world to my family. I can in no way repay your kindness. Thank you."

"Is there anything else you'd like me to deliver to your mother?" Samuel asked solemnly.

Why do they sound...sad? What's going on?

"Tell her I love her."

"She'll love hearing it."

Another "thank you" and Xhou returned from where he came. Ferdinan pushed the conversation from his mind and approached his General.

Coward.

"Ferdinan!" Tenalia's shout was disappointment personified. "What are you doing out of bed?"

^^^

"Go to bed!" Jon rubbed sleepy, unfocused eyes.

"Can't sleep." Wide-eyed and jittery, Ferdinan toyed with the machine he'd recently built.

"Do you have any idea what time it is?"

"4:26 in the morning," Ferdinan answered a little too quickly.

"Ughhh...having a tiny bit of energy doesn't mean it's time to start working. I'll be picking you up off of the floor again."

VVV

"It's a short walk to the boats," Ferdinan blushed. "I wanted fresh air too..."

"You'll get sick pushing yourself too hard."

Reddening all the more, Ferdinan bowed as far as his skin would let him. "Safe journeys, my General."

"Don't be so formal with your aunt." When she moved to hug him, he gasped and shrank away. "I'm so sorry..."

Defect.

"No! It's not your fault! I'm sorry, General."

◊

It was amusing watching the two dance back and forth in a never-ending quest for responsibility - until it became ridiculous. Oya cleared her throat, garnering both of their attention.

"My apologies, I'm stealing my friend when you're done." Oya grinned at the relief filling Ferdinan's face. Happiness flitted there for a moment before he pushed it away. *Why does he always do that? Why can't he let himself feel good?* Agitated glowing orbs vibrated in disapproval. *That's not it...?*

Tenalia smiled. "Thank you for caring for him. Make sure he doesn't overexert himself."

"Of course. He wouldn't do me any good sick." Oya gave her usual mischievous grin.

"It's time for me to board." Tenalia turned back to Ferdinan but kept a few feet from him. "I'll tell Zephyr about your injuries so he can make sure you heal properly."

Every ounce of color drained from Ferdinan - leaving him dizzy. "You don't have to trouble our Prince with such a petty thing."

"Petty? Your health is hardly trivial."

"There are more important matters pressing on him."

That concerned frown was something only Oya saw since Ferdinan kept his eyes on the ground, leaning forward as far as he could.

Unnatural green eyes glowed brightly. "Care of I'll make sure he's taken."

"Thank you, Oya."

With this they said a final farewell and Oya followed Ferdinan back to his suite.

Chapter 31

"Zephyr." A short, muscular woman with salted black hair walked in. "It's nice to see you're well."

A smile blossomed on his lips as he ran over and hugged her. "Aunt Tenalia!"

She returned the hug. "Are you up for a visit?"

Onyx eyes brightening at the thought of actual conversation. Just as Aguilla said, a week later a counselor came and evaluated him. But the woman said nothing beyond her little assessment. That'd been days ago. He was starting to worry... Zephyr shook his head. *That* was the last thing he wanted to think about.

Golden hands expressed emotions his words never could...even if she didn't know what the gestures meant. "Thank you, Aunt Tenalia. I was about to take up puppetry for something to do." *And someone to talk to.*

Tenalia laughed. "You look much better."

"I feel better. Thank you."

"I'm pleased to inform you, you've been cleared. Your mind's perfectly healthy."

Jumping forward, he squeezed her tightly again – thanking whatever deity decided to end his torture. His entire body shook. The idea of solitude never seemed intense. But this last month was torture. He never realized how much he needed people.

Guiding him to the lounging area, she motioned him to sit next to her. "Can you tell me what started all this?"

Shaking his head, he sighed, tapped his fingers together and turned his palms up. "There was Azuté...that was settling down then Ferdinan came back from some vacation or another. Next thing I know I can't sleep."

When Zephyr mentioned his cousin's name, his eyes dimmed. It startled Tenalia. "What's wrong?"

Leaning back, he studied her. "What?"

"You look sad. What's troubling you?"

A golden hand chopped at the air then turned palm up then down and back up. "I'm not sad. Bored yes...painfully bored."

"You don't look bored," she insisted.

Standing, he walked over to the mirror... *No...*

"Zephyr?"

Why are his *eyes here!? I'm not selfish! I'm not like him!*

The elf's words echoed through his head. *"You've noticed, it's the very thing inside you."*

"Zephyr, there's a number of things you need to know."

Why...? Closing his eyes, the Prince centered himself and painted on a smile before turning to his aunt. *I have to figure this out...* "About what?"

She studied him for a long moment. "Actually, why don't we take a stroll? The gardens are beautiful right now."

A pleased smile overcame the fake – allowing him to push aside the elf's words. "That sounds lovely."

* * *

Elbie knocked timidly at the door of his mentor's lab. He really tried. He asked everyone. Jon was even kind enough to study the disk with him, but neither of them could make any sense of it. The response Master Ludwick gave was less than inviting. The more Elbie struggled, the more he realized the man was right.

It was unbearably frustrating. He needed to "get the basics down and everything after," before bothering with the disks. But admitting defeat...

Ferdinan's voice welcomed him in.

I failed and he had to rescue me... Elbie felt even more useless and stupid. Worse. Ferdinan was seriously hurt. *How do I face him?* But...if he put this off any longer, he'd fall too far behind.

◊

"How may I help you, Lord Elbarrat?" Ferdinan gave Elbie his usual pleasant smile – keeping the weariness off his face.

"I tried this entire time! I really did. I searched everything. I asked everyone. I'm sorry, but...I couldn't complete the assignment."

^^^

Ferdinan turned a blank face to him. "How do viruses work, Jon?"

"Huh?" Jon raised an eyebrow. "I would've thought you'd know that one by now."

"They invade a host cell to replicate." Ferdinan spoke, though it was hard to tell who he was talking to. "They haven't evolved to learn magic."

"Uh...? Excuse me?"

Reinforcing his expressionless stone mask, Ferdinan continued. "Either they've found a way to disappear or the healers aren't giving me real samples."

"They're lying to you?"

"Feels like it." Still... What if? Something was off and it'd been eating away at Ferdinan. "Assuming they aren't...what would cause a virus to disappear from twenty samples in two days?"

"They were switched along the line?"

"Less conspiracy theory and more scientific explanation."

VVV

Ferdinan walked stiffly up to him.

Pathetic.

"But what did you learn?"

"What?" Elbie blinked away frustrated tears. "I wasn't able to *start* the assignment. How could I learn anything?"

"Where's the disk?" Ferdinan smiled encouragingly. He knew all the effort Elbie put into this. Now it was time to teach.

Taking the disk from Elbie, Ferdinan placed it on a work table.

"Show me how you tried working out the answer."

Making children cry. You're a great villain.

Elbie walked up and opened it.

"Show me everything you did to this disk."

ΛΛΛ

Dissecting the virus...

Learning the truth...

It made him sick.

How did I miss this?!

But even as he retched and berated himself, he saw what the thing was.

One step at a time he took it apart in his mind until all the pieces laid before him. Retreating into himself, he grabbed each piece - going over the best way to break it.

VVV

Like the virus from that memory, the disk's pieces laid out before him. It was taken apart multiple times, and not with the proper tools. "What did you do when you saw the inside?"

With this direction offered, Elbie told Ferdinan that when he couldn't find anything similar in his research, he studied the layout. Ferdinan asked him a myriad of questions - starting with how he figured out how to open it and ending with what responses he'd gotten from help requests.

"Please put it back together." Ferdinan walked to a table near the back of his lab.

Incompetent.

The disk was no longer usable. It'd suffered too much damage. Even Ferdinan had difficulty taking one apart with the proper tools. He developed those micro boards himself to be stronger and smaller to suit his needs, but there was only so much something that thin could take.

Once it was back together, he told his apprentice to turn it on. It didn't, of course. Ferdinan knew it wouldn't. But this was the last straw for Elbie who started crying and apologizing.

ΛΛΛ

Knowing what the virus was... Of course, nothing made sense. This was something man made. Even how it replicated... It wasn't too dissimilar from his bots. Only...these were created to hurt people. It was made to look and behave like a virus so it wouldn't be figured out. Why was I so blind...so naïve? I refused to see it...

VVV

Enjoy torturing children?

That voice pulled him out of the memory. Ferdinan couldn't understand half the things the young boy said. Forcing back a grimace from the sand rubbing under his skin, he lifted a flinching Elbie to the table - putting the boy at eye level. "Elbie. I'm impressed."

This shocked his mentee into silence.

"You accomplished more than I expected you'd be able to."

"But, I haven't..." Elbie trailed off with a stifled sob.

"I didn't think you'd get the case apart." He put down a small tool made specifically for sealing and unsealing the cases. "These are completely waterproof - perfectly sealed. I'm fascinated. You found a way to open it without destroying the case and breaking the circuitry inside. Do you know how amazing that is? And...important for me to know. I'll have to improve the design."

Ferdinan showed his apprentice how to use the tool by opening the new disk. "Look at the inside. You put every board back perfectly. It's wonderful!"

"Then why won't it work?" Elbie sniffled.

That sniffle egged on the cackling inside his skull - making him dizzy. Grabbing the edge of the table, Ferdinan steadied himself before continuing. "They are placed correctly, but the connections were destroyed upon removal. It couldn't be helped."

"I'm sorry I broke it," Elbie whimpered.

You're nothing but a burden.

"I wouldn't have given it to you if I needed it back in working order." Ferdinan mussed the boy's hair in an attempt to lighten the mood. "You've gone above and beyond my expectations,

Elbie. I applaud you. Now, you've told me all you learned concerning this disk. But what did you learn trying to complete the assignment?"

The young Tinkerer's mismatched eyes opened wide when he realized his mentor finally called him "Elbie." He'd been trying for as long as he'd known Ferdinan. "I learned it's frustrating when no one can help you. Even more so when they tell you not to bother with it."

"Did this stop you?"

"No! It only made me want to try harder..."

ΛΛΛ

Ferdinan stood in the middle of the room staring at the beautiful gardens outside the window. To anyone looking from the outside, they'd see a skin wrapped skeleton in fancy clothing standing peacefully in the middle of a sea of tranquility.

Any Telepath, however, would feel something vastly different.

Darkness closed in, stealing the vibrancy sunrise offered. It killed the life in everything around him. For as far as his eyes could see lay a desolate world of death and destruction.

And here he stood in the center of it all.

This was the work of his hands.

His blood soaked, guilty hands.

VVV

Swallowing hard, Ferdinan closed his eyes against that memory and the laughing voice. *Why is it back? Why won't it go away...?* "Good. What else did you learn?"

"I learned what failure feels like. I've always done things well...I'm happy working hard to learn...but..."

"It doesn't feel nice, does it?"

"No," Elbie blushed.

"Did you learn anything else, Elbie?"

His pupil gave him a strange look. "I learned you're scary smart."

^^^

"Do you honestly believe what you said or are you giving Evelyn someone to hate?"

Ferdinan closed his eyes.

"You didn't kill anybody. You stopped someone else from killing more."

Hiding behind his hands, Ferdinan leaned forward. "I'm not a child. I know the truth."

"I'm not lying," Jon insisted.

"My incompetence led to their deaths! How is that not murder?!" Guilt and anger screamed out as he leapt to his feet. "If I'd noticed sooner... All the data was right there! From the beginning! I missed it!! Millions, Jon! I killed millions because I overlooked the obvious, blatant discrepancies!"

VVV

No one as incompetent as him could be intelligent. "I'm no smarter than you. I only have more years of experience."

Ferdinan resealed the disk he'd opened. *What am I doing? How could I ever hope to teach anyone? I want this to be over. I want...* Swallowing hard, Ferdinan pushed those thoughts out of his head. "You didn't complete the assignment, but you learned what I wanted you to."

"What?"

"First, people will tell you all sorts of things. But in the end, if you want to do something then you should keep trying."

Selfish child.

Looking Elbie straight in the eye, Ferdinan continued on. "Second, failure, regardless of how it feels, is ok. If we only try what we know we can do, we'll never grow. We'll have no hope of discovering our potential. It's important...failing at something beyond us. It gives us a target, a goal to reach. Once we reach it, we should find another goal. Do you understand?"

Elbie nodded. "I think so."

"Good. Elbie, you're talented. The potential I see in you is astounding. I want you to reach it. You have to do the work, but I want to help you with what I can."

"Thank you." Elbie looked at his hands bashfully. "Will you teach me the lessons you were going to teach before break?"

"I'd be happy to."

"Um... Why're you finally calling me 'Elbie?' I've asked you to for forever."

Ferdinan blushed. "When addressing those higher or lower than us in status, isn't it polite to use the person's title?"

No one's lower than you.

"Yes."

"You've shown you're as capable as I am. You've figured out more about these disks than anyone else. This puts you easily on par with me. At least as far as the sciences go." That voice laughed uncontrollably. *Please! Leave me alone!* He'd have to start listening to music again.

Joy filled Elbie's heart. "Really?"

"Yes. Now concerning these disks and my other inventions, you won't ask about them again 'til after you've completed your apprenticeship. Then I'll be happy to teach you. Agreed?"

"Yes, sir!"

Ferdinan smiled. "We'll restart our sessions tomorrow. Do you need a new time or does the same one work for you?"

"The same time works for me." Elbie jumped down and ran out.

Ferdinan watched his pupil dash away, happy Elbie was more cheerful when leaving than arriving.

"That was amazing." Oya appeared out of thin air – tugging at the chain around her neck.

Oya... A gentle smile took over his lips. It was greedy...he was a terrible person...but...seeing her... The warmth her presence always brought... "Not really. I only told him the truth. Thank you for staying out of sight 'til he left."

"It wasn't the time to intrude. You know, it makes no sense."

His heart quickened. *I haven't offended her, have I?* Living without that warmth. That joy and sunshine. Living without her brightness... Even if it magnified his selfishness...he didn't want to do anything to drive her away. "What?"

"How someone who feels incompetent at everything can make others feel capable of anything."

Oya's comment caught him off guard and drained every ounce of color from him.

^^^

Off like a rocket, he shot through tall grass and soft ground.

Run!

Run faster!

Get away!

Escape!

He ran until he couldn't see the death – couldn't feel the blood. Picking up speed, he tried outrunning the pain and failure. Tried outrunning his self-loathing... But that companion refused to be left behind.

Continually it whispered in his ear.

You're a failure.

Your own stupidity stole her family.

It laughed at all he'd failed.

There was no redemption...no hope.

VVV

"Regardless of how you feel, I know exactly how remarkable you are. One day you'll see it."

I didn't know you were capable of anything, defect.

It was all Ferdinan could do to keep his stone mask in place. Her words hurt. They were physically painful! But... They felt like...they felt like something he'd always seen – always wanted – but never had. *Please stay with me... I know you don't need me anymore...but...please? Let me be greedy.*

Pink tinged his cheeks – slowly darkening until it consumed his face. Carefully. Uncertainly... *How do you say something like this? Can someone like me hope....?*

Looking away, Ferdinan crafted a smile he'd never worn before. It was small – smaller than he intended as if too scared of what she'd do for saying something so greedy – something that didn't take her thoughts into account. But he turned it to her nonetheless. Her warmth and light... Living without it... *I don't deserve her.* He knew it was true. Knew this more fully than any of his inventions. But...could he be selfish this once? Was that ok?

"Thank you... friend."

Epilogue

Tightening her grip on the silver strand, Oya pressed forward.

"You remember your promise?"

She almost laughed. *Of course, you'd arrive now.* "There's no need to worry, Fisherman."

"There isn't?"

"If anything happens to that woman, those she's working with will panic and disappear. I'll be able to find some of them, but not all. I need her unharmed."

"Then what're you planning?" The Fisherman straightened his spine, but it did little to intimidate her.

"I'll make her connections my own 'til I have them all."

"And then?"

"I don't know..." Oya laughed, but it wasn't funny. "By then I'm sure I'll have a plan that suits my promise."

"Just don't forget." The man removed his floppy fisherman's hat and waved it forward. "Did your mother teach you how to access the silver roads?"

"She didn't get the chance." Wicked green eyes flashed at him. "But she told me about them. Entering another's unconscious would be easier than dragging them to a dream I made."

Then she could set up a permanent connection between her friend and Evelyn's dreams. Oya grinned. *He finally called me friend. Can I get him to accept the family of giants as well?* She didn't mind dragging Ferdinan to Evelyn whenever he slept, but there were other things she needed to do...

The Fisherman pointed to the locket hidden under her shirt. "The door to the silver roads looks just like that."

Of course... A little giggle left her as Oya grabbed the locket and studied it. It was steel, rectangular and had countless lines etched every which way across its surface. The back...she didn't need to turn it over. The symbols written there were the dearest things to her – she knew them perfectly. Eyes closed, Oya cleared her mind and pictured the intersection of roads carved on the front of her locket. They came and went in every direction.

When those alien green eyes opened, she was treated with a sight only her imagination could top. "'For all who dared to dream a dream a road was built to take them there.'"

"Your father's words?"

"Mom wasn't the poet..." One bare foot stepped upon the starting path, then the next. All that existed in the pitch black were countless metallic roads webbing across it, herself, and the silver strand. The pulse was light, but she felt it. It was faint...but... That'd never stop her. Stepping forward, Oya followed that pulse, that draw of life from the one she was after. Each time a road intersected, she'd feel the direction she needed to go. Sometimes she continued on, sometimes she changed paths.

Until she stood in a mind that wasn't asleep.

Interesting...

Picturing a window, Oya reached forward and flung her arms apart as if throwing back heavy curtains.

Prominent veins snaked along the back of hands starting to show their age. There was nothing particularly distinctive about those hands, but Oya knew them. How could she not? *Finding you was easier than expected...*

Those hands scrolled through a screen before the view panned up and to the side.

All Oya wanted was to close the curtains and rip out that woman's heart...but she couldn't. Doing so meant failure.

So, she watched.

She watched a young man scream. Those pleas for mercy weren't ones that kōjomȁ understood. But Oya did. She knew every subtle image and nuance... The tautness and twitch of his eyes. The particular dance of his tongue and movement of his lips. Even the way his nose flared and his body tensed. All were things she understood. Every word he couldn't plead, she heard them...saw them.

Every. Single. Word.

Three deep breaths. Oya pushed aside the appeals and prayers for his sister's safety. She pushed aside the silver blade leaving oozing red tracks across his skin. She even pushed aside her own fury. It was the only way...

Delving deep, Oya found the cluster of connections the woman held.

Starting with the thickest...

The strongest...

That'd be the easiest to work with...

About the Author

Psychologist, writer, crafter, and colored hair enthusiast...when CR Saxon isn't coming up with new and terrible things to subject various characters to, she can be found attempting projects with more ambition than skill, getting lost in random research, or catching up on chores. Her life is generally one of chaos and glowy screens – all while mentally living many lives in the name of fun, adventure, and storytelling.

Cost of Victory

ISBN: 9781955644006

Made in the USA
Columbia, SC
15 August 2021

42893690R00191